ABOUT THE AUTHOR

Born in Brighton, in 1932, Roland Curram trained as an actor at the RADA. After repertory seasons in Carlisle, Nottingham and Worthing, he joined the Royal Shakespeare Company in 1967, for *Little Murders*, then the National Theatre for *Grand Manoeuvres*. His other West End credits include *Enter a Free Man, Design For Living, Noises Off* (1984-85) and *Ross* at the Old Vic. His films include *The Silent Playground* and *Decline and Fall*. He played 'Malcolm' in the Oscar winning *Darling*, and he has appeared in many television plays and series, including *Z Cars, Nana, The Avengers, The Crezz, Some Mothers do 'Ave 'Em* and *Holby City*. He was 'Harold Perkins' in *Big Jim and the Figaro Club* and 'Freddie' in *Eldorado*. Troubador published his first novel *Man on the Beach* in 2004.

The Rose Secateurs

Roland Curram

Matador
9 De Montfort Mews
Leicester LE1 7FW, UK
Tel: (+44) 116 255 9311 / 9312
Email: books@troubador.co.uk
Web: www.troubador.co.uk/matador

The characters portrayed in this novel are based upon actual persons now
deceased. The events depicted are from the lives of those persons. Although the
events have been dramatised for dramatic purposes, any resemblance to actual
persons or events other than those portrayed and depicted herein is purely
coincidental.

ISBN 978-1906221-225

Front cover image: 'Pot Pourri' by Herbert James Draper
Thanks to the Art Renewal Centre @ www.artrenewal.org

Typeset in 10pt Stempel Garamond by Troubador Publishing Ltd, Leicester, UK
Printed by TJ International Ltd, Padstow, Cornwall

Matador is an imprint of Troubador Publishing

In memory of my daughter, Lou.

Contents

Acknowledgements

I'd like to thank Paul Linn, the first reader, for his invaluable assistance and support, and Jan Waters for her insistence that I knuckle down and write this story. A big thank you, too, is due to Sally Mates for her constant encouragement and enthusiasm, and for her advice. To Caroline Smith, I owe a particular debt of gratitude for allowing me access to her library. Among the books from which I gleaned detailed knowledge of the Victorian and Edwardian period are: *Forgotten Children* by Christian Wolmar, published by Vision, of Satin Publications. *The Rise and Fall of the Victorian Servant* by Pamela Horn, published by Alan Sutton Publishing Ltd, surely the best book published on the subject. The *Imperial War Museum Book of The First World War* by Malcolm Brown, published by Sidgwick and Jackson. *The King in Love* by Theo Aronson, published by John Murray Ltd, and *Working for Victory* by Diana Condell and Jean Liddiard.

I'm especially grateful to everyone at Troubador Publishing for their help, and, once again, to the inestimable Jeremy Thompson.

R.C.
March 2007

Preface

Some years ago I went to the funeral of my great Aunt. She had died in an Asylum at the age of ninety-eight. Mine were the only flowers on her coffin, and apart from three nurses and a geriatric patient in a wheelchair at the back of the chapel, I was the only mourner.

In the car, as we followed the hearse to the burial, I asked the nurses what my aunt was like. "What was her conversation? What used she to talk about?"

"She had a mantra," one of the young nurses answered. "She used to mutter it all the time. It was, 'You must never have children. You must never have children.'"

Another nurse spoke up, "The other one was, 'The rose secateurs.' We all used to wonder about that one," and the nurses nodded in agreement. "'The rose secateurs should be put away properly,' she'd say. 'The rose secateurs should be put away.'" They smiled sadly and rather philosophically at each other, and I wondered what could have been going on in my poor aunt's mind to say such strange things.

As her only surviving relative, the Matron gave me her bundle of belongings, and when I requested to see her file, showed it to me. What I read there amazed me and seemed hardly credible, but the details were tantalizingly incomplete.

I subsequently researched her history and became even more intrigued. This is her story.

I have changed the names to avoid giving offence, and used my imagination to fill in the gaps. What follows is therefore fiction, but based on true events.

PART ONE

The Unwanted

Chapter One

Her birth coincided with that of the twentieth century, the first freezing night of the 1st January, 1900. A time when Queen Victoria, Empress of India, Grandmother of Europe was on the throne of England and residing in Osbourne House on the Isle of Wight.

Her Majesty was seated at her desk reading a report concerning the siege at Mafeking. She lifted her eyelids. Disconsolately she gazed into the glowing coals of the fire deeply worried about the Boer War. Behind her, through the thick plush velvet curtains and shuttered windows overlooking her wintry rose garden, across the grim and melancholy waves of the swelling Solent, over the mudflats and salt marshes of Lymington Spit, a light shone in a farmhouse window, from within came the unmistakable cries of a new-born baby.

"It's a lassie!" exclaimed Annie Oliphant, gathering up the babe.

The exhausted mother shut her eyes. "Don't ...don't tell me. I don't want to know."

Annie was not a professional midwife, simply a woman of good sense and kindness of heart who, in a modest way, enjoyed nursing, and in matters relating to pregnancy and childbirth, which, at that time, was fraught with danger and mystery, carried a certain authority. She'd been prepared for a reaction of this sort from the mother, but marvelling at the birth of a bairn as perfect as this, her emotions had taken over. *How can any woman deny such a helpless wee lassie like this?* "But she's beautiful!" she said.

"Take it away," gasped the mother. "Please," she pleaded. "You promised."

Determinedly ignoring the mother's eye, the square-jawed Scots girl cleaned the bawling infant and bundled it up in swaddling clothes. "What a treasure!" The baby quietened down. "There now, y'see."

"I can't keep her," anguished the mother. "You know I can't."

"Come along, I never heard of such a thing. A new-born baby is the most blessed gift in the world. Especially a bonnie love like this." The mother turned away in torment. Tenderly Annie placed the baby beside her. "Hush now. Just for a while."

"Oh, God, this is torture. We had an agreement, Annie."

"Just look at those blue eyes." Annie waited a moment, but the mother remained motionless. "Get to know her while I clean things up," she said, and she went about her business.

Alone, the mother reluctantly turned to look at her new-born. Tentatively she lowered the swaddling clothes to see its face. With the back of her finger she made to caress its cheek. Abruptly she checked herself. "Annie!" she called. "For God's sake, take it away!"

Outside the door Annie was hoping the mother would relent. Re-entering, she took the babe without a word and left the room.

The mother mutely sobbed.

Five minutes later, the former nursemaid bustled in again with a cheerful, "Here we are now. Have a nice cup of tea. Are we feeling any better?"

"Oh, Annie, don't," groaned the young woman. "Stop. Please."

Annie's smile faded. She placed the saucer and teacup – from her best china tea-set – onto the bedside table. "Have a sleep," she murmured, "and in the morning Fred will drive you home in the trap."

"I must give you some money," said the woman reaching for her reticule.

"Leave all that. Settle up with him later. Just you rest easy now." Tidying the bed covers she confided, "And don't you worry yourself. No one will know. I promise you."

The mother stretched out her hand.

Annie clasped it. "No one." With her free hand she smoothed away the damp locks of hair from the mother's brow. "There, now. Just you rest easy."

"I'll never be able to thank you. I'll see you're not the loser."

Annie handed her the saucer. "Here, drink your tea." Lifting the oil lamp she observed, "You'll have the light from the fire. Sleep now," and closing the door she left.

Noiselessly entering her own bedroom next door, she shielded the lamp light from the bed in the corner where, side by side, her two-year-old twin sons lay sleeping. The new-born baby was mewling in a washing basket on Annie's double bed. She set down the oil lamp and leaned over to look at her. *What on earth am I to do with you? I wonder who your Dadda was?* The baby opened its eyes. Annie smiled. "Well, hallo," she whispered. The baby gurgled, chomped its mouth, blinked and went back to sleep. Deliberating, Annie turned away. Pushing aside the cambric curtain and limp Nottingham lace covering the window, she gazed into the dark. Gusts of rain pelted the window pane. *We're hardly able to make ends meet as it is. Fred will throw a fit. Still, he's a bairn himself, bless him, he'll do what he's told. 'You'll not be the loser', she said. How much will she pay?* Distant thunder rumbled. Suddenly a bolt of lightning flashed from behind giant black clouds, illuminating a vast and forbidding heaven. *God is angry. 'Suffer the little children to come unto me, and forbid them not.' Mark 10, verse 14.* Searching the sky for a happier portent, she spotted a solitary morning star in the east. As a sign, it was good enough. Turning to the oak chest beside her sleeping boys she opened the top drawer. She removed a cardboard box and hairbrush, and padded down the clothes inside. Taking the baby from the basket, she placed it inside the open drawer. Then, collecting the oil lamp and basket, she opened the bedroom door. Looking back at the downy sleeping heads of her twins, a flicker of maternal joy warmed her unlovely doughy face. Silently she closed the door and went downstairs.

"What!?" cried Fred in the parlour, raising his black caterpillar eyebrows. "Another mouth to feed! Are you mad, woman? Tell her to look after her own brats. You never said naught to me about keeping it. What's in it for us, eh? How much is she gonna pay us?"

"Ask her yourself when you drive her home," Annie instructed her husband, as she cleared the table.

"I bloody will," he retorted, biting his fingernail and flinging his leg over the arm of the armchair. Fred was a wiry, athletic little man, younger than his buxom wife, with thick shiny black hair growing in curls round his ears, dark gypsy eyes and a dazzling white-toothed smile which belied a character that would gladly have cheated his best friend of sixpence.

"Ask her two guineas a week. And payable to me, mind. None of y'slipping it into y' own back pocket." Annie was sharp about money, too, or as her Ma used to say to her, "Y'short arms don't reach y'long pockets."

Fred guffawed in disbelief. "Two guineas! G'arn! She'll never pay that much."

"To buy our silence?" Shrewdly Annie regarded her husband. "Oh yes, she will."

And indeed she did. Every month eight golden guineas wrapped in tissue paper arrived in a thick velum envelope addressed to Mrs. Alfred Oliphant.

Being a woman of the deepest faith, Annie insisted the child be christened. She approached her local Anglican parson, the Reverend Ralph Ambrose. The young rector was well known to her and she respected him, for not only was he a nice-looking gentleman, the youngest son of a titled family, he had performed her marriage ceremony and christened her twins. She explained to him she'd found the baby on her doorstep and he appeared to believe her. "Even more reason to cleanse the child from sin," he intoned glibly. Annie had already thought of a name, and the following Sunday afternoon at St Thomas and All Saints in Lymington, the unwanted baby was christened Sarah Smith.

Chapter Two

*I*t is an indisputable fact that our lives are shaped by our upbringing. In Sarah's case, her future was so profoundly affected by the life changes forced upon Mrs Oliphant and the choices she made, that to ignore them would be to leave Sarah's story incomplete. So, while our heroine is growing up, we will stay awhile with Annie.

Annie had always been a strong-willed and resourceful character. She needed to be, for three months after Sarah's christening, her husband Fred announced he found the weight of fatherhood too heavy and was leaving her. Something of a musician with airy ambitions to travel and see the world, his frustration at what he saw as his failure in life was exploding.

"Being wed to you is like suffocating!" he shouted, banging his fist on the breakfast table, his face red with fury and flinching with nervous agitation. Reg and Stan, their eyes the size of saucers, sat watching their father fearfully as he strode round the parlour gesticulating wildly with his stubby, grubby, finger-bitten hands. "I want more outta life than this tinpot existence! Trappin' rabbits and birds to scrape a meal together's no life. I'm an artist, for God's sake! I'm twenty-four. Me life's been nothing but bein' a kitchen boy, coachman and cabby. Slavin' away for other people all me life. I've never 'ad no adventure, nothing! It's as if me life is finished already, and what I've got in me, I'm telling you!" Beating his breast, he repeated forcefully, "What I've got in me!

I'm stifled in this 'ere saltmarsh backwater. It's fit for naught but salt and fisher folk, which sure as hell ain't me."

"What of these children I've had to bring into the world?" answered Annie, trembling, but trying to stay as calm as she could as she nursed baby Sarah, "and the trouble we've had to keep them, what's to become of them if you go?"

"You're a canny, savvy girl," he tossed carelessly at her, "you'll manage. I'm leaving' you five sovereigns in the pot o'er the mantel, and you'll get the money for the girl, so there's no need to fret. Me, I'm off to the Continent to seek me fortune. I'll board a boat at Southampton. First stop, Paris." Taking in Annie's aghast expression, he softened his tone. "Sorry gel, I've just had enough. Wish me luck!" So saying, he slung his accordion over his shoulder, up't and left.

Annie was devastated. Fred had been her first and only love. They'd been married for just two-and-a-half years. She'd tried not to make a scene, what would have been the point? If that was how he felt, what could she say? It wasn't as if there was another woman involved. She'd always recognised his immaturity, but to waltz off and leave her and the twins, and now wee Sarah, to face life without a breadwinner! Cursing her misjudgement of his character, she reached for the pot over the mantel. Counting out the five sovereigns, she wondered how on earth she was going to cope when they ran out. Gathering up her boys and Sarah, she sat with her arms round her little family on the cosy, but broken, three-legged sofa trying to comfort them and gazing round her parlour as if lost.

It was a snug parlour, too, with a dresser, armchair, a photograph of Queen Victoria over the stove, and a painting of Jesus above the sideboard. *How life can change in a moment!* Wistfully, she recalled her courting days when she and Fred had been in service... the passion of their lovemaking. *That side of things was always best... made me blush sometimes, he did... his gypsy blood, I daresay. Said as his father was a gypsy who'd deserted his parlour maid mother. Talk about history repeating itself! Still, we did have fun. That happy time up in London celebrating Queen Victoria's Diamond Jubilee. Squeezed up against the railings outside Buckingham Palace. Waited hours, we did. When she appeared, what excitement! Her white widow's veil cascading behind her in the wind, all in black, she was... alone in that open landau. How we cheered and waved our flags... I swore blind she looked right at us when she waved ... I'm sure of it. It was that very evening, in that rowdy parlour in "The Wheatsheaf" in Soho, over his tankard of Reid's stout, he smiled that wicked smile of his and proposed... and I, blooming lovesick fool that I was, accepted. But then, I was two months gone. Well, you live and learn.*

Annie pulled herself together and got up to clear the dishes. Never one to appear needy, she prided herself on her practicality, and with three mouths to feed, not to mention her own ample frame, she had to come up with something. They could hardly survive off the land behind the cottage, which already supported a horse for the trap, a goat, four sheep, three pigs, and some chickens, all of which had to be looked after and housed at night in the barn. With her firm belief in the Almighty, Annie went to St Thomas' to pray for guidance.

The Reverend Ralph greeted her after the service. Peering into Sarah's pram he enquired, "And how is our new young Christian this morning?"

"She's grand, Father. Not a tack of trouble."

"And Mr. Oliphant? Not off sick, I hope."

"No. He's not off sick exactly," said Annie, chewing her lip in anger.

"Whatever is it, Annie?" quizzed the perceptive Reverend.

Sensible to the scandal-loving ears of the parishioners waiting behind her, Annie lowered her voice and reluctantly confessed, "I'm afraid, y' reverence, he's gone off. He's deserted us."

"Oh, Annie, I am sorry! You have my sympathy. Indeed you do." The rector regarded the toddlers at her side thoughtfully. "Would you mind remaining a while. I have an idea. I may be in a position to help."

Annie ushered her boys into the graveyard, and gently rocking Sarah's pram, waited. Gazing at the ancient headstones crookedly sticking up through tufts of grass like uneven bed-heads, she had an urge to straighten them. Peering at the weathered engraving on one, she made out the date, 1310. She thought about the lives of those lying beneath and it occurred to her that her problems were small beans compared to the hard way they'd had to live in those days. Watching the Reverend chatting with his departing congregation she wondered about his life, too. Slim and dark-haired, his cassock rather suited him, she thought, she knew he was a bachelor. At that moment he concluded his pleasantries and beckoned her over. Leading her back inside the church, he ushered them into the back pew. Standing before her, with well-born confidential tones, he came straight to the point.

"The bishop has recently approached me with a proposal to open a local Church of England Home for Waifs and Strays. Would you be interested in looking after it for us, Annie?"

Taking Stan onto her lap and urging Reggie to keep still, she wasn't sure she'd heard him correctly. "Look after waifs and strays, y' say?"

"Let me explain." Earnestly, he elucidated, "Apparently the authorities of the Port of Southampton have become increasingly concerned about their rising population of street children. Old-fashioned large institutions are no longer thought ideal for the saving of souls, something more personal, comparable to the work of Dr Thomas Bernardo is now thought more suitable. A parish cottage and farm such as yours would be ideal, a property with a barn that would lend itself to a conversion. I suspect these good evangelists are motivated by visions of the bucolic life," he smiled, as if he knew the truth to be otherwise, "but whatever the case, they are a sincere group of philanthropists, members of the gentry, some of them, who are genuinely committed to financing such an orphanage. They believe that by removing these trouble-some urchins from the streets they are saving them from vagrancy, begging, crime, drunkenness and loose morals. Now do you think, Annie, that you could possibly handle such children? Be 'a house parent' to them? It would be demanding and a great responsibility."

Annie was staggered. "Begging your pardon, sir, but what sort of remuneration would such a position carry?"

"Sufficient, I would say. Probably rather more than you're used to as a cabby's wife. The church committee would, of course, meet the expenses of running the Home, and your annual rent to the parish would be annulled. What do you say? May I have your consent to propose you as a candidate?"

"Well sir, I'm strong. Never been afraid of hard work. How many children would I be expected to look after?"

"As I recall a specific number wasn't mentioned. But I had the impression a largish family unit was envisaged. Maybe eight or ten."

"Ten! Goodness! I'd need help with ten."

"I imagine the children themselves would be encouraged to become domesticated."

She looked at him doubtfully. "I'd need a cook. And a man around for the heavy work and help handle the rougher boys."

"Ah yes, of course. That might prove a problem. However, we can try. I'll write to the bishop immediately."

Three weeks later, by appointment, he brought a committee

of bible women and do-gooders in white starch and black worsted to inspect her cottage, the barn, the field, and herself. Preoccupied, as they were, with the Victorian virtues of cleanliness, diligence, honesty, sobriety and civic pride, charity to them, did not mean love, but the dutiful support of the deserving poor. Holding baby Sarah, Annie stood with her sons defying them to find fault as they scrutinised her spotless parlour. Knowing full well that if they approved, her future would be secure, she smiled politely. But as the group were crossing the courtyard to inspect the barn, she plucked the Rev Ralph by the sleeve. Something had been bothering her.

"Begging your pardon, Reverend, but can I speak private, like?"

"Of course, Annie, what is it?"

"Well... What happens if Fred comes back? He'd not take to any of this carry-on."

"Ah yes, I've thought about that. I should have explained. When a marriage breaks down, it is now morally acceptable that it is right to grant custody to the mother. I happen to be familiar with the Matrimonial Act, and Chancery can award custody as it sees fit. So don't worry, by doing nothing for the next three years, you will have a divorce and Mr Oliphant will no longer have any rights over you or your children."

That gave Anne something to think about. After the inspectors left, as she fed baby Sarah, she mulled it over. *Do I want a divorce? I want him back something terrible... don't I? Feel his body next to mine. Welcome him back with open arms, I would. Yet... am I still in love? Maybe not ... maybe it's just the lovin' I miss ... the loneliness ... But I'll love him for always. How can I not? He was my first love. He'll be in me heart forever.*

She waited for a week, then the postman delivered a thick envelope.

'The Governors of the Lymington Church of England Home for Waifs and Strays are pleased to inform Mrs Annie Oliphant that her application for the position of House Mother has been successful.' Included was a paper to sign concerning the lease on the cottage and barn, which would be converted into living accommodation for sixteen. Annie gulped! All she could think of was washing sixteen pairs of sheets every week under the cold-water pump in the kitchen. A ground plan was enclosed. Never before having seen such a document, she studied it carefully. Two upstairs dormitories were proposed, separated by a single room for a supervisor. It stipulated that the main water pipe from her cottage be extended to supply water to an upstairs wash room – with a bath, and four showers – and a downstairs kitchen. A fortnight later a team of builders arrived to lay pipes and convert the barn. After six weeks Annie couldn't believe the transformation. Her old barn had become a modern, spick and span Children's Home, considerably smarter and better equipped than her own humble cottage next door. Members of the committee returned to inspect the work. Over Annie's best teacups they "Ooh"ed, and "Ah"ed and congratulated themselves on their munificence.

When they'd departed, the Rev Ralph installed himself before the hearth. Coolly he produced a purse from his cassock, saying, "I have been instructed by the Governors to hand you this to purchase the necessary furnishings. They urge you to use all possible frugality and economy when making the purchases and not to exceed the sum of sixty guineas."

Dumbfounded, Annie accepted the purse and counted out the guineas.

The Reverend watched her with a countenance of studied benevolence, a hint of amused condescension discernable in the occasional pursing of his lips. This expression was quickly wiped from his face at Annie's question.

"Now then. What about the education of these children? And their medical welfare?"

"Ah yes," he responded vaguely. "I shall have to make enquiries."

In due course the headmaster of nearby South Baddesley School agreed to accept children over the age of six, and Dr Eccles, the local medical practitioner, agreed to inspect all new arrivals. Things seemed to be falling into place. *Miraculously so,* thought Annie. A suspicion dropped into her mind. An outrageous unchristian suspicion. *What if the Reverend Ralph isn't looking after us as a representative of the Lord, but as representing himself? What if he's Sarah's Dad?* Guiltily, she dismissed the irreverent thought. Yet it kept returning. *Why not? He's an upstanding enough fellow. And he's certainly being the good angel solving all of our problems. But banish the thought! He's sure as honest a God-fearing Christian as any in the county.*

A local acquaintance, Clara Woods, a jolly widow whose sons had recently left home, was engaged as cook. So too, on Reverend Ralph's recommendation, and no doubt after judicious enquiries concerning a young unmarried man's sleeping quarters, was a six-foot-four, broad-shouldered, affable fellow called Albert Cox.

"Named after Her Majesty's late husband," he said with a bright friendly smile, towering over Annie as he shook hands. "Glad to make your acquaintance."

"Likewise, I'm sure," assented Annie. "To put you in the picture, I have to furnish this Children's Home from top to bottom. Can you advise me?"

Albert said he knew a man called Wally. "He owns 'Wally's Emporium' in Lyndhurst. He'll help us strike some good bargains."

So, leaving the children with Clara, she put on her bonnet and shawl and set off beside Albert in the chaise-cart for the ten-mile drive to Lyndhurst. Valuing his viewpoint, she confided, "We need everything." From her shopping list she read out, "'Nineteen beds.' They should be second-hand, but I'd like the mattresses to be new. 'Linen, blankets, cots, kitchen stuff, dining table, benches, dresser, crockery, cutlery, towels...'"

"Linoleum," interrupted Albert.

"Ah yes." She fished for a pencil to add 'lino'.

"And books. 'Robinson Crusoe', maybe, and 'Treasure Island'. Got to think of their minds, too. Wally's got heaps of second-hand books."

Annie glanced across at him, "You're right," she said. "Always supposin' they can read. I've been thinking, we'll m'be have to learn 'em." Nevertheless she added 'books' to her list, grateful for his advice. *Different from Fred, who was a handsome devil, but as practical as porridge on a washing line.* "Clothes, too, smocks, boots and such. Will this place supply them?"

"Wally clears out old houses. He collects all manner o' stuff. I helped him many a time, to earn meself a tanner, like. You'll have to dig deep, mind, to find what you want. How about a piano? Would they stretch to a piano, you suppose?"

"I dare say. If it's second-hand," said Annie. "What a grand notion. Do you play at all?"

"Part-time organist at St Thomas's, me. Thought you knew. I spotted you there often."

Annie would never forget the three hours they spent at "Wally's Emporium". A huge warehouse with four floors full of every conglomeration of furniture and household article you can imagine. With Albert and his friend Wally's help, everything on her list was purchased, and at cost price. Wally even threw in a box of second-hand children's clothes for gratis when he knew who they were for, and he promised all would be delivered the following week.

When two loaded-down horse-drawn vans arrived, Albert took charge of the piano and furniture, Clara organised her kitchen, and Annie set about transforming the upstairs dormitories. By the evening, the three of them flopped into the armchairs by the newly lit fire, exhausted.

"Looks real dandy!" commented Albert, lighting his pipe. "Just like a pukka home."

"That dresser," observed Annie, "with its plates and mugs, just finishes it off. It's as handsome a parlour as any in the land. I thank you both sincerely. Indeed I do."

Albert grinned, for it was he who'd arranged the dresser. That night he moved into the supervisor's room between the two dormitories, and in the morning painted a sign in white across the black barn door, "OPEN ALL NIGHT".

Then came the children. The first were two bedraggled sullen lads of nine and ten who arrived at the door with a constable. "Morning, ma'am," he said cheerfully. "Mrs Oliphant?"

"Yes, " she said, taking in the boys' scowling faces.

"We got a notice up at station saying as how you're the new C of E's Waifs and Stray's Home. That right?"

"That's correct, constable."

"In that case, these 'ere ragamuffins are for you," and he handed her an envelope.

Putting the letter in her apron pocket, Annie ushered the boys in. "Come in, lads. Come on in. Thank you, constable."

"Sign 'ere, ma'am, if you please," said the bobby, handing her a receipt and his pencil.

Annie signed her name.

"Ta. Good luck to you, ma'am," he said, with a cheery twinkle, adding, "I'm thinkin' you'll be needin' it."

Undaunted, Annie welcomed the wary lads with a smile and led them upstairs to the bath. After giving them a good scrubbing, clean clothes and a bowl of Clara's hot leek and potato soup – which they devoured most appreciatively – she opened the envelope. 'I am anxious,' she read, 'to get these lads into your home. Both boys are pickpockets. Frank has been in prison 13 times and flogged 4 times. Sam's father died of a heart attack. Mother not strong enough to work. Family owed a horse and cart but horse became lame and could not be sold. Signed, S. Griffiths, sergeant at arms. Brockenhurst.'

The following morning a tribe of eleven children arrived in a horse-drawn van, they included five little girls. Scruffy, destitute urchins with runny noses, thieves and beggars with filthy hands and even dirtier hair, some shy, some noisy, all thin, troubled and abandoned.

The beadle accompanying the driver held nothing back as he handed them over. "All destitute and rescued from street," he announced. "Sign here, please." Annie signed, and he gave her an envelope. In it were eleven application forms from the 'Waifs and Strays Society. 23rd October, 1900', signed (illegibly) by a representative of the Authority of the Port of Southampton. Under every application was a potted history of each child: 'Mother died of cancer, father worthless drinking man.' 'Family disowned him, mother pawned child's clothes.' 'Pickpocket. Mother, charwoman and alcoholic, father sent to prison.' 'Orphan in temporary care of aunt', and on and on the sorry catalogue continued.

For the first time, Annie had doubts, but firmly hid them. With calm determination she promised herself she would do her utmost to give her charges the opportunity of a fresh start in life. At first she was unclear how to organize things, but her earlier training as a nursemaid came to the fore, and, slightly to her surprise, she discovered she had certain principles. Deal with every child as if it were your own, she told herself; give them three healthy meals a day, prayers, and top-to-toe washing. To reinforce her opinion, she decreed that her own children and baby Sarah should no longer be separated from the orphans in the cottage, they should all live together under the same roof. In the event – rather than take up two beds in the boys' dormitory – Reggie and Stan retained their bedroom in the cottage, but Annie insisted they all ate and lived in the orphanage.

It soon became apparent that a rota was needed for using the bathroom when the children got up and went to bed. By her matronly common sense this was achieved, and the children responded – as in most matters, they were grateful for some sort of discipline and affection in their lives.

Annie instinctively understood that the success of the Home and her own well being were mutually dependable, for to help young human beings grow and fulfill themselves is a wonderful undertaking. She guessed, though, that mighty challenges lay ahead.

Over the following weeks and months, babies were brought to her by lone mothers or fathers unable to cope, by nursemaids and nannies because their charges were unwanted, cast out through deformity, or abandoned because they were illegitimate. By the time the new year approached, when they were snowed in and the milk froze, one-year-old Sarah Smith had been joined by nineteen other young souls for the Christmas feast. 'Mister Albert' organized games by a roaring fire, there was music and singing, and a rowdy, jolly time was had by all.

Then on the 22nd January, the eighty-one-year-old Queen died. Millions mourned her passing and St Thomas' church bell tolled from the Georgian cupola in the High Street for one whole day. But a new age lay ahead. Goodwill throughout the Empire surrounded the new King Edward VII and his Queen. Hopes were high.

Chapter Three

By March, the day-to-day running of the orphanage had settled into a routine and Annie's days became less hectic. One windy morning, while baby Sarah was with the other young ones being looked after by Clara in the barn, and the older children were at their lessons (South Baddesley school was across the field and a mile along Snooks Lane), Annie was hanging out washing in her garden. She noticed Albert emerge from the woodland, he'd been cutting logs and was limping. As he approached she saw his trouser leg was torn and there was blood on his knee.

"Been trying to saw me leg off," he joked as he reached her. "Peg-leg Pete!"

"You great booby! However did you manage to do a thing like that? Here, let me." Placing herself under his arm she helped him stagger to the kitchen. "Sit yoursel' down. Rest that leg up here," she said, placing a chair under his calf and examining his knee. "For pity's sake, how on earth did this happen?"

"Me saw slipped. Awkward bloody branch snapped. Damn thing!"

"There's no need to swear, now," she chided, fetching her medical box.

"It's sure as hell a bloodied branch now. I'm telling you. Same as these 'ere trousers."

"Mm. Well, you'd better take 'em off. I can't clean the wound with that... bloody trouser leg flapping around, can I?" she grinned.

"She ticks me off for swearing, then orders me to take me trousers off!" Albert declared to the wall. "There's contradiction for you."

Annie pursed her lips. "Och! Keep your precious pants on. I'll cut round the trouser leg." Which she proceeded most carefully to do. "There. Now the dog can see the rabbit." She cleaned the gash and disinfected it, but the torn flesh still seeped blood. She applied antiseptic cream and covered the wound with lint. As she bandaged it, Albert watched her intently. When she'd finished, he reached up and kissed her on the lips. "Bless you," he whispered.

"Get along with you!" she said, flapping her hand at him. But she was not displeased. She'd found him primitively attractive from the first moment she'd set eyes on him, and certainly his light-hearted banter over the months had been a boon. Many a night as she lay in bed exhausted she'd had cause to thank the Reverend Ralph for recommending him. 'A warm, God-fearing fellow,' he'd said, and so he had proved. Albert had since made himself indispensable. "Better keep that leg up a while," she said, moving away to tidy away the scissors and ointment jar. "It's not a deep cut but you should rest it. I'll make us a cup of tea."

"I'd prefer another kiss," he said.

"You're getting as cheeky as yon boys over there," she said, indicating the barn.

"You wouldn't deny a wounded man comfort now, would you?"

"Albert Cox, you're full of blarney and that's a fact. You're a one, indeed you are!"

"Annie," he said, catching her wrist. "You're the best one in the whole wide world." Gently he pulled her to him. "Come now. How about a kiss?" He stretched up and kissed her rather more passionately than either of them had expected, unleashing starved and sublimated desires in both of them.

She looked at him confounded.

"I'm wanting you, Annie," he whispered. "Ever since I first saw you."

Playfully she answered, "Would that have been while you were playing the organ at St Thomas's?"

"It's true. And the good Lord answered my prayer. I came here to work with you."

"Albert, I...I'm.. "

"You're married, I know it. But without a husband. Where is he, eh? I'm here, woman, before you. Feel my arms round you. My flesh. The good Lord understands. It's a fine and noble love I'm havin' for you, Annie. Let me take care of you."

Annie caressed his face thoughtfully, her finger lingered on his lips.

Albert kissed her hand and reached up to kiss her again, his hand fondled her hair. He stood up, enfolding her in his arms.

Annie's whole being flooded with emotion. She broke their kiss and looked up into his eyes with astonished happiness. "Albert," she murmured.

"Annie," he breathed into her ear. "Can we go upstairs? I'm wanting you so."

Breathlessly Annie nodded.

Injured leg or no, Albert managed the stairs to her bedroom surprisingly swiftly. Once there he reminded Annie how much she'd missed being made love to, and how magnificent a fully-grown naked man's body was.

With a man back in her life, and an alpha male at that, stronger and more romantic than Fred had ever been, Annie's confidence grew. She felt more able, and her workload seemed to lighten. She'd always got on well with children, but in these numbers discipline was essential. At meal times the noise was sometimes deafening, it got so bad she had to insist on a silence rule. She became more strict, though punishments seldom exceeded being sent to bed with bread and water; only occasionally was there a thrashing.

Five evenings a week she taught Household Management. "The only way any of you will make anything of your lives is by becoming good servants. So listen well," she instructed. "Finding a place is a matter of vital importance to all of you." Annie's mother had been a housekeeper on a grand estate where Mrs Beaton's 'Book of Household Management' had been a highly-championed possession. Annie had inherited the copy. To these ragamuffin children unacquainted with even the names of kitchen articles, how to carry out delicate tasks like dusting china ornaments was anathema. She taught them everything, from cooking to manners, how to behave to employers, how to gain the confidence of tradesmen, and crucially, the importance of dress and speaking well – for all, her lessons were to prove indispensable. Annie hadn't been so busy since she'd been a scullery maid of fifteen on a wage of £6 a year. Now on a salary of £50 a year from the Lymington Waifs and Strays Church Committee, plus £104 a year for baby Sarah, she thought herself rich. Plus there were the 'sweeteners'.

Under the auspices of the Church of England, these forgotten children saved from destitution and vagrancy, begging, crime, drunkenness and loose morals were recycled and sold on as servants. For each sale, 'sweeteners' were offered. Along with the buyers of servants, sometimes barren married couples arrived at Annie's door wanting to adopt, these foster parents who came to inspect them, mostly preferred fair hair and chose the youngest and prettiest. Once, brown-haired, blue-eyed Sarah was chosen. But Sarah was worth more to Annie than any foster parent could afford in sweeteners. It didn't take her many seconds to redirect the couple on to another child. "Oh no," she laughed, "she's m'daughter. You can't have her." Her conscience never troubled her about this. When it occurred a second time, her proprietorial greed won through once again and Sarah was denied the promise of a better life.

In some instances, under the guise of foster parents, paedophiles would take Annie's charges away to their homes to abuse. These shop-soiled children were eventually returned to stock permanently damaged. Annie was learning from experience that caring for these children she had to be better and even more inflexible than parents at protecting them from harm. An adherent to the 'regular-bowel-movement' school of training, she used her fierce brand of religiosity to turn her charges into God-fearing and disciplined drudges. She became both feared and respected as she metamorphosed into a procurer and purveyor of children.

The three years that the Reverend Ralph had stipulated for an automatic divorce passed, and after the relevant papers were issued and signed, Annie became free. Though to be a divorced woman would have meant becoming a social pariah, Annie's situation was slightly easier. Her position as a deserted wife was well known in the neighbourhood, in truth, it had given rise to a certain amount of sympathy for such an obviously useful citizen. Her reputation was growing. Clara's opinion was typical of many. "She's a woman of remarkable strength of character," she confided to her local biddies. "She devotes herself to those children day and night, and all for the public good, for without her they'd all be on the streets."

When the popular church warden, Albert Cox, announced his intended betrothal to Annie, there was general approval and few detractors.

On the summer afternoon they returned from Lyndhurst Registry Office dressed in their Sunday best as Mr and Mrs Albert Cox, the boys had put out trellis tables in the field overlooking the Isle of Wight, the girls had covered them with white table cloths and laid out sandwiches, crumpets and tea. As a surprise, Clara baked a two-tiered wedding cake which she proudly brought out to hearty cheers. Friends, neighbours, orphans and

South Baddesley schoolchildren alike, joined in the merrymaking. As evening fell, lanterns were lit, a fiddler appeared, there was singing, beer and cider for the grown-ups, and, at a separate table, lemonade and ginger pop for the children, a convention the younger boys subverted by a cunning combination of bottle-swapping teamwork and hiding under tablecloths.

That night the bed in the supervisor's cub in the dormitory was unoccupied.

So it was that Annie Oliphant changed her name, and, among her band of little unfortunates, acquired the sobriquet 'Ma Cox'.

Chapter Four
June 1908

Sarah's toes were plainly sticking out of her scruffy boots. Annie stood, arms akimbo, frowning down at them. "However did you get them into that state?"

"I grow'd," said Sarah.

"She really should have new," said Annie, addressing Albert, whose immense frame lay sprawled across the sofa reading 'The Hampshire Chronicle'.

"It says here," he said, "'The Fourth Olympic Games are to open in London on the 13th July.' Wouldn't mind going up to see some of them. Take the boys. What do you say?"

"Be far too expensive for the likes of us," dismissed Annie. "What about this girl's shoes?"

"If she has new, then why not Reggie?" reasoned Albert, winking at his stepson behind the newspaper. "The boy's so down at heel he has but a tenth of an inch left."

"'Cause one twin can't have new unless t'other one does."

"So be it, then," reasoned Albert. "There's a tidy enough sum in the pot over the mantle. Come Saturday, let's buy 'em all new. These two stout souls deserve a pair of good stout soles!"

Annie pursed her lips and flapped her hand at him. "Albert Cox, you'd persuade the King of England black was white!"

Reggie and Stan flung themselves on top of Albert laughing, while Sarah stood in her smock grinning up at Annie.

On such minor decisions can the direction of our lives depend. So it came about, that the following Saturday, on a fine blue-sky summer morning, eight-year-old Sarah, wearing her brown floppy beret, clambered aboard the wagon with Reggie and Stan, to sit behind Albert as he took up the reins alongside Annie, for the two mile shopping trip to Lymington High Street.

The mature lady in the shoe shop – of grand proportions and confident manner, suitable to the serious business of shoe-fitting – having helped Annie fit up her boys, turned her attention to measuring Sarah's foot. Noticing her pretty apple-pink face and sparkling eyes staring at a pair of red-buttoned shoes on display, she addressed Annie. "Such a dainty foot. Narrower fitting than her brothers'. Can I show madam these?"

Annie allowed Sarah to try on the red, but considered them far too showy and expensive. Instead, she purchased a pair of practical black lace-ups.

Sarah was never one to sulk. She skipped outside the shop showing off her new shoes to the bustling bonneted ladies on the pavement, enjoying the quantity and quality of the people passing to and fro, the horseback riders, cyclists and carrier's wagons crossing and recrossing the busy High Street. Outside a Georgian house, a sign announced, 'School for Young Ladies. Misses Noake & Banks'. Sarah pressed her nose to the window and looked in.

Annie joined her. *This is the school we should be sending her to.*

Inside, a girl with ringlets and frills looked at them, she poked out her tongue and haughtily tossed her curls.

"What a horrid girl," said Sarah, not in the least piqued. "I'm glad I don't go to that school."

Annie smiled to herself. "Come," she said. "We have to go to the butcher's."

After making their purchases from Mr Dickinson at No 6, and

gossiping about the recent freak hailstorm, they wandered back to the wagon. Sarah ran ahead with the boys to look into a sweet shop window. Suddenly she stopped. She'd heard music and turned to see where it was coming from.

"Look!" she called. "A gypsy man."

They all looked in the direction of her pointed finger.

By the roadside stood a busker playing an accordion.

"Her brow is like the snowdrift," he sang.

"Her throat is like a swan,

Her face it is the fairest,

That ere the sun shone on."

Annie screwed up her eyes and peered at the fellow. There was something familiar about his brows. Drawing nearer she examined him closer. Unshaven and haggard, with hair down to his shoulders and tramp-like clothes he looked nearer forty-two than her first husband, Fred Oliphant's thirty-two years. A stab of pain hit the pit of her stomach at the memory of his traumatic departure from her life eight years ago. Her eyes focused on the man's bitten fingernails playing the keyboard. It was then she was certain.

"Oliphant!" she cried. "What do you think you're doing?"

"Hallo, gel!" he grinned, as he continued playing. "How goes it?"

"Me?" replied Annie. "I'm just dandy. It's you I'm thinking needs some vitals inside o'you."

"Ah, well. Didn't 'ave much luck with the Froggies. Came over to see these 'ere Olympic Games. Thought I'd stop off 'ere, like," and he picked up his song again.

"And dark blue is her 'ee

And for bonnie Annie Laurie

I'll lay me doon and dee." Flashing his white-toothed grin, he added, "Thought I'd come back to where I'd been happy, like." One by one he scrutinised his ten-year-old gawping sons in their knicker-bockers, caps and new boots. "Be those our Reggie and Stan?"

"They certainly are," said Annie, unyielding.

"And yon girlie?" he frowned at Sarah. "Is she the one the madam left?"

"You'll get my toe in your rear end if you don't watch y'mouth," said Annie squaring her jaw and firmly locking her arm through Albert's. "This is my man, Albert. He lives with us now. All legal. We was wed three years back."

"Howdy do," said Albert, manfully grasping Fred's hand and shaking it. "Glad to know you. Heard a deal about you."

Fred's mouth gaped.

"Close y'mouth," said Annie, "you look like a string of dripping standing there. Don't seem to have collected much in yon hat o'yours. It's a square meal I'm thinking you need. Where y' staying?"

He shrugged. "Wherever the Fates land me."

Regarding him ruefully she chewed the inside of her lower lip. "Better fetch up with us, then?" Flashing a glance up at her husband for reassurance, she asked, "Right, Bert?"

"Why not?" said Albert. From his superior height he considered his predecessor. "Like a bit of music round the house. Play piano meself. Y'welcome," and he slapped him on the back. "Just got in some steak and kidney. Makes a fair pie, she does."

Fred gave him a wary smile and picked up his hat from the pavement to pocket the change, "I remember," he said.

Annie indicated the horse and wagon ahead, and ambling nonchalantly towards it, as if picking up an ex-husband of a Saturday morning was a casual affair like picking up the fish, said, "That's our wagon. New since your day."

"The mare too," observed Fred.

Into the wagon they all bundled. Reggie and Stan sitting in

silence at the back staring up at their scruffy father, while Sarah studied the accordion at his feet and wondered how the music played. In front, Annie put her hand on her husband's wrist and whispered, "Sure you're all right with this?"

Albert flicked the reins to urge the mare forward, "'Course," he murmured.

The wagon trundled across Lymington River Bridge, and after a mile's drive up the dirt track lane they reached home. A rather different home to the one Fred had deserted eight years ago.

"What's all this?" he asked, looking up in amazement at his old barn, now rebuilt with a chimney stack, upstairs windows, and on the door, Albert's sign, 'OPEN ALL NIGHT'.

"We're an orphanage now," answered Annie, brusquely, collecting up her packages as Albert turned the horse from the track into the shingle area by the barn. During the drive, a combination of anxiety and anger had replaced her initial confidence in issuing her invitation. "Had to make ends meet somehow after you did a bunk." The wagon came to a standstill. "Save young'uns from crime, drunkardness and loose morals, we do. Daresay you might know a bit about that?"

Albert glanced at his wife and hid a smirk. "Reggie," he called, "help y' Ma down."

Reggie jumped down and held up his hand.

"Ta, luv'," said Annie, taking it and alighting.

"Who paid for it all?" asked Fred.

"The Parish," answered Albert. "Authorities of the Port of Southampton, and charitable gentry folk. Mind the stable doors, Stan," he ordered, leaping down.

"Here," said Annie, handing her food parcels to Sarah who'd just alighted. "Take these to Mrs Woods. See if you can help her with the children's lunch."

Sarah obeyed and the boys ran towards the stable doors.

Annie took the path to the cottage. "I'll take you over there later," she called to Fred, who was gazing up at the barn with his accordion over his shoulder. "Once you're more presentable."

Albert caught the bridle to lead the mare into the stable. From between the animal's ears, he thoughtfully watched his wife lead Fred into their home.

Before matters went any further, Annie decided there were a few personal and delicate matters she had to clarify: like a scrub-down, a haircut, a change of clothing, and, crucially, the sleeping arrangements. Swiftly, she made the position clear. "I'll give you a square meal and you can kip down on the sofa, but only for tonight, mind. After that, you're on your way."

Albert loaned him his shaving kit, trousers and a shirt – which hung on him very loosely – and Annie gave him a haircut. She felt curiously pleased to have him around her again. It was only when she spotted the covetous look in his eye as he peered round noting the changes in the cottage – the least of which was Edward VII's gilt-framed photograph hanging over the stove instead of Queen Victoria's – she guessed his intention.

"You're not staying," she said firmly. "This is only a one night thing."

Come Sunday morning, Fred joined the family and all the children in the orphanage for breakfast. Chastley, he asked, "All off to church, are we? Time with the Lord is time well spent."

Whether he was sincere, or whether his words were said to oil his way in, Annie didn't wish to look into.

"Like to come with us?" offered Albert.

"Very much," said Fred.

Annie had a secondary interest in attending church on this particular Sunday morning. During the week she'd been surprised to learn that the Reverend Ralph had married, and it was assumed that this Sunday, his new wife would be in church.

The church was full. Obviously the vicar's parishioners were just as curious as Annie to make their assessments of his new bride.

After the service, the Rev. Ralph, as was his habit, greeted his congregation outside under the entrance porch. Today, his wife stood at his side. There was ne'er a blush in sight, for Mrs Christiana Ambrose turned out to be a forthright, wellborn 'blue stocking' of thirty-five years or so. Annie knew her slightly. She was the sister of a gentleman to whom she'd once been in service. There were introductions and pleasantries, and the Rev. Ralph greeted Fred with an ease of manner and bland expression as if he'd been absent from his congregation for merely a fortnight. Though Annie noticed one or two of her neighbours eyeing Fred curiously.

Walking home by the field holding Sarah's hand, with the other children running alongside, she observed her husband chatting side by side with Fred up ahead. She admitted to herself it was going to be a wrench to turn him away. Then, after lunch, watching him from the kitchen window play football in his loose-limbed way with his sons, Albert, and some of the orphanage boys, she relented. *He fits in with everyone. Albert seems to like him. Just one more day,* she thought.

That night Fred slept with his sons in their bed.

In the next room, Annie sat up in bed plaiting her hair. In a low voice – for the walls were thin – she said, "Just as well we never asked Reggie and Stan to call you 'Dad', eh? We was thinking of doing so in the beginning, remember?"

"Do indeed," answered Albert, standing in his socks and unbuttoning his collarless shirt. "But no one can replace a boy's true Dad."

"I'm thinking you've been doing a mighty fine job of it. And I don't mean just my two."

"You too, 'Ma Cox'," he grinned, clambering into bed beside her. Leaning his head on the back of his bare arm, he said, "You know, it's my belief, if he had some proper work to do, if he had an anchor, like, he'd batten down, turn over a new leaf. It's no Christian act to turn the lads' Dad out onto the street."

"I know," murmured Annie, resting her head on his chest. "Sometimes, Bert, I think you're too good for me."

"Gertcha!" he said, wrapping his arms round her and giving her a hug.

The following Monday morning, on the third day of Fred's stopover, Annie faced him.

"If you want to stay, you'll have to earn your keep. We could do with an extra hand to keep discipline in the barn." Doubtfully she regarded him. "Are you up to it?"

"Told you, I always been happy at Lymington, Annie."

Meekly, he followed every instruction Annie and Albert gave him, from cleaning out the stables and pigsty, to mopping down the dormitories and cleaning the children's washroom. By the end of the week he'd established himself in the supervisor's cub upstairs in the barn.

Fred Oliphant was back and on the parish payroll.

Chapter Five

arah was not told of Fred's previous marriage to Annie until she heard of it from the twins.

"Ma said he was our Dad!" said Reggie. "We had to share our bed with him!"

"Gosh!" said Sarah, impressed. "Well, at least you know who your Dad is. Wish I knew who mine was."

From then on she looked at Fred with more interest and a certain amount of sympathy. She also studied Albert more closely, for she was sensitive enough to realise his situation was an odd one.

If Albert did experience any pang of jealousy at Fred's presence, he certainly disguised it well. For not only did he treat him with respect, and work alongside him with humour, but on the Saturday night music-making ritual, he invited him to join him at the piano with his accordion to play duets. So big was Albert's heart and so great was his confidence in Annie, that not for a moment did he exhibit one jot or tit of envy at the return of his wife's first love.

The resentment Fred had initially harboured toward him gradually melted before Albert's warm-hearted and disarming generosity, but it was not long before a stronger, more insidious rancour grew in him. Until now, Fred had never relished the role of father, but over the weeks and months that followed, as he tried to get to know and win round his sons, as they reluctantly agreed to call him 'Dad', it became clear to him that they much preferred

Albert's company to his own. A pain welled up in his breast. His boys clearly worshipped Albert. He watched enviously as they pleaded with his rival to play with them when they returned from school, as they fought to sit next to him at meal times, as they clambered over him as he sat in his armchair in the evenings by the fire. Knowing himself, and aware that his jealousy, unless controlled, might turn to vindictiveness, Fred took pains to control himself, for penniless and without a home, he badly needed Albert's approbation.

He took to competing for popularity among the children by singing comic songs and ballads in the evenings and telling stories of his adventures – the repeatable ones – in foreign parts. His description of seeing a magical moving picture show called the cinematopraphe in a Paris Music Hall had them all amazed. Reggie and Stan always sat with Albert as they listened; Sarah sat either at his feet or curled up on the sofa beside him. She listened goggle-eyed as he told his tales. He told of playing his accordion in cafes on the Left Bank, of having to paint the interior of one of them to pay for his lodgings; of visiting Amsterdam, where everyone wore clogs and he worked in the tulip fields; and while in Rouen, he'd seen the very spot where Joan of Arc was burnt at the stake. When he played 'The Grand Old Duke of York' and 'Bill Bailey Won't You Please Come Home', Sarah's voice was always the first to join in, but her favourite was 'In the Good Old Summer Time', which, once she'd learned the words, became their party piece.

"Ma," she asked Annie, after one such jolly evening, as she was helping with the drying up in the orphanage kitchen. "Is Mister Fred's second name, Mister Smith?"

"No. Whatever gave you that idea?"

"I wondered if he could be my Da, as well as Reggie and Stan's?"

Annie stared at her in astonishment. "Good heavens, child, you get the strangest notions. You know well enough Reggie and Stan are not your kin. You're a foundling."

"Yes, but Mr Fred said he said he knew me when I was a bairn."

"Aye, that's true enough, but that's not to say he's your Da. No more than I'm your Ma."

"Who was me Ma, Ma?"

"What a question!" Annie looked at her hard. "Ach, maybe I should have explained earlier." Drying her hands, she sat herself at the kitchen table. "Come here, lass. Sit down. It's time you knew about yourself."

Sarah's big blue eyes never left Annie's face.

"No. Mister Fred's not your Da, child, that's one thing you can be certain of. It's just that when I took you in, he and I was wed. As to who y' Da really was, I've not a notion. I thought of the name Smith, 'cause that was my Ma's name. As to *your* Ma's name, well..." Annie considered with knitted brow and saw no reason to deviate from the story she'd told the Reverend. "I've not a notion of that either. You were a gift from God, that's certain. We found you on the doorstep."

"Didn't me Ma want me?"

"She gave you to me. Think on' t that way, pet. And mighty glad I am that she did, too, 'cause since you came into my life, it's been a blessing and that's a fact. You were the very first of my new big family to arrive. So you forget your mother, pet, just pray daily that her sins be not visited on you. There, now dry your tears, that's no' so bad, is it?"

But Sarah's eyes were dry, and she was still no nearer answering the question that had occupied her thoughts for as long as she could remember. The question she'd spent so many solitary hours wondering about, sitting on the shingle beach withstanding wind and rain, staring out over the mud flats watching the foaming waves and passing sailing vessels. *I wonder who they were? I wonder what happened to me Ma and Da?*

Lying in her dormitory bed that night with the other girls, she wondered again. *Still, till the day I find out, Mister Fred, with his black curly hair and his songs and lovely voice, is the bestest person I know.*

For the August bank holiday treat, Annie and Albert decided on an outing to the Woodbury Fair, thirty miles away. But the carrier's wagon only sat ten, so six people were going to have to stay behind.

"I seen Woodbury Fair dozen o' times," said Clara. "I'll stay home wi' the young'uns."

"I don't mind either," said Fred. "I'll take t'others on a row boat trip. We'll explore the estuary up to Brockenhurst." He winked broadly at his sons. "Who'll come with me?"

Sarah's hand shot up, then five others.

But Reggie and Stan's hands were not among them.

It was a magnificent day. One of those perfect summer afternoons one dreams about in childhood, in old age, too, come to that. The sky was blue and cloudless, the larks were singing high above the trees, and dragonflies skimmed the water as Fred rowed up the peacefully flowing glinting river. Fred sat amidships, four small boys sat fore, and aft, facing him, sat Sarah and Robert – a bigger boy who'd tried and failed to kiss Sarah two days before, but who was now exceedingly glad to be sitting next to her. Holidaymakers were hiring boats when they'd started out, but as they progressed up river, they lost them and seemed to be quite alone. Once, they waved to a couple on the bank who waved back, and a trout fisherman scowled as they passed, but otherwise all was still and summery. The magical sylvan setting lulled Sarah and Robert, each little boy, and even Fred – who, with all his shortcomings, could appreciate a good view – into their own secret, almost holy, state of bliss. Each bend in the river revealed more leafy oaks and beeches, further sunny reeded banks, with endless fields of ripening cream-coloured corn beyond.

"A kingfisher!" cried Fred, catching sight of a blue bird swooping ahead. They all turned and saw the kingfisher dive into the water and emerge with a fish in its beak. "Supper for his family tonight!" he laughed, opening his shirt, letting the breeze cool his hairy chest. Pulling on the oars, he revelled in his strength, the stretching sensation in his muscles, the exertion in his loins and legs as he strained to propel them forward. He noticed the hairs on the back of Sarah's slim arms gleaming in the sun. Brushing the sweat from his brow with his forearm, he grinned at her. Shyly she smiled back, the tips of her white teeth peeping between her sweet pink lips, her peach-like cheeks dimpled. *Albert may have my sons, but I've got sweet Sarah.*

At the Woodbury Fair, standing by the carousel, Annie and Albert watched the brightly painted wooden horses with barley sugar posts going up and down, and round and round. The fairground music from the paper rolls blared out gaily as they waited for their charges to finish their ride. Outside one of the booths Annie noticed a gaudy poster-painting of a mermaid swimming: 'SEE THE ONLY LIVING MERMAID IN CAPTIVITY'.

She grabbed Albert's arm. "Sarah can't swim. I forgot to tell Fred, Sarah can't swim."

"Not to worry," Albert reassured her. "She's a sensible girl."

"Yes. And Fred's a strong swimmer. It's just, I suddenly felt she was in danger."

"Now, can everyone swim?" Fred asked as he spotted a wooden landing platform ahead.

"Yes," the lads cried in unison.

Fred tied off the boat and the boys clambered onto the bank, immediately stripping off. Five naked skinny little boys ran and splashed into the green water, shouting with joy. Fred, too, slipped off his trousers and underpants and dove in.

Sarah took off her shoes and socks to paddle. Taking care not to get her smock wet, she tucked it up into her bloomers. Stepping into the cool water with waving tresses of green weed beneath, she wrinkled up her nose as the mud squelched up between her toes. Young Robert splashed her. Frowning, she shied away from him.

Eventually, when they'd all had enough, the boys came out and modestly put on their knickerbockers to lie on the bank, drying themselves in the sun.

Fred just put on his underpants. "Should have thought of bringing a picnic," he said.

There was teasing talk of bread and dripping, cakes and lemonade.

Robert asked, "Where does that path lead to?"

"Brokenhurst," answered Fred, lighting up a Woodbine, "where there's a bun shop!"

"Hurrah!" they all chirped. "Can we go?"

"'Long as you bring one back for me," he said.

"Me too," shouted Sarah, as they scampered off.

Fred, glowing from his swim, lay back sunbathing and blowing smoke rings.

Sarah watched him. "How do you do that?"

Fred chuckled.

"Mr Albert does it with his pipe."

"Does he indeed?"

Sarah brushed her feet clean and put on her socks and boots.

Fred tossed his cigarette butt into the river and pulled on his trousers. Flipping his braces over his bare shoulders, he carried his shirt and jacket. Following the boys along the pathway he called, "Coming?"

Sarah joined him, and side-by-side they walked in silence. Casually he put his hand round her shoulder.

Annie's mouth opened in a silent scream as she slid down the helter-skelter grasping an excited Reggie sitting on her lap.

Albert was waiting for them at the bottom. Scooping them up into his arms he laughed, "No more, Reggie. Your Ma's gone green!" Clasping her to him, he laughed, "It's grand to see you enjoying yourself!"

"M'be it's time we made tracks. I'm feeling guilty. Worried about them all on the river."

"Fred knows what he's doing. He'll take care of them. Stop fretting, woman. Look, there's a gypsy tent. Fancy having your fortune told?"

"Why didn't you come in for a swim?" Fred asked as they walked.

"Can't."

"Can't swim? You should 'ave said. I could 'ave learned you."

"Got my smock wet," she said, squeezing out a wet patch from her skirt.

"Proper little lady, aren't ya? So which of those lads up ahead is your boyfriend? Young Robert, is it?"

"'Course not," she answered indignantly.

"Don't tell me a pretty girl like you don't have a sweetheart?"

"Don't be silly."

"Who are you calling silly?" he said tickling her.

Sarah wriggled away. "You."

"I'll get you for that," he shouted.

Weaving out of his grasp she ran into the wheat field next to the path, jumping and enjoying the feel of the high stems lashing against her body.

Fred was gaining on her.

On she ran, laughing.

At last he caught up and they tumbled over into the wheat breathless. Rolling on top of her, he lifted himself on his palms and looked into her eyes.

Sarah laughed but her smile faded as she took in his expression. She tried to smile but couldn't.

"You smell wonderful," he said.

Cautiously she said, "You've got a very hairy chest."

Fred grinned and flipped down his braces.

Timidly she extended her fingers to stroke the smooth black chest-hair.

To her surprise he suddenly kissed her on the side of her neck.

"The corn stalks are sticking into my back," she said trying to wriggle away.

"Give us a kiss," he said.

"Get off,' she said. 'You're heavy."

"Relax," he grinned. "Leave everything to me." Opening his flies he bent down.

Hidden in the high ripe wheat, they were both lost from sight.

The warm smell of dry earth and the silence of satisfied summer hovered like a haze over the sunny field. If you listened very carefully, the perpetual buzz of bees could be heard. High in the blue sky a lark sang.

Suddenly Sarah's scream cut through the warm air.

The lark stopped singing for a moment, curious perhaps, then continued.

Bing! rang the bell high above the fairground.

"Hurrah!" Reggie and Stan shrieked. "Knew you would."

Annie clapped her hands and Albert set down the wooden mallet, grinning. "Just as well! The shame, if I hadn't!" Just as he was putting on his jacket, the stallholder handed him his prize. A big fuzzy coconut, and the children cheered.

"Our secret," said Fred, pulling her up by her arm.

Sarah allowed herself to be stood up. In great pain she staggered through the corn field back to the riverbank. Once there, she sank onto the grass, nursing the ache in her uterus and staring into the green water.

Fred stripped off again and dove into the water. "Come on in," he shouted. "It's beautiful. Don't be afraid, I'll hold you."

Sarah stood up and obeyed.

Before Fred could reach her, she'd sat down fully dressed in the water and was crying.

"I knew there'd be an accident," said Annie as she washed through Sarah's dress that evening. "I had a feeling. I was worried sick you'd fall in and drown. What's this mark? Is this blood here? Did you hurt yourself?"

"She fell on her knee," said Fred, looking at Sarah, "but she's fine now, aren't you, pet?"

Sarah puckered her mouth and made a face.

Annie glanced at her. "Well, before you go out on any boats again, my girl, you make sure you learn to swim. Fred! That's something you can do. Teach her to swim."

That night in the dormitory Fred winked at her as he passed her bed before dousing the oil lamp. She lay in the dark nursing the pain between her legs and remembering. *This has been the horridest day of my life. What did I do wrong? How did it happen? How could I have stopped him? How did I ever like him?*

He's nasty and wicked and I hate him. Wish he was dead. I thought he was my friend. Sobbing quietly she fell asleep.

A door slowly swung open. The room was filled with sheaves of wheat.

"Spin all this straw to gold," said Ma Cox, "and you'll marry a king."

"But I don't know how."

"I'll help you," said the goblin. "Here, sit on my knee and stroke my hair."

Sarah sat on his knee and stroked his goat-like hairy chest.

"Guess my name," said the goblin, "And I'll turn the straw to gold."

"Rumplestiltskin!" she cried.

The goblin became furious and transformed into Mister Fred. He pounced onto her, squeezing her tight... so tight.

Sarah awoke in pain. Fred was twisting her toe at the bottom of her bed. 'Into my cub," he whispered.

Disoriented at first, she didn't understand. But as she watched him in the dim light tiptoe past the other girls' beds back to his supervisor's cub, she realised. She shut her eyes tightly and tried to go back to sleep – but not to dream.

The next morning she avoided him, but when she came back from school and was sitting having supper, he passed on the other side of the table and winked again.

Later, in the stables, while she was standing on a box grooming her favourite horse, he sauntered in. "Why didn't you come to me?" he asked, grinning and sidling up beside her like a hairy satyr. "Y' like being with me, don't you?"

Sarah carried on brushing the horse, wanting to answer 'no', but not daring to.

"Why not, eh? We could have 'ad a good time." Fred stroked

the animal's flank as he searched her eyes.

"Didn't want to," she barely breathed. "Was sleepy."

"Come tonight."

She stepped off the box to get away from him.

"Come here." He pulled her into the corner.

"I got work to do."

"It can wait, can't it?" He took the brush from her hand and threw it to the ground. "No one can see us here. Here, feel me."

She tried to pull away.

He put his mouth to her neck and pressed himself against her. His chin was bristly and he smelt of beer. "You're a little peach, ain't ye? Don't go. Here, feel this." He unbuttoned his trousers and, taking her hand, put it inside.

Sarah froze, staring up at him in horror.

"Come on, now. Don't look at me like that. I'll tell Annie what you did, if you're not careful. She'll throw you out on the street, she will. Chuck you out with nowhere to go. What would you do then, eh? Come on, now. We're friends, ain't we? Just kiss it for me. Go on." He put his other hand on her head and pushed her down. "There's a good girl."

Terrified, she did what she was told.

Three days later, it happened again. On the way to the beach, Fred took her arm and led her into the woodland. When they got to a clearing, he laid his coat on the ground, and there, he raped her again.

Despite what Fred had told her, Sarah just knew she had to tell Ma Cox.

Feeling wretched and fearful, she waited till she was sure she'd catch her alone.

Come Saturday morning, while Annie was chopping up vegetables in the cottage kitchen, Sarah crept in and closed the door.

"Ma," she said shyly. "I want to tell you something."

"What's that, luvvy?"

"I don't like Mr Fred playing with me."

"Tell him to leave you alone, then."

"He lifts my skirt and does nasty things."

Annie turned to her with the knife in her hand and looked at her hard. Her face was tense with fury and her eyes flashed as her nostrils flared. Then her eyes closed, as if she sought to control herself. Sarah didn't know what to expect, for a moment she thought Annie was going to go off like a bottle of pop, find Mr Fred and stab him. Then she put the knife down and advanced toward her. "Now look here, missy," she said steadily. "You stop that. Don't you dare come to me with wicked lies like that about your elders."

"But he does, Ma!"

Annie turned away. "One more word and I'll beat the living daylights out of you."

"But it's true, Ma."

Annie picked up the birch rod she beat the carpet with, and grabbing Sarah, thrashed her within a inch of her life. Sarah had never known her so angry.

The following week, Fred lead her into the woodlands.

Again she did as she was told.

Sarah went on doing what she was told for the next six years.

On the 6th May, 1910, just nine years after succeeding to the throne, Edward VII died, and his second son became King George V, and Sarah grew up, as thousands of others of her kind before, abused among the forgotten children.

Then in August 1914, at the height of another summer, the Great War broke out, and Fred Oliphant and Albert Cox, in a mood of high-spirited patriotism, volunteered to 'Put the Kibosh on the Kaiser'.

Chapter Six

Determined to do well, Albert, and, by now his 'mate', Fred, joined a specially formed "Pals' Battalion" and sailed to France with the Royal Hampshire regiment.

Annie had a letter from Albert saying how he loved the army. It's like a game. I've not seen action yet, I dread it, but army life is grand, though I shouldn't like it in peacetime. His second letter after the battle of Marne in September was very different.

I hate this business with all my heart. This beautiful countryside has become a desolate wasteland, like one great cemetery, dead bodies wherever you go. Thousand upon thousands of men robbed of life, and thousands more wounded. I look on peace and home life with you as a dream of summer. All I want is to be able to live quietly with you and the children and tend our garden. I am sorry to be writing such a gloomy letter, but I can no longer look upon war from a cheery point of view.

Fred didn't write at all, but then, he never had.

In the sky over the Isle of Wight, Reggie and Stan, who were now teenagers, saw marvelous patterns at night made by ships' searchlights on the lookout for Zeppelins. Immediately they wanted to join up. Annie forbade them. But a year later when they turned eighteen, she could no longer prevent them. They too sailed to France, from where they wrote, enclosing three photographs of themselves in uniform.

These cost a tanner. Our faces look white with

the electric photo lights, but really we are both very brown. Let us know how you like us in uniform. We have not got our belts yet so the tunics look something long. We had it a bit rough last week but it's done us no harm. It is quite exciting and surprising what we can take.

Love Reggie and Stan.

With the men away fighting, both orphanage and village became a woman's enclave with the sight of the post-woman on her bicycle becoming feared as the new harbinger of death.

Sarah joined the Women's Forestry Corps. Timber being a vital commodity for the war, great areas of the New Forest were felled for fuel, for construction, paper, for packing cases, ammunition boxes and duck boards for the trenches. At sixteen she'd become a very pretty girl, with large blue eyes, a full mouth, and a sprinkling of freckles over her tup-tilted nose, her golden brown hair, she wore coiled up in a bun at the nape of her neck. Tanned and thin, she laboured in unglamorous heavy corduroy breeches and a canvas smock as she felled trees, stripped bark, ground axes, and undertook all manner of manual work, but she only worked in the forest part-time, for Annie needed her help more than ever at the orphanage.

On a Spring morning in April, 1916, early, before the clouds had cleared and the sun was struggling to shine through, Sarah, as was her habit on a Monday morning, was scrubbing the hearthstone and front steps of Annie's cottage. The daffodils and bluebells she'd planted by the door and alongside the barn were in full bloom. Perhaps because Spring was in the air, perhaps because she had the percipience to know her life was soon to change, she felt unaccountably happy. For, despite her undernourished childhood and the abuse she'd endured, her personality had about it a sweetness – a stoic, almost noble, tractability. Inside, though, she still hurt, Fred had scarred her deeply. She'd come to despise herself for her early willingness to please a man she now feared and abhorred. Deeply shamed, not wanting to make trouble and afraid of not being believed, she'd kept silent. Since Annie had thrashed her for "making up such wicked lies", she'd lost trust in her and felt more alone than ever. Had it not been for the constant companionship of younger children, children far worse off than herself, helpless, needy children wanting comfort and love, her tenderness of heart, which might otherwise have numbed, remained intact – at least, directed as it was towards children and animals. She'd not forgotten what had happened to her, but she had learnt to live with the memory, and more recently, sharing confidences with girls her own age in the Women's Forestry Corps, she'd managed to focus her self-preservation. Whatever ancestral genes were working within her they were of a pragmatic nature, for she had successfully achieved a more healthy, optimistic approach in the two years since Fred had left. By reading, too, she had broadened her mind and encouraged a resolve not to look backwards, nor to ruminate on past negatives.

Rubbing a bar of shale oil soap onto the scrubbing brush (for Annie did not approve of whitening the hearthstone), Sarah's attention was caught by the sound of an automobile coming along the lane. She looked up to see a magnificent silver grey motor vehicle drawing up outside the gate. A uniformed chauffeur got out and walked round the front bonnet to open the passenger door.

An elegant lady in black stepped out. She wore a shoulder-wide brimmed velvet hat with a heavy veil, a long fur wrap and a matching muff. Descending the running board, a breeze caught her veil. As she walked it billowed out drifting behind her, outlining her profile like a cameo silhouette. Her neatly-gloved hand reached out from her muff and opened the picket gate. It squeaked, for since Albert had gone to war, no one had bothered to oil it.

Kneeling by her bucket of dirty water, Sarah watched the gliding figure approaching. Never before had she witnessed such poise, such grace.

The lady stopped and looked down. "Good morning, child."

"Mornin' ma'am," she murmured respectfully.

"Could you tell me if Mrs Cox is at home, please?" The lady's voice was low and cultured, her manner, Edwardian.

"Yes, ma'am," answered Sarah, admiring the pair of polished buttoned boots before her.

"Would you be good enough to take me to her?'

"She's across in the Home, ma'am." Pushing her hair away from her eyes with her wrist, she wiped her hands on her apron and stood up. "This way, ma'am."

But the lady remained stationary, her hands in her muff. "A minute," she said. "It's Sarah Smith, is it not?"

Sarah turned and looked into the lady's face, which was difficult through the heavy veiling. Feeling as if she were standing before the Head at South Baddesley School, she answered, "Yes, miss. I mean, ma'am."

The lady carefully lifted her veil. "And do you know who I am?"

Sarah looked at the powdered once-beautiful middle-aged face. The lady's eyes were a penetrating steel blue, but there was a sadness about her expression. Her lips were quite without colour. "No, ma'am."

"I'm one of the Governors here. I've noticed you before." She looked her up from top to toe.

She's thinking how tall I am. Everyone always says how tall I am.

"You're the Head Girl here, I'm told."

"Yes, ma'am."

The lady turned and started along the path by the cottage leading to the courtyard. "Tell me, what work do you do here?"

Cheerfully scurrying in her wake, Sarah explained, "Maid of all work me, ma'am. Scrub, clean, cook, mend, look after the bairns. Scrub and clean them, too! Look after the animals. Joined the Women's Forestry Corps, too, last year, I did."

"Did you? How patriotic. I approve. How many children are there at present?"

"Twenty-two, ma'am."

"As many as that? They are all at school, I take it?"

"Yes, ma'am. 'Cept the bairns and toddlers."

"Education is of vital importance. You have finished your schooling?"

"Nearly two years back."

"What were your favourite subjects?"

"Numbers, the mathematics."

"Excellent. That will be most useful."

"And stories."

"Stories?" The lady stopped in her tracks. "You mean literature?"

"Yes, ma'am. I read the bible stories, and last month I read 'Jane Eyre' by Currer Bell."

The lady blinked. "I'm surprised you found the time." Continuing her perambulation, she added dryly, "I'm told it's rather depressing."

"Oh no, ma'am. But it is a tad sad."

"Tad! Ah yes. Well, life is, life is. So tell me, do you enjoy all this work you do?"

"Like looking after the animals best, ma'am."

"Ah yes, the pigsty. I thought I could smell something."

"Wind's a bit breezy this morning ma'am."

"Indeed." The lady looked around vaguely. Her attention caught by the waving daffodils and bluebells by the barn wall, she murmured, "Delightful combination. Delightful."

"Thank you, ma'am."

"Why do you thank me?"

"That's my bit of the garden, ma'am. Ma Cox said I could do that bit."

"Ah! Why did you choose to plant flowers?" Abruptly she stopped to look at her. "Why not vegetables in time of war?"

"Vegetables are at the back, ma'am, by the stables." The lady remained looking at her, seemingly requiring an answer. Sarah shrugged, "I just like flowers."

The lady's eyes softened as she studied her. "So do I, so do I. Well. It seems you do a good deal around here, Sarah Smith. You speak nicely, too." Turning to proceed across the courtyard, she said, "Would you like to come and work for me at The Hall?"

"Oh, ma'am!"

"Oh, ma'am what?"

"No one's ever asked for me before."

"Well, I'm asking you now."

"What would I have to do, ma'am?"

"You could help me in my garden. I have a large garden but with all the young men away at the war, I need help. I'm particularly fond of roses, but alas, my back doesn't like the bending when I have to prune them," and she smiled at her self-deprecating pleasantry. "You might help me dress in the morning. We could train you to be a lady's maid. Should you like that?"

"Oh yes, miss. I mean, ma'am. I'd try very hard. Would I be paid at all?"

"Certainly. You may have five shillings a week and all your food. Is that satisfactory?"

"Oh yes, ma'am."

"Good. So while I have a talk with Mrs Cox, you wash your hands and pack your things." Having reached the entrance to the barn, where there was a bicycle parked, she lifted the brass knocker with her gloved hand and knocked. "When you're ready, wait with Powell over there. He'll drive us home. Off you go now."

Sarah stood dumbfounded.

The door was opened by Annie, wearing a full-length white apron over a black dress with the sleeves rolled up. In her beefy arms she clasped a baby to her shoulder. She had become a rather generous-bosomed matriarch over the years, her hair was drawn up towards the back with the ends falling down in an old-fashioned, so-called 'Cadogan style'. With a grave expression of concern, she said, "Oh, y' Ladyship! I'm that sorry."

"Annie! You received my note, then?"

"The boy who brought it is just having a drink. Please to accept our deepest condolences." Her sharp eyes flicked to the watching Sarah. "Do please come in, y' Ladyship."

"I had to see you," said the lady stepping over the threshold.

Annie shut the door.

Sarah stared at it. *A pound a week! Golly Moses, that's a fortune. Be a lady's maid for a fine lady like that. What sort of house could she live in, I wonder? S'pect it's a palace. She was ever so nice. Wearing silk and velvet, she was. Knew my name an' all. Knew Ma Cox's name, too. Only ones who called her 'Annie' were Mister Albert and Mister Fred. Don't think 'bout him, he's gone, thank goodness. Won't be back neither, if I get my wish. A lady's maid! Can it really be my turn? Never thought the day would dawn. What will it be like? 'Pack my things', she said. Wonder if I could take Polly? Yes, I'll take Polly.*

And Sarah ran behind the barn out of sight.

Polly was a newly born lamb. Sarah's greatest joy, as she'd hinted to the lady, were the stories she read in books and the comfort she derived from the animals she tended. At the moment, her favourite was a lamb she'd christened, "Polly". The only other consolation Sarah had known in her short life had been the changing faces of the children she'd huddled together with at night when Ma Cox or Mr Fred turned out the light. But they all left. Everyone left, except her. She had seen so many children come and go, occasionally even made friends, but they had all disappeared. Sometimes at night when she put out the light (for now, as Head Girl, it was she who slept in the supervisor's cub), she wondered if they had ever existed at all. Before the war broke out her world had been Ma Cox, Mr Fred, Mr Albert, Jesus (of course), school, clouts and cuffs, cod liver oil and chores – she'd learnt to know her place and be eternally grateful. At South Baddesley School she'd had her struggles with randy teenagers, and lately, a couple of boys at the orphanage had tried to kiss her, but she'd not wanted anything to do with either of them. Now, at sixteen, she longed to be out in the world. Working and talking with the Forestry Corps girls had encouraged her yearning to explore life, conquering her earlier trepidation and distrust of adults. Long ago she'd decided that animals were nicer than grown-ups – dogs and rabbits, but best of all were the lambs. It was sad when they went away to be slaughtered, but that, she had learnt, was life. She'd promised herself that one day, when she was grown-up, she'd have a lamb all her own, and she would never let it be taken away to be killed.

In the backfield she made for Polly and picked her up. Returning past the barn the thought occurred to her that she should ask Ma Cox's permission before taking the lamb. The boy who'd brought the note, a sparky shaver of sixteen or so, was balancing on one leg by his bicycle hitching up his knickerbockers. It was Henry Walsh, a boy she recognised from South Baddesley School, the boy who'd sat behind her and put straws down her back. He looked up and grinned.

"Sally Alley!" he called out pleasantly.

His use of her school nickname irked her. She'd liked the 'Sally' part, but not cared at all for the 'Alley' bit. She'd not cared much for Henry Walsh either, though judging by his beaming expression her feelings had not been reciprocated.

"You still livin' 'ere?" he asked in a surprised tone.

She ignored his question. "Who's that lady in there?"

"Lady Isabel from Kingsford Hall. His lordship pegged out last night. Me Mam's in service there. 'Ere," he said, swaggering towards her. "Fancy comin down the harbour tonight?"

Sarah shook her head. "Too much work."

Mounting his bike, he said, "One day, eh? I'll get you one day, Sally Alley." Grinning he pedalled off shouting, "See ya."

Lady Isabel Kingsford! Of course, I should have known. Everyone for miles around had heard of Lady Isabel and the General, they were the richest and most respected folk in the county. Sarah peered in at the barn window. A full view was denied her, but she could see the back of Ma Cox's head as she sat feeding the baby, and glimpse a black-stockinged ankle flexing beneath skirts as Lady Isabel sat talking. The window latch was open slightly, with her forefinger she pushed it wider and listened.

"I intend to put Kingsford Hall at the disposal of the medical authorities. My friend Constance, the Duchess of Westminster, has set up a hospital in her chateau at Le Touquet, and I thought I should follow her example. Now with Thomas gone, and the boys all away... Oh, certainly the house is inconvenient from a medical standpoint, I appreciate that, but I must do what I can. No doubt I shall have to use my network of influential contacts to carry it through. But the point is, the household is severely scaled down,

I've lost over half my staff. All to work for victory, of course, but what with the men away, and even the girls now joining up, I have no one. Esther, so they tell me, has even become a bus conductress! So I need staff.

"*Staff? That means a housemaid.* Sarah remembered having once been rejected for that post by a buyer and Ma Cox's comic-but-bitter tirade describing the job. "Stop grizzling, girl," Annie had scalded. "Don't let the others know it, but the life of a housemaid, let me tell you, is no better than being a slave, and that's a fact. You're up from six to eleven, and drudge without stop. You tidy grates, lay fires, light 'em, sweep, dust, polish, serve morning tea, and carry cans of hot water upstairs." Annie had reeled off the tasks, comically gasping in a lungful of air to make her point. "Make beds, empty slops, scald chamber pots, wash windows, paintwork, carry coals, clean bedrooms, put away clothes, change towels, check soap. Answer doorbells, run errands, serve meals, turn down beds, draw curtains, prepare warming pans, water bottles, carry up more hot water." Another deep breath. "Then you have to tidy up downstairs, and you 'ave to do all that without being seen by the master, 'cause if you do, you gets dismissed, or worse, seduced. And if not by him, then his sons. And if you get pregnant, you get thrown out. So think yourself lucky they never choose you, lass. I even married Oliphant to get meself out of it!"

Sarah thoughtfully nuzzled her lamb, enjoying its warm earthy meadowy smell and walked toward the car. She noticed it had been turned around in preparation for the return journey and the chauffeur was smoking a cigarette as he waited by the wheel. She approached him warily, as she did all men.

"The lady said I was to get in."

Powell looked at her dubiously. "You're not bringing that animal into this vehicle, miss." There was more than a hint of hostility in his voice.

"Why?" said Sarah. "What's so special about that old thing? I seen tons of 'em."

"Have you, miss? In that case you'll recognise this as a 1912 Silver Ghost Rolls Royce."

"Don't look much like a ghost to me," she said, sitting on the verge cuddling Polly.

"Seen tons of them too, have you, miss?"

Sarah had never been called 'Miss' before. She rather liked it. "Yeah. There's one right behind you now!"

Powell was impervious. "Don't catch an old soldier out with the likes of them old jokes."

At that moment the contrasting matriarchs re-emerged into the courtyard. Lady Isabel turned to her hostess saying, "Annie, my dear. Thank you."

"Likewise, I'm sure, y' Ladyship."

"Do you have any news of your boys?"

"Not for weeks. All we know is they're together and in France somewhere. You read about these terrible battles in the newspapers. What with them, and both Bert and Fred away, I dread the arrival of every post."

"Oh, Annie, I know exactly how you feel. I feel just the same. This dreadful war! But they say there is a Big Push coming soon. So we must pray for them all."

"Oh, we do that every night and morning, m'lady. And we saw one of them German Zeppelins flying over the other evening. Everyone was in the road screaming, they didn't know what to make of it. One of the boys said The Kaiser was going to jump out and take us all. I said he'd want a bloomin' big Zeppelin to take all the people of Lymington. Did you see it yourself?"

Lady Isabel murmured, "No, no, I didn't." She glanced at the car and observed her chauffeur talking to the girl. "Ah, there she is. I'd best be on my way. I have much to do."

"Of course. And you know you have our deepest sympathy," said Annie. "His Lordship was the grandest gentleman ever, and I know Fred and Albert would say the same." Silently they clasped hands for a moment. It was clear they had an understanding. "I'll come and say goodbye to her," said Annie, and they set off toward the car.

Powell was watching them. He timed extinguishing his cigarette and walking round his vehicle to open the rear door for her Ladyship to perfection.

The two matrons reached the automobile and stood regarding the crouching girl cuddling the lamb.

"So, Sarah," said Annie. "You're going to work for Lady Isabel at Kingsford Hall. That's good news. You're a lucky lass. Let me take Polly for you," and she held out her arms. "Take off your apron now."

Truculently Sarah nuzzled her nose further into Polly's furry coat.

"Do as Mrs Cox tells you," said Lady Isabel. "We have many dogs at Kingsford Hall, I'm sure you'll grow to like them just as well."

Sarah looked up at the lady, who smiled. She smiled back, but still held on to Polly.

"And we'll find you a smart new apron," said Lady Isabel passing her and occupying the rear seat of the Rolls.

As Powell closed the door behind her and walked round to switch on the trembler coil below the dashboard, Annie, with a severe expression Sarah knew only too well, hissed, "Don't be so stupid. Give me that lamb."

For a moment Sarah was still. *Oh dear, this is important.* She whispered into Polly's ear. "I have to go. But I'll always love you. Always." She stood up and kissed the lamb, reluctantly handing her over to Annie. She untied her apron, folded it in half and spread it blanket-like over Polly.

"Don't worry," said Annie softly, "I'll take care of her. Good luck to you, pet."

Sarah realised this really was goodbye. Like the ones she'd witnessed so many times before. So many times when she'd wished it had been her that had been chosen. *At last it's my turn. It's me that's found a home.* Now the same height as Annie, she turned to look her in the eyes.

"Don't forget us," said Annie.

Forget? I'll do everything I know how to forget. Forget Mister Fred slobbering over me with his smelly breath, forget the times he forced me down in the woods, jabbing and prodding himself into me. Forget the times he swore he'd put me out on the streets if I didn't. The time I tried to tell you, and you whipped me for making up lies. Unable to feel sorry, sad, or any emotion other than relief and excitement, she kissed and hugged Polly for the last time, but some half-forgotten instinct made her open her arms wide enough to include the woman who had once been the centre of her world.

"Sit up the front with Powell," called Lady Isabel from the back seat.

Sarah experienced the nearest thing to heaven as she opened the car door and sat on the red leather upholstery next to the chauffeur's seat. For despite what she had told him, she had never seen a car quite like this before, let alone ridden in one. It was even better than the Woodbury Fair.

Standing before the bonnet, Powell rotated the turning handle, and the engine fired. He stepped in beside Sarah and the Silver Ghost Rolls moved forward.

Sarah was so excited she laughed as she waved goodbye to Ma Cox, who called out, "Be a good girl. Don't forget to say your prayers," which was typical of her, being as nice as pie in front of the visitor. With no regrets, Sarah turned her head away from the only home she'd known, and faced her future.

Annie stood by her cottage gate holding the lamb and watching the car. Over the years she'd become hardened to the emotional comings and goings of her charges. Yet Sarah's case was exceptional, so much of her own life had been bound up with the child. Recollections crowded her mind as the car disappeared down the lane on its journey back to Kingsford Hall. Once there, Annie guessed, the whole current of Sarah's existence, and that of Lady Isabel, would turn into a new channel and alter them both past recognition.

PART TWO

Kingsford Hall

Chapter Seven

"George," called Lady Isabel, addressing the chauffeur whom she'd previously referred to as Powell. "May we have the hood down, please?"

George Powell stopped the Rolls and stepped out. Sarah watched him, intrigued. He twisted a wing screw above the windscreen and moved to Lady Isabel's side-window. Loosening another screw, he murmured, almost inaudibly, "Home soon, y' Ladyship."

"I'm fine, George. Fine," she answered, extending her hand onto his and patting it. "It's such a beautiful morning. I thought we'd enjoy it with the roof down." He moved around to the other side, and, after more unscrewing, folded the roof down. Lady Isabel held on to her hat and leant forward to allow him to complete the task.

"Look at the ponies," said Sarah, opening her door preparing to join them.

"Careful, miss!" warned Powell. "They might look gentle, but these New Forest ponies are not tame y' know. They kick and bite."

Sarah took heed and shut her door.

Powell leant in to switch on the coil, then, bending down before the front bonnet he rotated the handle. The engine turned, he resumed his seat, and the Silver Ghost hurtled off once again.

With the wind in her hair and exhilaration in her heart, Sarah hugged herself with glee. *A new life. A new life. I'm going to a new life.*

Now that the clouds had cleared, the morning sunlight was catching the full spectrum of contrasting hues in the forest landscape, amber green tree tops, lime and yellow, olive and hazel to shades of deep black purple. Ahead, a herd of deer, some with giant antlers, nibbled leisurely, then turned to stare at the dashing silver monster that was disturbing their morning munching. On they travelled, over Hackett's Heath – where Powell had to slow down to allow a score of wild ponies to gallop across the track – past rolling farmland, through pretty villages with thatched cottages that Sarah had never seen before, and onward where the track almost disappeared. Just as she was beginning to wonder how much further they were going, they turned in between a pair of tall iron gates by a lodge.

Under an arch of ash and oak, through dappled shafts of sunlight, past seas of bluebells beside the winding half-mile driveway, eventually, between a wilderness of beech, birch and giant rhododendron bushes, Sarah caught her first glimpse of Kingsford Hall. It was a Grimm's Fairy Tale vision of turrets and battlements that looked even more romantic than the palace she'd imagined.

"But it's a castle!" she gasped.

"Built in 1790," said Powell. "In the Gothic style, so they say."

One of the finest estates in Hampshire, Kingsford Hall was rivalled only by Beaulieu – which Sarah knew had once been a monastery dissolved by Henry VIII in 1538. The castle had become known as 'The Sleeping Beauty house', for its heyday had been in the last century, when the great men and women of the day had filled its 250 rooms for weekend house parties, shooting parties on the glorious 12th August, and that favourite of the Victorian era, fancy dress balls. It boasted electric light, a generator (which frequently broke down – possibly because it had been installed in 1898), central heating, hot and cold running water in the main bedrooms, and there was even a telephone (installed in 1881). The Kings and Queens, politicians and potentates who visited must have been delighted by its reassuring grandeur. Its panoramic views of sheep-cropped sward to the north, arable fields to the east, lawns, statues, flower gardens, lake and fountains, spoke of wealth, culture and sophistication.

The lavish parties had ceased with the death of Lady Isabel's mother-in law, Lady Emma Kingsford, who, as a member of the Marlborough House set, had been part of the witty and worldly circle of pleasure-loving friends of the Prince of Wales before he became Edward VII. It was Lady Emma who had been the great hostess and had spotted young Isabel as a potential daughter-in-law while presenting her own daughter at Court. The castle had been inherited and was at present owned, or at least it had been up until the early hours of this morning, by her son and Lady Isabel's husband, General Sir Thomas Kingsford, one of the great warriors of the last century.

The General, who had died of a chest infection, now lay supine between a pair of ornate oil lamps – their light mysterious and subdued appropriate to the gravity of the occasion – on the monumental four-poster bed in which generations of his family had endured the kicks and kisses of their privileged lives. A lion-hearted man of bravery, hero of the Boer War, his once ruddy face was now melted to a fleshy porridge blob on the pillow. Only his flamboyant white whiskers, that had once inspired awe and terror in his subalterns, remained. The earlier person had quite vanished, for, just three hours ago, the surly boatman of Hades, Charon, had ferried his soul across the river Styx to the gloomy realm beyond.

His youngest son, Edmond, a boy of fifteen, with blue-black hair like his father's had been at his age, was kneeling at the foot of the bed in pyjamas and dressing gown attempting to pray. In this endeavour he was doubly distracted, by his father's pet dachshund Frou Frou, who snuffled up to his side and licked his ear, but, more significantly, by his thoughts, namely his father's dying words.

"I've left you a letter," Papa had wheezed. "Remember our talk?" Raising a finger he'd indicated the doctor. "Roberts. He knows. Important letter. Our secret." Then, with finality, he'd demanded "a Scotch!" and an hour later had died.

Frou Frou slipped away from under Edmond's hand and waddled over to his master. Lifting his two front paws he tried to reach up to the bed. Edmond picked him up. "Say goodbye to Papa, then," he said, and placed the dog beside his father's body.

Edmond regarded his Papa's closed eyelids. *What exactly had he meant? 'Important letter', and 'our secret', and what was the 'talk' he'd referred to?* The only important talk Edmond could remember ever having with his Papa was the one that had taken place on the eve of his departure for Eton. It had coincided with one of the General's rare visits home, but had been no Polonius-like advice speech. "Absorb life and educate yourself," he'd said, which Edmond thought odd as Papa was paying for him to be educated at one of the most expensive schools in the land. "Have courage. Be a credit to your family and to yourself. You're clever and a good-looking lad, you'll have the girls eating out of your hand, but watch yourself, do not indulge in pleasures of the flesh too much, lest you damage your health, and beware other men, they'll be jealous." *Jealous of what*, Edmond had thought. Curiously he studied his father's profile. Even in death he was still a little afraid of him. He felt he should cry, but couldn't. Unsure where his emotions lay, for Edmond had barely known his sire, he grieved that now he never would, and at the same time cursed the constitutional law of progenitor that would exclude him from any inheritance.

At that moment he heard the sound of the automobile. He lifted Frou Frou and went to the window.

Papa's Silver Ghost Rolls was drawing up outside the front steps. He watched as George got out and opened the rear door. Mama stepped out. *Where could she have been so early?* A girl stepped out, too. *Who on earth is she?* Mama spoke to her. The girl turned back, sat next to George and the car moved off round to the stables.

Edmond opened the bedroom door into the arcaded gallery that surrounded the first level of the central hall. As he did so Mary O'Reilly, a girl with black Irish good looks was passing with a tray of used tea things. Immediately he recognised her, for she was the prettiest and youngest of the under-housemaids, the one he'd had the dream about. She stopped.

"Oh, master Edmond, there you are. 'Morning, sir, I thought you was in your room. My condolences, sir. T'is a sad day, indeed it is."

"Thank you, Mary," he said, setting Frou Frou down on the floor.

"Begging your pardon, sir. There are two undertaker gentlemen waiting in the library for her Ladyship."

"Oh! Thank you. I'll tell her. She's just arrived."

Mary blinked at him. Two seconds later the echoing sounds of barking dogs came up from below confirming his words. Mary peered over the marble balustrade. Her Ladyship was just walking through the main portico, slapping the flanks of her favourite grey-coated Great Danes. Assorted King Charles Cavalier spaniels joined them, barking and wagging their tails in welcome. Mary lowered her eyelashes at Edmond, said "Sir", and continued on her way to the servants' back staircase.

Edmond regarded her retreating figure with appreciation, savouring the memory of his dream when he had pulled off her perforated apron to reveal her naked breasts. He tightened his dressing gown cord, and, lame, limped to the top of the staircase. Frou Frou's claws made tiny tapping noises on the corridor floorboards as she waddled behind him.

Lady Isabel, pinching her glove fingers off one by one, crossed the hall to a large ormolu mirror. Dropping the gloves and her muff onto the refectory table, she lifted both her arms to remove a giant hat pin, and thus her hat and veil, which she also placed on the refectory table. Adjusting her greying hair back into style with her fingertips, she glimpsed Edmond's reflection in the mirror as he negotiated the stairs behind her. Her heart went out to him as she watched him deftly place his shortened right foot and tiptoed onto each carpeted step. At the time of his birth she had regarded his deformity as God's retribution for her sins, but if it were so, the Almighty had compensated by blessing him with a gentle nature and almost feminine beauty. With his cornflower-blue eyes, straight nose and well-sculptured mouth, he somewhat resembled her younger self. Yesterday, on his return from Eton, she'd noticed how he'd filled out, his height and pronounced Adam's apple announced pubescence, though on his cheeks the innocent down of youth still bloomed. As a child she'd taken him to many specialists, their advice had all been the same. His legs being of an uneven length he would have to wear a built-up boot for the rest of his life, but this morning he was barefoot.

She turned to him. "Darling boy. You're still in your pyjamas!"

"I couldn't get back to sleep. Where have you been, Mama? The undertaker people are here."

"Heavens! Already. I was hoping to rest."

A white-haired conservative gentleman of middle years, came out of the library. Dr Roberts had helped Edmond and his two elder brothers into this world, and only last night had seen their father out of it. "Good morning, your Ladyship. Edmond. The funeral directors are awaiting your instructions."

Lady Isabel sighed in dread.

"Would you like me to speak to them, Mama?"

"Would you, darling? I really don't think I'm up to it at the moment," then turning to Dr Roberts. "I've not had one wink of sleep since you left this morning."

"Hardly surprising, your ladyship, with so much on your mind. I have a sleeping draught in my bag, if you wish?"

"No, no. I'll be fine now, thank you." Then to Edmond, "You know what is required, dear. I'm sure whatever you decide will be correct. Thank you for all your help, Roberts. Excuse me, but I really must retire." Languidly she ascended the great marble staircase to the upper gallery, passing enormous paintings in elaborate gold frames, portraits of ancestors, masterpieces by Gainsbourgh, Millais, Burne-Jones and Reynolds. When she reached the top, she rested her hand on the balustrade and turned back to regard the commodious hall. Her eye rested on the handsome portrait of her late mother-in-law, Lady Emma Kingsford by John Singer Sargent. *Twenty-four years ago I came here as her house guest... for a shooting party... and met my darling Thomas. Just twenty-four years ago. For twenty-three years I have been chatelaine. And now Thomas has gone. However shall I survive?* Looking down over the antlers and hunting trophies, past the fifth century B.C. painted Egyptian mummy standing guard by the double doors leading to the library, and ahead into her drawing room, packed with massive furniture, antique cabinets, white lace curtains, oriental art, photographs of royalty and enough bric-a-brac to fill a pantechnicon, every item held a memory. *My beloved home. Now it all belongs to Harry, and he's not here. No Arthur, either. Only dear Edmond. Ah well, no doubt we will endure. We must.* Poignantly she turned away to continue along the corridor to her bedroom, pausing briefly to smile at Frou Frou lying guard outside the General's bedroom door.

In the library the Great Danes sat suspiciously eyeing the sombre funeral directors, causing the gentlemen no little unease as they waited for Lady Isabel.

"Good morning, gentlemen," said Edmond, confidently advancing to shake their hands. "Excuse my dressing gown, but, as no doubt Dr Roberts has explained, my father only died a few hours ago. Now what has to be decided upon?"

The undertakers, denied their interview with the famous beauty, looked askance at the little boy with the deformed bare foot. Dr Roberts saved the moment.

"Gentlemen. Edmond. If I may? As senior next of kin, naturally Sir Henry, as he now is, would have the responsibility of making the funeral arrangements. But as he, and indeed his brother, are both on active service in France, in his absence the task falls to young Edmond here. Do you have any special instructions, Edmond?"

"Yes," he said, firmly. "I should like an open coffin."

"That would be appreciated, I'm sure," said the baldest of the directors, making a note. "We will certainly make the preparations. That would be for the lying in, or extended vigil?"

"The vigil," said Edmond. "In the chapel."

"That is St Edward's chapel," added Dr Roberts. "Across the courtyard of the west wing."

The directors nodded simultaneously, like Chinese dolls. Naturally there was a chapel.

"I think it unlikely," continued Edmond, "that the military people will insist on a full martial funeral at this time, but we would like a casket and ceremony in keeping with my father's position, for he has served the Crown and Empire with great distinction. Preparations should be made for certain dignitaries to attend, the local tenants, of course, and the household staff. The burial will be an internment in our family vault. It should be concluded as soon as is practicable, for I have to return to school, I have exams. Do you think that is in order, Roberts?"

"I think that would be just grand, Edmond," said Roberts, smiling proudly at the boy.

"Oh, and will you make an announcement in 'The Times' newspaper, please?"

"Certainly, sir. With Dr Roberts' help we already have that in hand."

"Thank you," said Edmond.

"Right, then, gentlemen," said the doctor after a moment. "So, unless you have any other questions, I'll accompany you to the deceased." The directors looked at each other, inclined their heads to Edmond and, grateful to be led away from the Great Danes, allowed themselves to be ushered into the hall. As Roberts passed the boy, he patted him on the back.

"Roberts. Did Papa leave you a letter for me?"

"He did indeed. Last week. The fact is he asked me to post it to his lawyer, but forgive me, with all my other duties I quite forgot. When I arrived home this morning, I remembered." Withdrawing a wide vellum envelope from his inside breast pocket, he handed it over. "Here."

Edmond read his name on it, but curbed his curiosity. "Thank you."

"Oh, and I meant to give this to your Mother," said Roberts, handing him a ring. "It's your father's signet ring. I'll look after these chaps from now on," and he followed the directors out.

Edmond looked at the ring. *He must have removed it whilst laying Papa out.* It was heavy, with a worn gold lozenge engraved with intials. 'B' for Belle – his father's pet name for his wife – interwoven with 'T' for Thomas. Thoughtfully, Edmond climbed the stairs to his bedroom. Frou Frou immediately nosed past his feet through the bedroom door to curl up in the chair by the newly-lit fire. Edmond opened his letter.

Stamped at the top was the family crest, "To D'ey Nikato." Let Right Prevail. But the paper was crumpled and the writing unrecognisable, totally unlike any writings of his father's he'd seen previously. The General had obviously been very poorly at the time of writing.

> My dear boy,
>
> I had expected to be done with this dying business years ago on the battlefield, now I grow more irascible daily. My mind has been much taken up with thoughts of the past. The longer I live, especially now when I dare to feel the approach of death, the more I feel moved to express what I feel.
>
> Throughout your childhood I was frequently ~~away~~ abroad on manoeuvres, and much regret not knowing you while you were growing up. Having been a second son myself, I anticipate your feelings concerning Henry becoming the seventh Baronet while you inherit nothing. When your grandfather died and your uncle David inherited, I, too got nothing and was hopping mad, I recall. By the time David died and I had to take over, I had embarked on a military career (I realise no such option lies before you because of your health) and thus avoided the onerous task of having to manage Kingsford. In truth I would not have enjoyed taking the estate into my hands and setting a good pattern of farming among my tenants. That responsibility fell to your dear Mama, who has had to manage the whole kit and caboodle

alone, but all agree that she has set a magnificent example.

I trust it will not displease you to learn I have arranged ~~a divertissement~~ an adventure for you. Despite our separated lives I wish to assure you, my dear boy, that I have always held you in the greatest esteem, my respect, pride and love for you remain unqualified.

Your Papa.

Though not around to hear you gasp
Treasures abound within your grasp.
Search for a box that is not square.
There lies the clue interred there.

Chapter Eight

Miss Vines, a brisk, wonderfully neat housekeeper in her late thirties, with a centre parting and polished hair scraped into a bun, regarded Sarah suspiciously across her desk in the basement office. "I take it this is your first post?"

Sarah nodded. "Yes, miss."

"Vines. Miss Vines. And your name?"

"Sarah Smith."

"The tradition here is surnames, so you'll be called Smith. Take this," and she thrust a list of rules at her. Sarah glanced at Rule 1. 'Housemaids are never to go out without leave from the housekeeper'. "Learn them," uttered the housekeeper, "and take note of Rule 4. 'No men friends allowed on the estate'."

Not at all likely, thought Sarah, but smiled sweetly.

"Now, come with me." Miss Vines looked down. "Did you not bring any luggage?"

"No, miss. Thought I'd start off new, like."

"Well," she said, pursing her lips, "this way, then."

Sarah followed her out of the kitchen and up the narrow servants' staircase. "You've arrived on a difficult day," commented Miss Vines as they climbed the worn wooden steps, scooped out by the toil and tread of a hundred servants' feet. "A sad day. His Lordship passed away this morning, we're all somewhat at sixes and sevens."

At the top of the house, from the hand-me-down spares in the servants' clothes cupboard, she held up a plain V-neck black dress, it had a black bow and cream lacy cuffs. "That'll fit. Suitable for mourning too. And take these." She handed her a cap, apron and stockings. "Try on these house shoes. Do they fit? They don't squeak, do they?"

Sarah tried them on. They did fit, and they didn't squeak.

"Good," said Miss Vines locking up the cupboard. "When I have more time, I'll kit you out properly. The cost will come out of your wages. Follow me and I'll show you to your room. Change, then come down to the Ironing Room. You can sew, I hope?"

"Yes, Miss Vines," replied Sarah, clutching the dress and shoes. "I make up all me own clothes, and for the other girls at the orphanage."

The housekeeper's eyes dropped to Sarah's thin worn grey dress. "Well. You won't find it hard to sew up mourning bands, then," and she opened a door. "This'll be your room."

Sarah stepped in. After sleeping sixteen years in a ward full of girls, toddlers and babies, the sunny little attic bedroom Miss Vines revealed, seemed like a shrine of refuge. She turned to thank her, but Miss Vines was already halfway down the corridor.

After changing, Sarah looked at her reflection in the mirror. To her surprise the dress fitted perfectly. Never having worn such a fine frock, she felt very lady-like and not like a servant at all, not even after she'd tied on the apron. An ivory-backed brush and comb lay on the dresser; she brushed her hair, and coiled it up at her nape, then attached the white lace cap with satin ribbons. Though the cap was pretty, it immediately branded her a servant. Eagerly, she found her way back to the staircase and descended to the Ironing Room. For two-and-a-half hours, under the beady eye of Miss Vines, she industriously sewed up, and ironed thirty black armbands.

Twenty-four staff members came by to collect them. First,

was an old white-haired butler called John, who looked so perfect in his immaculate tails and stripped morning trousers, it was difficult to imagine him wearing anything else. George Powell was next. Without his chauffeur's cap, his cropped grey hair and bullet head immediately stamped him as an ex-military man. Recognising him, Sarah smiled, but he grimly examined the armband and walked away. She wondered what she'd done to offend him. A plump woman with a good-natured smile introduced herself. "Mrs Walsh. Cook," she announced, taking one of the armbands. "Ta, dear."

That must be the mother of Henry Walsh, from school.

Other staff members welcomed her with a nod or casual smile, but they all seemed solemn and sad. Mary O'Reilly was last to arrive. "Sally Alley is it?" she exclaimed warmly. "What be you doing 'ere?"

Seeing a friendly face, Sarah beamed. "Mary O'Reilly!" Mary had been at the orphanage; she'd left about a couple of years ago. "Didn't know you were here. I'm to be Lady's maid to madam."

"'Blige me!" cried Mary. "How d'you manage that?"

"Her Ladyship," corrected Miss Vines, addressing Sarah. "And you'll be a Housemaid, under my jurisdiction while you're training. You can take that ironed blouse up to her Ladyship's boudoir when you're done. She's had her rest now, and is out and about in the garden."

"The boudoir?" asked Sarah, bewildered.

"I'll show her," said Mary.

"You can take up her hat, too. Here," said Miss Vines holding it out. "And the other things she left in the hall."

"Yes, Miss Vines." Sarah took the gloves, muff and hat (it was the one with the veil, Lady Isabel had worn to the orphanage), and holding a coat hanger with the blouse on it in her other hand, she followed Mary up the back stairs.

"Don't you be worryin' about 'er," said Mary in her lilting Irish brogue. "She's fine. No more a tartar than Ma Cox was."

On the first floor corridor, as they passed the fifth doorway, Mary nodded. "That's 'is Lordship's room. The one comin' up is 'er Ladyship's. The one after, is 'er boudoir and bathroom. Peep in 'ere, you never saw such a fine room. You can get through to 'er boudoir this way, too, through the archway. Toodle-Oo!" and she went on her way.

Sarah knocked. Silence. Tentatively she turned the crystal doorknob and opened the door. Lady Isabel's bedroom was a dream oasis of luxury – sunny, spotless, still and pink. Sarah gazed mesmerised by her first sight of such sumptuous comfort. The room was panelled in pale oak with a tall cream and gilt painted wardrobe, a Louis XVI Boulle chest in tortoiseshell and brass, and by the pink marble fireplace stood an elegant chaiselongue upholstered in satin rose. Sarah thought it the most beautiful room she'd ever seen. The centrepiece, the gilt wood four-poster bed with mounds of cushions and hangings of rose silk tabernet, faced French windows, which opened up onto a terrace. Although the room was deserted, these doors, framed by wafting white voile curtains, were wide open. Sarah stepped on the rich pile carpet and walked across to the balcony. Beyond the balustrade was a breathtaking view overlooking the south-facing garden. To the right, a shallow brick staircase overgrown with moss and yellow lichen, led down to a patio beside the lawn. On each windowsill, window boxes were filled with yellow trumpets of daffodils. One of the boxes must have fallen down, for it lay on its side, yellow blooms were strewn across the terrace. A trowel was stuck into a pile of scattered earth. Sarah looked about wondering if a gardener was nearby. *Maybe I should replant them. They'll die if they're left out in the sun.* Then she heard a muffled voice: "I say, is that someone there, please?"

Looking around mystified, she returned to the bedroom. Assuming the door to her right, led to His late Lordship's bedroom, then the one to the left, through the archway was to the boudoir and bathroom. She hesitated. "Hallo!" she called.

"I'm in the dressing room."

Wondering if she should knock first, she called again. "Hallo."

"Come in. Come in," urged a young voice.

What she saw as she opened the door was a little boy balancing precariously on the back of a wobbly chair clinging to the top of a wardrobe. "I'm stuck!" he cried.

"Whatever skylarking are you up to?" she said, setting down the blouse and hat on a stool by the dressing table.

"Do you think you could help me, please?" panted the boy.

"Hold on a tick. If I push the chair nearer, maybe you can step down. What on earth are you trying to do?"

"The trouble is, I might overbalance the wardrobe if I take my feet off the chair. It skidded away from under me, you see."

Sarah went to him. It was only then she noticed the boy's right foot was encased in a built-up boot. Stretching up to him, she said, "I've got you. Can you reach my shoulders?"

"If you don't mind taking my weight, I think I could jump."

She held him firmly by his waist, but he didn't jump. He bent to grasp her shoulders and eased himself down beside her. Face to face, he grinned. "Thanks. Well done."

"That's alright. I'm well used to rescuing lads like you down from trees." *What a beautiful boy! What eyelashes,* she thought, turning to collect the hat. "What were you trying to do?"

"Reach those hat boxes up there," he answered, pushing back his floppy fringe.

"Why? Are you dressing up or something? This one's got a veil. Want to try it on?"

The boy appeared to stiffen. "Who are you, please?"

"Sarah Smith. I'm her Ladyship's new maid. Who are you?"

"Edmond Kingsford. You're the girl who arrived with George this morning."

"You mean Mr Powell, the chauffeur?" A second sense warned her not to share her opinion that he was a grumpy old codger, so tactfully she said, "He seems all right."

"George is about my best friend round here."

Just as well I fibbed, then.

"I saw you from the window," said Edmond.

"Did you want to try on those hats, then?"

"Actually, I don't try on my mother's clothes. I'm trying to solve a riddle."

"A riddle? Oh! I love riddles. What is it?"

"It's private. Well, kind of," he sighed. "Actually, you might be able to help. What's a box that is not square?"

"Ah, I see. Yes, I get it. A hat box."

"Exactly."

"Could be a shoe box, though. A pillar-box. A music box. A... what else? A box on the ears. A horse box. Jack-in-the-box. Matchbox. A chocolate box. A box of tricks!"

"Hey, you're good. I didn't think of half of those things. I only got to 'window-box'."

"I know, a boxing ring? No, that's square. A coffin? Oops! Sorry."

"That's all right. I thought of that one, too, but it didn't signify."

"Signify?"

"Follow."

"Follow what?"

"It's a verse. Oh, you might as well see." He fished in his trouser pocket and handed her his father's letter. It was folded so that only the verse showed. "I'm trying to solve this."

Sarah read it. "What's 'interred' mean?"

"Buried. That's what made me think it was a window-box."

"Ah! So it was you dug up those daffs from the window-box?"

"Mmm," he nodded thoughtfully. "A round chocolate box? That's possible."

Studying the verse Sarah asked, "Who is it, who's not around to hear you gasp?"

"My father. It's a letter from my father."

"Oh, I see. Well, that's private," and she hastily handed it back to him. "But if there's treasure around, maybe you should find it before anyone else does."

'Mmn.' Edmond looked wistfully up at the hatboxes on top of the wardrobe. "Would you mind helping me?"

"Of course. I'm supposed to put this hat away, and that's where it belongs. So let's see."

"But how can we reach up?"

"There must be a ladder somewhere." So saying she opened the wardrobe doors. Nestling inside was a folded ladder-chair. She grimaced at Edmond, who raised his eyes to heaven and made a silly face. They reached inside and unfolded it. Sarah climbed up and handed him down a hatbox. Kneeling on the floor, he took off the lid. Inside was a luxurious great feather-brimmed hat wrapped in tissue paper. He took it out and looked inside. There was nothing, certainly no secret message. Together they stuffed the tissue paper and hat back and Sarah took the box up the steps again, swapping it for another one. This box was empty, apart from clouds of tissue paper. Edmond removed it. Lying on the base, under the last flat layer of tissue, was an envelope. On it, in his father's handwriting, was one word:

Congratulations

"Ace! A1!" cried Edmond, tearing the envelope open. Inside was a card.

Though mummy may say no
At her feet say so.
A chesty condition,
Long in remission,
Not out at the end.
To you I descend
Gifts from afar,
Your loving Papa.

Edmond handed it to Sarah. "What do you make of that?"

"A chesty condition?" she mused. "That would be a cough."

"Too easy," commented Edmond, looking at the letter again. "'Not out?' Well, that's 'In'. 'At the end'?"

"'Cough In'. Back to a coffin again!" Sarah exclaimed.

"But Papa's in the coffin. It can't be."

"What did your Dad die of?"

"Tuberculosis."

"Sorry. Do you have any other coffins around?"

"Dozens. In the family crypt."

"But they must be ages old."

"Of course. 'Long in remission'. That must be it. Let's go!" he cried.

"You should really replant those daffodils first," said Sarah, putting the hat with the veil into the hatbox and climbing up to replace it on top of the wardrobe. "They'll die, otherwise."

"Let the gardeners attend to that," said Edmond, impatiently making for the door to his mother's bedroom.

"Your Mama said all the gardeners were at the war. You ought to do it, really."

"Oh well. Alright."

Sarah hung up the blouse, and followed Edmond onto the terrace.

He'd already lifted the window box and was straightening it onto the window ledge.

Picking up the trowel, she started scooping the earth back into the box.

Edmond contemplated her. "You're quite bossy, you now."

"Sorry! I'm used to bossing children around in the orphanage."

"The orphanage! Our servants always seem to come from there.' He contemplated her in silence for a moment, then said, 'I'll go and find George. Maybe he can help. Oh, there's Mama. I say, keep hush-hush about the letter, won't you?"

"'Course. What do you think I am?"

"I think," he said teasingly, "you're a jolly good sport, and..." But whatever he was going to say, he thought better of it, for he abruptly left, saying, "Excuse me," and made his way down the steps into the garden.

I wonder what he was going to say? Hoping it was something nice, she grinned to herself, then recalled Ma Cox's warning about master's sons making you pregnant, and shuddered with disgust. She put him from her mind, and completed re-planting the daffodil bulbs. The earth felt dry, so she fetched a jug of water from the bathroom and watered them.

A Great Dane bounded up the steps towards her. Quite unafraid, Sarah greeted the huge animal affectionately, stroking him and fondling his velvety ears. "Hallo, you soppy great thing. What's your name?" The dog replied by licking her face.

Lady Isabel was standing at the bottom of the garden steps regarding her in a mildly interested fashion. She'd changed out of her black and was now wearing pearls over an oatmeal lace gown with a small train, a wide straw hat and a pair of gardening gloves. She carried a wicker flower basket, inside it nestled a pair of secateurs. "Blitzen," she called lightly, "leave her be. Come here."

Blitzen obeyed, then romped off to join his brother, who'd discovered some fascinating smell on the lawn.

"Should I close the doors, y' Ladyship?"

"Thank you," said Lady Isabel drifting away. "Come. Join me."

Sarah shut the French doors and tripped down the steps to catch her up. Behind the Lady drifted a halo of perfume. Never before having smelt such a fragrance, Sarah wondered what it was. (Later, she espied the Lalique perfume bottle on the Lady's dressing table. It was called 'Ambre Antique' by Francois Coty.)

"How are you getting on?" Lady Isabel enquired. "I approve the Battenburg cap, it suits very well."

"Thank you, y' Ladyship. What are their names... the dogs?"

"That one's 'Donner', the other there is 'Blitzen'. They may look a fearsome duo, but believe me, they're quite harmless."

"Funny names. How old are they?"

"Nearly three now. They're the names of Santa Claus's reindeer. The other ones are 'Dasher', 'Dancer', 'Prancer', 'Vixen', 'Comet' and 'Cupid'."

"I never knew that. I'll try and remember."

"At one time we thought we'd try for all eight, but, alas, there were only two puppies."

"Maybe these two will have puppies." Then Sarah spotted that both dogs were male. "Oh no! Sorry."

"Lady Isabel inclined her head in a faintly amused manner. "Did I see you talking with my son?"

"Yes. He was looking for Mister Powell."

"Ah yes, he would be," she sighed. "He's most fond of him." She walked on in silence, then, as if awoken from a daydream, added, "As indeed we all are. Powell was my husband's batman. He was wounded at Mafeking in '99. But my husband couldn't do without him, so we adopted him. He's been with us ever since. A member of the family, really. He's known Edmond since he was a baby, of course. Taught him to swim in the lake over there. We had a diving board put in for the boys by the summerhouse. Years ago, of course, years ago."

Sarah glanced sideways at the Lady. Her expression was one of the deepest melancholy. *She's grieving. I expect she's remembering her husband.*

"If it hadn't have been for George," the Lady continued, "I doubt Edmond would have the confidence." Again she walked in silence. "To swim, I mean. To swim... yes," she mused. "George is a comfort to us all, a great comfort." She caught Sarah examining her. "You've distracted me," she reprimanded lightly. "I came out here to prune the roses. I usually prune them in March, but with my husband's illness these last weeks and this dreadful war spiriting away my gardeners, I fear they've gone untended. I confess, though, I rather enjoy pruning them myself." At this instant her foot caught in a tuft of grass. "However, I don't enjoy mowing the lawn. As you see, it's in a frightful state!"

"I'll cut it, if you like," said Sarah.

Astonished, Lady Isabel looked at her. "Hardly an appropriate occupation."

"Why not? I've been felling trees in the New Forest. A lawn will be nothing."

"Well. If you think you can manage it. The mower looks a monstrous thing to me. Although it is a petrol-engined affair. It's a Ransome, with a grass collection box."

"Is there a compost heap?"

"Behind the kitchen garden. Well," she said, inclining her head and smiling, "it would seem as if I've found myself a gardener. I noticed you watering my window-boxes, too."

"The earth was dry."

"Do you know how to prune roses?"

"Not properly. I just snip off the spindly branches."

"That's good, but there's a little more to it. It's an art. I'll show you. Here." Reaching a statue of a cherub in the centre of the pathway, they turned into a secluded rose garden, protected on all sides by a square design of tall hedges. Lady Isabel bent down to a rose bush, tucked her train under her knees and took up the secateurs. "First the secateurs should be sharp, like these, so a clean cut is made. As you say, remove the dead wood, and any damaged or weak shoots. Then make a clean cut slightly above the new-growth bud. Like this one here. Look. Cut to an outward-facing bud. The angle is crucial; it should be down and away from the bud. Like so," and she cut off a twig. "These are Mary Rose, they have double blooms and their scent is quite lovely. They bloom from June to autumn. They're robust, so I'll shorten last year's shoots to six, maybe four buds. If they're weak, like that one there, two or three buds. Would you like to try?"

Sarah crouched down and accepted the proffered rose secateurs. "Thank you."

"Careful, they're very sharp. See that root there," said the Lady pointing to a stiff young sucker without buds. "Cut it off. It's absorbing too much energy. It'll never flower. Mind you don't scratch yourself, now."

Sarah positioned the secateurs and squeezed. Snip – the offending sucker fell off.

"Satisfying, isn't it?" said Lady Isabel. "Quite pleasurable."

Sarah agreed. "Can I try again?"

"Of course."

Enthusing to the task, she pushed a thorny branch aside to reach a diseased twig. In doing so she pricked herself. "Ouch!" Immediately she popped her finger into her mouth.

"Oh dear!" exclaimed Lady Isabel. "Is it bleeding?"

Sarah looked at it. A drop of blood began to seep onto her fingertip. "Yes."

Lady Isabel clasped her hand to her mouth. "Oh, I am so sorry."

"It's all right. It doesn't hurt," said Sarah wrapping the edge of her apron around her finger. A tiny red stain appeared.

"I tell you what," said Lady Isabel. "Keep them. The secateurs. I make you a present of them. To commemorate your first day with us. Then whenever you feel you'd like to do some gardening, you can come out here and prune the roses. Would you like that?"

Slightly bemused, Sarah replied diplomatically. "That's very kind of you, y' Ladyship. Thank you."

As Lady Isabel went chatting on about how the yellow roses looked fine in her bedroom, Sarah glanced at the secateurs in her hand wondering at the odd gift. The handles were covered in buckram with a lever notched into position to keep them shut. The blades, shaped like a parrot's beak, were of stainless steel; the light caught their sheen and revealed that they were engraved with roses.

"But, on the whole," Lady Isabel was saying, "red petals are more suitable for making pot-pourri. When there are sufficient blooms and we have the fixative – that's orris root, or oak moss works very well – we might try to make some."

Edmond, meanwhile, had tracked down George Powell to St Edward's Chapel.

"George!" he called in a hushed voice. "There you are!" His rubber-soled boot squeaked on the tiles as he walked up the aisle. "I've been looking for you everywhere."

George was sitting on the altar steps with a huge brass candlestick lying across his lap. He was polishing it in preparation for the General's lying in.

In God's house, Edmond didn't think it appropriate to use his normal tones, so, whispering, he excitedly read out the contents of his father's letter, and related how he'd found the clue. Triumphantly, he revealed the card with the verse on it. "We thought, 'A chesty condition, long in remission, not out at the end,' was a cough-in. Get it? Maybe one of those old stone coffins in the crypt. What do you think?"

"Treasure hunting, eh?" said George, re-folding his polishing cloth. "Well, now. First off, who might 'we' be?"

"The new maid you brought from the orphanage this morning. Sarah Smith."

"Ah!" George stared at a spot on the floor, weighing whether to speak his mind. "Master Edmond, you're telling me you showed this new maid – someone you only just met, someone you don't know from Adam – or Eve, come to that – your Papa's last letter?"

"Only the verse. She's all right don't worry. She suggested tons more round square things than I'd thought of. She's super, really bright."

"Mm, well, let's hope she's not *too* bright." Taking the card from Edmond, he resumed. "Let us consider. Your Papa had been ill for some time. Correct?"

Edmond nodded. "Mmn."

"So it's unlikely he'd have been up to marching down that there crypt, opening up one of them vaults, lifting one of them heavy tombstones, or coffins as you call 'em, to hide away treasure trove for you. Correct?" He paused and glumly regarded the boy. "It's only a suppose, mind."

Deflated, Edmond agreed. "Mmn, I do see." He glanced at the verse again. "He certainly wasn't well when he wrote it."

"Oh, he knew his number was up, right enough," said George handing him back the card.

"Someone must have helped him. Did you?"

George shook his head.

"Mama, maybe?"

"Maybe. But judging by that first line there...'Though mummy may say no', that would seem unlikely."

"Mm. So where do you suggest we look?"

George blinked thoughtfully. "Hold on," he said, extending his hand. "Let's see that again." He examined the verse, thought awhile, then.... "I think I might know something about this."

"What?"

George was silent.

"What?" Edmond repeated. George continued studying the verse. "Your Papa was a good friend to me. I flatter meself I knew something of the way his mind worked." He nodded his head. "Yes," he muttered, "I think I see what he was getting at."

"What? Tell me."

"Patience, lad, patience. Listen here. What with the vigil, then the funeral Saturday, there's too many folk around for treasure hunting. Best wait till after the ceremony."

"But we won't have the time. I have to go back to school after the funeral."

"That'll give us more time to consider. You'll see. Slowly, slowly, catchy hairy monkey."

Chapter Nine

*A*t all funerals, a story comes to an end, but, at all funerals, a new story begins.

The configuration of St Edward's chapel was such that the congregation – about a hundred of them at this solemnity – sat in the main body of the chapel facing the altar. Situated behind them, the raised pews in the nave faced each other and, by tradition, were occupied by the family. Opposite them sat the clergy: today, the Bishop of Winchester, the Right Reverend Edward Talbot, assisted by the Reverend Ralph Ambrose from St Thomas' in Lymington. Further along by the doors, the pews were reserved for the staff – for even in church, the classes were separated. Sarah was thus able, with only a turn of her head, to gaze upon the grieving faces of the Kingsford family without apparent intrusion. Lady Isabel, heavily veiled, was flanked by her two eldest sons, Sir Henry (now the seventh baronet), in the dress uniform of a First Lieutenant, and his brother, Arthur, wearing the uniform of a Second Lieutenant. Next to him was Edmond, formally dressed in his Eton suit and waistcoat. Studying him, Sarah thought his face perfectly angelic. He seemed to her, not only vulnerable and sensitive, but quite the handsomest lad she'd ever come across. She'd not had occasion to speak to him since their talk on Lady Isabel's terrace, so her gaze included a certain curiosity as to the outcome of his search.

For Edmond's part, when he lifted his eyes from his prayer book and, by chance met hers, he did not immediately remove them. Their eyes remained locked for longer than the statutory two seconds, and only broke after their shy smiles threatened to become grins, thus endangering the solemnity of the occasion. Their glances became more frequent, and created in Edmond a recklessness, indeed an intensity bordering on passion, so that by the time they stood for the final hymn, both parties had developed a heightened sensitivity toward the other.

After the service, the family, accompanied by the Bishop and the Reverend Ralph, descended to the family vault under the chapel for the internment.

Outside in the fresh air there was a good deal of milling-about as the mourners drifted to the dining hall for the wake. Distinguished khaki-uniformed officers with medals up, conversed in low tones with sombre-suited old-fashioned Edwardian gentlemen and their grand ladies wearing great wide brimmed hats gleaming with black goose and ostrich plumage.

"Fancy getting a letter from the King!" Mary O'Reilly whispered to Sarah.

"Shush!" answered Sarah, spotting Annie Cox wearing a new black hat, peering around looking for someone. Guessing it might be her, she ducked. "Quick!" she nudged Mary. "Let's get back," and off they scampered to the kitchens to bring forth the funeral-baked meats.

By the time the lids on the collation were removed and the all sauces and pies were laid out in the dining hall, the family had re-appeared.

The noble bearing and handsome presence of young Sir Henry and Arthur, provoked Mary to another of her irreverent sallies. "Couple of handsome buggers, them two!" At that precise moment the vicar and his wife passed (Sarah was certain they heard).

"Sarah!" said the Reverend Ralph. "Good to see you. And

Mary, too. How are you?"

"Very well, thank you, Reverend," they answered in unison, both bobbing.

"Christiana, these are two of our orphanage girls. Sarah used to come and borrow some of our Mr Dickens."

"Sarah and I are old friends," said the forthright Mrs Christiana Ambrose, smiling pleasantly, but nevertheless giving both girls a look of appraisal. "We used to discuss the books when you returned them, didn't we?"

"Yes, ma'am."

"'Oliver Twist', I remember, was one of your favourites." Sarah grinned. "Oh yes, ma'am."

"Excellent choice," announced the Reverend Ralph. "An author who really understood men. A Social reformer, too, in his way. Profoundly missed, profoundly missed."

"I'm so glad you've found employment here, Sarah," said Mrs Ambrose. "I wish you success."

"Indeed," added the Reverend. "If you have any worries, don't hesitate to come to me. God bless you, child. Bless you both," he added, moving away.

Mary turned to Sarah and raised an eyebrow, as if to say, well fancy that! But what she actually said was, "She's the General's sister... well, was."

"What, Mrs Ambrose? Gosh! I seem to have known her and the Reverend Ralph ever since I can remember. So that would make them Edmond's uncle and aunt, then."

By early afternoon the funeral feast was demolished. The wake finally disbanded with the departure of Sir Henry and Arthur, who'd only been granted compassionate leave and were due to return to their units in France.

Just as Sarah was clearing away the debris with the other

servants, Lady Isabel came by. "Oh, Smith," she said casually, "see the leftovers are packed up in tins, will you? They should be distributed to the poor, but make sure the dogs are fed first. I'm going to my room. Tell everyone I'm not to be disturbed. Thank you," and she drifted away.

Edmond, too, went to his room, but not before requesting a bath.

Miss Vines addressed Sarah and Mary in the kitchen. "I'm afraid the dynamo has broken down again. You'll have to fill his bath with water from the cauldron."

So the girls made four trips up the back stairs lugging buckets of hot water to Edmond's bathroom.

Wearing his navy-blue dressing gown, he watched them. "That'll be enough," he said, standing with his withered foot on tip-toe. "Thank you." Regarding Sarah evenly, he asked, "Would you stay and help me, please?"

She exchanged a look with Mary, who, hiding a smile, swiftly turned tail and left. "Why?" she answered with a grin. "Do you want your back scrubbed?"

"Mama said you used to wash the children in the orphanage. Would you wash me?"

For an instant, Sarah, like Mary, suspected his motives, but looking into his amazingly clear blue eyes that seemed to look into her soul, she was assured of his innocence and answered, "Certainly."

"Getting in and out is the hard part."

"Couldn't you sort of perch on the edge and swing your legs round?"

"That's what I usually do, but it's more fun if I have someone to help."

Rolling up her sleeves, she smiled. "I reckon you're one spoilt little boy."

He threw off his dressing gown and she saw his creamy naked body. Except for his withered right foot, a shrivelled approximation of a heel and toes, his body was perfect. Quite unlike the thin weedy bodies of the boys in the orphanage she'd had to scrub, Edmond's arms and chest were muscular and well developed. But she couldn't stop her eyes straying to that cruelly wasted foot. She deliberately avoided looking at his genitalia.

"My bad leg doesn't take my weight properly, you see," he said, holding out his hand to her. "When I go swimming, I balance on one foot and just dive in."

She grasped his elbow. Balancing on his good leg, he lifted his withered leg into the bath. Gently she lowered him into the tub. "Has it gone cold?"

"No, it's super. Oh, that's better," he said, sliding down letting the water cover his body.

"Hand us the soap and brush, then," she said, kneeling on the bath mat.

Edmond grinned and passed them to her. "Back first, please."

Sarah soaped up the brush and scrubbed his back as he leant forward. Then he lifted up his arms and she scrubbed under them, too. "Aren't you ticklish at all?"

"No. I like the feel of the brush on my body."

Setting aside the brush, she rinsed the soap from his back with her hands. He felt creamy and smooth, without a blemish.

"That feels nice," he murmured.

She soaped up the brush again and scrubbed his shoulders and arms. He held them out to her as if used to having someone brush his wrists and hands. Leaning back he closed his eyes. "That was the first funeral I've ever been to."

"Me, too."

"Strange, wasn't it?"

"How do you mean?"

He opened his eyes and looked into hers. "Us looking at each other while everyone else was being so serious."

Sarah's colour rose. She blinked and reached out. "Other arm."

Edmond obeyed. "I was sad for Mama, of course, but somehow I couldn't feel anything. I suppose it was because I hardly knew him. Papa, I mean. Are your parents still alive? No, sorry." Instinctively he put his hand out in apology, touching her wrist. The wrist of the hand that was holding his arm. "That was tactless of me. Sorry."

As his hand was sliding into her soapy palm, the thought flashed through her mind of the hundred times she'd wondered about her parents. Wondered who, what and where they were, if they were still alive, and if one day, she'd ever find them. She watched his fingers entwine with hers quite dispassionately, as if they belonged to someone else. Not moving, she said quietly, "It doesn't matter. I never had any parents to miss."

Edmond, too, was staring at their hands. "You must have wondered about them, though." Both his hands were now clasping hers.

"All the time when I was young." Breaking away, she reached for a towel. "Not anymore, though. After all, everyone's on their own in this world."

Edmond studied her as she dried her wrists. "That's a very grown-up thing to say."

"It's just something I know," she shrugged.

"I hadn't thought of it like that."

Sarah rested her hands on her knees and thought she should ought to go.

"Well," said Edmond cheerfully, "you've not missed much. I've always known my parents, yet the one I miss most is my Nana." He leant back in the bath covering his sex organs with his flannel. "She died when I was ten. I wasn't allowed to go to her funeral. I always thought of her as my real mother, 'cause I hardly ever saw Mama. Papa never. They were always far too busy. George was around, of course, and my brothers sometimes. Seeing them last night was grand. They're terribly worried about the war in France, you know. They said the whole show out there is crazy, the slaughter of men, just hellish. They said it was just as well I'll never have to join up. It's funny, I never used to think about death. Now, I think about it all the time. Sorry, that's depressing. Looking at you in the chapel made me forget all that. You made me feel happy."

In Sarah's heart, which was beating very fast, she understood him and wanted to say so, but conscious of her menial position and unsure of the words to use, she just said, "That letter the Bishop read out from the King about your Papa was wonderful."

Edmond murmured his agreement as he gazed into her eyes.

"Did you find your Dad's treasure?" she asked quietly.

"No. George said we should wait. Too many people around, he said. But I have to go back to school tomorrow, so I won't have a chance to look."

Sarah absently picked up the bar of soap. "You'll have to wait till your school holidays."

I can't ask him to stand-up to soap his lower half like I did the children at the orphanage. I'd better leave.

An uneasy excitement hovered between them.

"If you find it while I'm away," said Edmond in an undertone, "look after it for me, wont you?"

Sarah nodded and murmured, "Of course."

Without smiling Edmond looked at her lips. Slowly he extended his hand toward her neck, with his other hand he adjusted the flannel to fully cover himself.

Sarah looked down, she knew what he was hiding. In that one

second everything changed. A flash of the old fear returned, all she saw, all she imagined was Fred's engorged organ. The memory overwhelmed her, flooding her being. *I will not allow this to happen. I know what he wants. I will not allow it.* Abruptly she pushed him away and stood up. "You can get out by yourself. I have work to do." She turned her back on him and fled.

"Whatever's the matter?" It was Mary's voice intercepting her upstairs in the servants' corridor. "Sarah!" she persisted. "What is it?"

Sarah tried to pass her. "Nothing, nothing," she muttered.

"Something is. What's upset you?" Mary's eyes narrowed. "Don't tell me he tried it on?"

Sarah turned her head to the wall.

'The little bugger! I knew it! I just knew it! Come in. Come on, tell me all about it.' She opened her bedroom door and ushered Sarah in.

"No." Sarah held up her hands neither wanting to talk or to be touched. "Let me be."

"Oh, come on in." Mary took her by the elbow and bundled her in, shutting the door firmly behind her. "Here, have a cigarette. Nothing like a fag to sort you out. No, you don't smoke, do you? Never mind. Sit down. Now, what did he do? Did he grab you? Tell. Did he kiss you?"

Still breathing heavily from her run up the stairs Sarah hovered by the door.

"What, then?" Mary lit a cigarette, still holding the burning match she examined Sarah's flush face. Just before the flame touched her finger she blew it out. "Well, it couldn't have been that bad. He's only a baby." Putting the match in the dustbin, she said, "His eyes used to pop out at me before you appeared on the scene. Oh, he looks like butter wouldn't melt in his mouth, but behind those baby blues I always suspected he was a randy little sod. He's going to be a proper heart-breaker that one when he grows up, despite his funny leg."

Sarah was still refusing to meet her eye.

Mary, her rosy face wreathed in smiles, regarded her friend. "Calm down, pet, you're quite safe. Sit down. Tell me what happened. What did he say?"

Sarah took out her handkerchief and blew her nose. Suddenly she dropped onto the end of the bed. "Nothing, really." She was beginning to suspect she might have made a fool of herself. "Wasn't what he said exactly."

"Well, what's the fuss about then?"

Sarah was beginning to wonder, too. *Perhaps I overreacted.*

Mary leaned back grinning. "What was it? Don't tell me he got a stiffy?"

She nodded.

Mary laughed. "Bless his wee heart! Did he really?"

Now that Sarah came to think about it, she wasn't sure. *Maybe I imagined it.*

"Take it as a compliment, lass!"

"He wanted me to... well, you can guess. I could have, too. Wouldn't have meant nothing to me. Well, it's nothing, is it, sex? Like... well, like going to the lavvy."

"The lavvy! You're a bit mixed up there, lass, if that's what you're thinking." Mary pulled on her cigarette and laughed. But her expression altered as she took in Sarah's unhappy tight expression. "Lassie! Sal. Here, look at me."

Sarah turned to her defiantly.

"Did you never have a boyfriend, Sal?"

"Tons."

"Who?"

But Sarah couldn't bring herself to say. Neither able to bluff, nor tell the truth, she sulked.

97

"At the orphanage, was it?"

Sarah shut her eyes. "'Course."

"Well, it couldn't have been Reggie or Stan," said Mary, enjoying herself, "'cause they would have said." Then with a flash of insight, "Not Mister Fred? Don't tell me the old bugger tried it on with you, too?"

Astonished, Sarah looked at her. The surprise, that not for one moment did she anticipate that Mary, too, had shared the same pain as herself, seemed scarcely credible. Mary had never been the closest of her friends at the orphanage, never been one to cuddle up with at night. Sarah had always thought her noisy and rather tough, up to no good, flirting with the older boys. "You mean... you, too?"

"Oh, Jesus and Mary, yes!" Mary perched on the washstand with a wry smile on her face. In her palm she held a round tin top, which she was using as an ashtray. "Would you believe it? The bugger!" She inhaled her cigarette thoughtfully. "I'm surprised he had the nerve. You were always Ma Cox's favourite."

Sarah frowned. "What made you think that?"

"It was obvious, you had it so easy. All of you. None of yous knew how lucky you was. That place was a palace compared to the cesspit I'd come from."

"Where was that?"

"I never liked to talk about it. Still don't much. Still..." and she gave a great sigh, "it's all under the bridge now, thank God!" In matter-of-fact tones, quite at odds with her words, Mary unfolded her story. "I was in a workhouse run by the Sisters of Mercy in Dublin. We had to scrub floors barefoot and in rags, starved and beaten, we was. We were so hungry sometimes we had to eat from the pigswill bins and drink from the lavvies. They treated you worse than dirt. We had to thread rosary beads onto wire, but the wire cut your fingers, see, and they bled, but there was never any let-up. God, they were wicked those women, really cruel. I'm illegitimate, see, so they thought I was evil. Beatings, you wouldn't believe! Still, I suppose it made me strong. I got the hell out of it. Ran away with a lad when I was fourteen. We was picked up in Southampton and packed in with you lot and Ma Cox. She was a saint, that woman, a saint."

Sarah frowned, totally surprised.

"Leastways, compared to the cows I'd come from. Thought I'd fallen into a pot of jam till that bastard Fred Oliphant started mucking me about. I told his son Reggie about him, y'know. We had a bit of a thing going, Reggie and me. He was livid! One night we set a trap for Mr Fred we did. I was waiting in this part of the woods where he usually tried on his nonsense and Reggie was hiding behind the bushes. 'Cause we knew every bush and tree in those woods behind the Home like the back of our hands, as I s'pect you did. Anyway, up he comes all smiles, bit the worse for hop juice, and starts mauling me, as per usual. Out comes Reggie from behind the bush with a shillelagh the size of this washstand leg. He bashes his Dad round the head like there's no tomorrow. Calls him all the names under the sun, he did, fecking this and fecking that! Off the old bugger staggers, bloodied and bowed and that was the last trouble I ever had from him. Reggie was grand. I had a letter from him t'other week. He's at the front with his brother in France, you know."

By now composed, Sarah had listened to these revelations riveted. Of all the questions tumbling about her brain, the one that bubbled uppermost was, "And Reggie set about his Dad ?"

"I'll say. Bloody fantastic, it was! Served the wicked sod right, too."

"I knew he never cared for his Dad much, but... And Reggie and you had a thing? You mean a romance?"

"A romance!" repeated Mary, comically teasing Sarah for her

choice of word. "I'll say! Didn't you know? We thought you'd all guessed. And his twin, Stan. Oh, yes," she rolled her eyes, "we had some right times the three of us."

Sarah looked at her friend quite unable to understand her.

"Oh now," said Mary, "don't look so shocked." She stubbed out her cigarette in the tin top and crouched on her haunches before Sarah, holding her hands. "I'm thinking you're still suffering from what that bastard Fred did to you. There's fellas in the world who'll love you for yourself, y'know. And the nookie bit can be the best fun ever, believe me." Smacking her lightly on the knee she added, "Fix your hair, you look frazzled. Ma Vines will be after us. There's tons more clearin' up yet to do."

Preoccupied with her thoughts, Sarah moved to the mirror tidying her hair behind her ears. "I pushed Edmond under the water."

"Shouldn't think that'll qualify you for the sack. Here, let me," and she arranged the ribbons of the Battenburg cap down the back of Sarah's hair.

Sarah looked at herself in the mirror, then at Mary's merry face. Comparing herself to the older girl, to her obvious experience of life, she felt an odd sort of admiration. Realising their experiences with Fred had affected them so differently, she thought... *She's so relaxed about sex, boastful, even. I feel numb about it. But if that's true, why did I react that way to Edmond?* "What do you think I should I say to him?"

"Edmond? Nothing. Just be polite. And being a bit stand offish wouldn't hurt none."

Sarah bit her lip.

Mary noticed. "How old are you?"

"Sixteen."

Mary raised her eyes to heaven and turned Sarah round to face her. "Just keep out of his way. And whatever you do, don't flirt."

Sarah tried to smile.

"Now don't tell me you don't know how to do that! Oh, I can see I'm going to have to take you in hand. Come on, lass," and with her arm round Sarah's waist she ushered her out of her bedroom into the hall.

On their arrival in the kitchen, Miss Vines snapped at Sarah with, "Her Ladyship's been asking for you. She's in her bedroom. And Mrs Cox left you that." She pointed to a brown paper parcel on the sideboard.

Sarah swiftly made up a tea tray, taking care to place a pink and yellow flower she'd saved for the purpose from one of the wreaths into a silver rose holder. Wondering if Edmond had reported what had happened, she mounted the servants' stairway to Lady Isabel's bedroom. After setting down the tray on the marble mosaic table in the hall, she knocked.

"Come in." Lady Isabel's voice sounded cold.

Sarah opened the door then retrieved the tray.

Lady Isabel was lying in bed. "At last," she said, sitting up. "Wherever have you been, Smith? I like my tea at four o'clock, it's nearly half past."

"Sorry, m'lady, I was busy with..." It was only then, when she was halfway across the room, that she noticed Edmond curled up in his dressing gown on the chaise longue with Frou Frou on his lap. He was regarding her with an amused smile on his lips. She tried not to stammer as she completed her sentence, "...with something."

"Oh, an Epimedium!" gasped Lady Isabel, delightedly holding the flower from the tray to her nose. "They're known as 'Bishop's hat', you know. Apt, Smith, most apt. No scent, of course, but most appreciated."

Sarah flipped down the side legs of the tray and carefully placed it on Lady Isabel's lap.

"Thank you. Remove Edmond's dirty tray, would you?"

"Y'Ladyship." Not daring to meet Edmond's eyes, she skirted various King Charles spaniels lying around, grasped the tray next to him with both hands, and made for the door.

"Allow me," he said, rising from the chaise longue and following. Opening the door for her, he inclined his head mockingly. As she passed him, his blue eyes very close, he whispered, "Sorry if I frightened you," and closed the door behind her.

Sorry for frightening me! He's laughing at me. I'll show him. Making for the servants' stairs, she stopped at the top of the main marble staircase. Forbidden or not, she boldly descended them. *Careful now! Can hardly see the steps with this great tray in the way. Well, if he liked me before, he certainly doesn't now. Probably thinks I'm some stupid ninny running away from him like that. Which, I suppose, I am... even though I am older. Still, he is a nobleman, better educated and all. Not as experienced about sex, though, I bet. Bet I know a lot more about that than him. Maybe... maybe it was just me. Maybe I imagined it. But Mary said he used to flirt with her. She'd never have run away... and she was raped same as me. She'd have laughed at him. That's what I should have done. Laughed at his silly stiffy. We were having such a nice talk, too. But I don't want all that sex stuff. I want him to like me for me, not that. We'll never be friends again now. Ma Cox said you never can be friends with gentry folk. Still, he is nice, and I know he liked me in the beginning. He'd never have talked like that about his Nana, if he didn't. How can I make him like me again? If I could find his Dad's treasure... Yes, that would be grand. Then I could present it to him when he comes back from school. He'd have to like me then. How did that rhyme go again? 'Though mummy may say no. At her feet say so. A chesty condition, Long in remission. Not out at the end. To you I descend Gifts from afar. Your loving Papa.' But what does it all mean, and where would I start looking? Mummy may say...?*

Sarah had now reached the bottom of the staircase. Meeting her eyes, staring right at her, was the seven-foot-tall painted Egyptian Mummy, the 4th Dynasty Egyptian pharoah Khufu. She'd passed it before, of course, had known what (but not who) it was from the pictures in her history books, but only now, at this very instant did she connect the word 'mummy' with the verse. Walking up to it with her tray, she gazed at it curiously, examining it in detail.

The ancient doll-like eyes gazed back at her smugly, daring her to invade its cocooned secrets. Four-and-a-half thousand years ago it had been richly painted in black and gold, now the plaster and resin that covered the recycled cloth was chipped and faded, but it still exuded an hypnotic power. The fact that there was a dead man inside, a dead King, made it even more compelling. The wrapped cartonage stood on a three-inch plinth. Looped round the chest, ensuring it would not topple over, was an unsightly rope tied to a ring set in the wall behind. Around the body were depicted a complex design of birds and snakes, creatures half-man, half-crocodile, wide-spread feathers and one single staring eye. It was The Eye of Horus, but Sarah didn't know that yet. The painted lips smiled enigmatically. From the chest to the feet was a three-inch-wide design, a strip of Egyptian hieroglyphs. *At her feet say so.* Sarah bent to study them. Above the toe area was a snake-like sign that could, at a pinch, be an S on its side, and an oval one that might be described as an 0. *Say S O.* Sarah bent down further, balanced the tray on her knee, she put out her hand to press the S. The material gave way slightly under her finger. Then she pushed the O sign. The material gave way even more, causing a gap to appear between the plastered cloth and the upright panel facing the toes. Sarah could clearly see rough string-like stitches threaded through holes in the arched panel.

"Smith!" called John, the old butler, as he entered the hall to attend to the grandfather clock. "What are you up to?"

"Nothing," she said, getting up. "Just dropped something," and she scurried away to the kitchen, where she opened the parcel Ma Cox had left. Wrapped up in her best summer dress was a toothbrush, a pair of worn boots and a wooden bird on a spring that she'd won at the Woodbury Fair two years ago, with it was a note.

'Dear Sarah, Hope you are keeping well and happy in your new employment. In the excitement of leaving we forgot to pack these, I thought you would like them. We all miss you. All good wishes, Ma Cox.'

That evening in Lady Isabel's boudoir as Sarah was tidying away her mistress's clothes, the Lady entered from her bathroom tying the cord of her full-length pink and beige peignoir. Wearily, she sat before her dressing table. "What a day!" Closing her eyes she murmured, "I pray to God I never have to go through another like it." Unpinning her hair, she addressed Sarah in the mirror. "Mrs Cox was asking after you. Did you see her? She said she'd left you a parcel."

"It was just a summer dress, y'Ladyship, and a toy she thought I might like."

"A doll?"

"No. I never played with dolls."

"Really? Well, I suppose you had real little girls to play with."

Sarah nodded. "I certainly used to dress them up and read them bedtime stories."

"Fairy stories?"

"I must have read every fairy story ever written."

"Here." Lady Isabel held up her silver-backed hairbrush with 'I.K.' engraved on the back. "Brush my hair, would you?"

Sarah took the brush and with her left hand scooped up Lady Isabel's long greying tresses. Slowly, in steady strokes, she brushed.

"You're used to doing this, I can tell. But with darker hair than mine, I daresay."

Sarah smiled at Lady Isabel in the mirror. "You have lovely hair, m'lady."

"Thank you, Smith. Time was, time was." Gazing at herself thoughtfully in the mirror, she said, "I was once told it was 'the colour of beech leaves in autumn.' Golden brown, it was. Not unlike yours."

Sarah dipped her chin in embarrassment.

Lady Isabel smiled. "Never be discomposed by a compliment, Smith. Accept them gracefully and gratefully."

"I'll try, y'Ladyship." Busy with her thoughts Sarah continued brushing the Lady's hair in silence. Minutes passed. She became aware that the lady was watching her in the mirror.

Lady Isabel abruptly put her hand to her head. "That'll be enough. You must be tired. It's been a hard day for all of us. Run along now."

Sarah put down the brush. "Are you sure that'll be all, y' Ladyship?"

"Quite sure, thank you. Good night, Smith. Sleep well."

But sleep for Sarah did not come easily, not until she had completed her plan was she able to finally doze off.

The following morning when she saw old John coming down the staircase carrying Edmond's suitcase and handing it to George, she ran up the servants' stairs to a high window.

Watching Edmond, dressed in his school uniform, board the Rolls, she waited till it disappeared down the drive. She pondered about his mysterious treasure and the verse, and became more determined than ever to find it. In her mind's eye she pictured his sweet smiling face when she triumphantly presented it to him.

Chapter Ten

"*Mirror, mirror on the wall,*" demanded Lady Isabel, "*who is the fairest of them all?*"

The ancient painted mummy in the mirror answered, "High in the castle lives a maid with hair the colour of beech leaves in autumn. Her name Sarah Smith."

Lady Isabel stood tall and haughty. George Powell knelt at her feet.

"My faithful huntsman," she said, "take her deep into the forest. Cut out her heart with this," and from the folds of her purple cloak she produced the rose secateurs.

"Flee as fast as you can," said George. "Run deep into the forest."

*Sarah ran. Branches clawed at her cloak. Through the leafy undergrowth appeared a pretty thatched cottage. Upstairs slept seven little men, their names carved on the foot of their beds. 'Edmond', 'Reggie', Stan', 'Henry' (his bicycle was parked by his bed), 'George', 'Albert' and 'Fred'. **The rose secateurs** magically appeared in her hand. She pulled back the bed covers and with a merry snip, snap, snip, cut off each one of their morning stiffies.*

Sarah woke in a very strange state of mind. *Stupid, stupid! Silly dreams.*

In the darkness, the house was deathly quiet. *I'm going to do it,* she thought. She struck a match and lit the candle. The bedside clock said ten minutes past two. She got out of bed. Over her nightie she put on the pink and brown checked dressing gown Miss Vines had given her, and, taking the rose secateurs from her bedside drawer, put them into her pocket. Into the other pocket she put the box of matches. Then, carefully taking a stout needle she'd previously threaded with string from the china dish on her dressing table, she stuck it through the lapel of her dressing gown. She grasped the candle holder and quietly opened the door. The sound of her heart beating thumped in her ears as she tip-toed down the corridor, then a snore from behind a door made her smile. She ventured on, biting her lip. Down the servants' staircase she stepped, her bare feet noiseless on the worn treads. There was no handrail to these stairs, unlike the grand marble banister by the staircase on the other side of the wall. The candle flickered and cast threatening shadows on the wainscot, eerie noises seemed to issue from the plastered passage walls. Excitement and fear vied within her, but the thrill of adventure was uppermost. Purposefully she moved forward, confident that she could now find her way about all the parts of the castle that concerned her in the dark. From the staff area, she pushed open the door leading to the Grand Hall. A draft gutted the candle. Panic!

In the pitch black her courage faltered, but her eyes gradually became accustomed to the light. Dim watery moonlight filtered from the glass dome above, bathing the statues and marble busts in a ghostly phosphorescence. To re-light the candle she had to put it down. She made out the refectory table by the stairs and set the candle-holder onto it, fumbling for the matches. The sleeve of her dressing gown caught a protruding wing of an art nouveau butterfly on the table. It crashed to the floor.

Instantly dogs started barking. Sarah pressed herself against the side curve of the staircase. From the library door Donner and Blitzen, senses alert, gruffly padded into the hall. Approaching her, their ears flattened, grateful for her companionship in the dead of night, they wagged their tails and Blitzen licked her hand. She patted their heads with relief.

Listening for a moment, wondering if anyone had heard, she struck a match and re-lit the candle. She carefully replaced the metal art nouveau butterfly. Mercifully it was unharmed. The ancestral portraits stared down at her in horror, a maidservant in a dressing gown had not been seen in this part of the house for centuries. She made her way to the four-and-a-half-thousand-year-old Mummy. It stared impassively, even more alien and impenetrable in the candlelight. She placed the candle holder at its feet and knelt down. Donner and Blitzen watched, their eyes glinting. Sarah remembered the soldier in the story of 'The Tinder Box', finding caskets filled with gold in the hollow tree guarded by dogs with eyes the size of dinner plates. She looked over her shoulder to make sure there was no waiting witch watching her – in the shadows she noticed nothing.

Had she looked higher, up to the first-floor landing, she might have noticed a stealthy figure in a nightgown arriving with a rifle.

Sarah pressed the snake-like S sign on the foot of the mummy, then again, the oval O. Once again the cloth gave way slightly, indenting the material. A tiny gap appeared at the edge, stretching the stitches holding the upright arched panel against the toes. She took out the secateurs and inserted them into the gap. Snip, snap, and again, snip. The stitches gave way. The arched panel fell half open, hinged at the base it left an opening in the foot of the cartonage. Sarah reached for the candle and peered inside. There was something that looked like bandaged feet, but in the area above the toes, something else was squashed up. She pulled at it. But it was imbedded. She tugged again. It moved. Carefully she withdrew it. It appeared to be a purse or bag filled with something lumpy, about the size of a large potato. On close examination it proved to be a man's woollen sock. It felt as if it was stuffed with marbles or some such. She looked inside, but couldn't make out what they were. They didn't seem to be coins. Blitzen drew near to investigate, he sniffed the sock and sneezed.

Sarah stuffed the bulging sock into her dressing gown pocket to look at later. She took hold of the needle she'd threaded with string and proceeded to sew up the fallen panel, carefully placing the needle into the same holes as before. When she'd completed the task she cut off the remaining string with the secateurs and returned them to her pocket. She tucked a short protruding piece into the crack and carefully examined it to check it looked the same as it always had. It did. She dusted away some dirt, patted the dogs and returned to her bedroom.

In the shadows upstairs the watching figure retired.

Back in the attic, Sarah emptied the contents of the sock onto her bed. Ancient jewelled amulets, gold and silver cartouches, startlingly blue and green jade scarabs poured out onto her counterpane. Though unaware of what they were, she was able to recognise gold, silver and precious stones when she saw them. She put them back into the sock, wrapped it up in a towel and tucked it in her bottom drawer. Pleased with her night's work, she got back into bed and soon fell fast asleep.

Up in his bedroom, George Powell returned his rifle to its home under his bed and considered what he'd witnessed. At first he'd been unsure as to the identity of the figure in the dressing gown, for his sight was not what it used to be. Relieved to discover it wasn't an intruder, but a member of staff, he'd screwed up his eyes in an effort to recognise the female. Deducing – by the hair colour – it was not the cheeky Miss Mary O'Reilly, but the new girl, Sarah Smith, he'd recalled his conversation with Edmond in the chapel, and watched her every movement carefully.

Now, as he sat on his bed, he was extremely vexed. *Discovered by a bloomin' servant girl! And after all the trouble and care we took. My dear old General will be turning in his grave. He thought he was being so ingenious, too. Like a great school kid, he was. "What an adventure it'll be for the boy," he beamed. "He'll never guess. We'll have to leave him some artful clues."*

George's mouth softened into a grin as he remembered how the plan had come about.

It was two years ago, just as I was taking up the morning newspaper to his room. "George!" He roared. He might have been ordering one of his regimental charges.

Lady Isabel came into the hall from her bedroom wearing her peignoir. "Ah, there you are George. He's in a rage because he can't find his socks. I don't know where he keeps them. Do sort him out will you. He's in his dressing room."

"Certainly, your Ladyship." I answered. "Certainly."

The General stood in his bare feet and underwear rummaging through his sock drawer. "They've all got holes in!" he bawled, his great white moustache quivering.

"Allow me, sir."

"Shot through, every blasted one. Why does no one mend them or buy me new ones? Suppose they think 'cause I'm no longer in service, I'm not worth bothering with. I'm not standing for it, I tell you, George. I'm going to damned well be joining this war if I have to go up to London and start one in the bloody War office itself! Damned cheek! Too old!"

As I looked in the back of his drawer, he broke into one of his terrible coughing fits, and I gave him some whisky from his flask. "You've had that cough a week or two now, sir. Better call in Dr Roberts."

"It's nothing," he choked. "No time for that paraphernalia!"

Wish I had called in the old Doc, he might have helped. "I'll be sure to buy some new socks when we next go to Southampton, sir," I said. "Ah, now, here we are" and I pulled out a tartan sock, "but where's the other?"

"That's what I'm telling you, man. There aren't any. Hold on!" he said, looking at the sock in my hand. "Let me see that." He took the sock from me and examined it. "Well, I'll be damned!" he chuckled, "there's a story behind this sock, or rather it's partner."

"What's that, sir?"

"Find me a clean pair, and I'll tell you. Silk ones, mind, none of those thick woolly things!" He padded through to his bedroom and opened the bottom drawer of his bedside cabinet. "Should be in here somewhere. Ah yes," he said, "here we are!" and he pulled out the partner to the sock I'd just found. "Come and see this," and he stretched open the top of the sock so I could look inside.

"Whatever are those, sir?"

"Egyptian artefacts. Lazuli, Beryl, and that one's Carnelian. Amulets, they're called. Pal of mine, Flinders Petrie gave them to me, along with old King Khufu back in '84. It was payback, 'cause I'd backed his expedition. Grand fella, he was."

"Artefacts, sir? They must be worth a fortune. Shouldn't they be in the bank, sir? A museum or something, somewhere safe?"

"I was saving them for the boys. Forgot I'd put them here, till I recognised that tartan sock just now."

I handed him the clean pair of socks I'd found. "Here we are, sir. Nice and fresh."

"But they're black, man. They're for evening Mess kit. Oh, better than nothing, I suppose." He sat on a chair and put them on.

"So what's the plan of action this morning, sir?"

Raising his eyebrows and with a gleeful look in his eye, he said. "Maybe we should hide it away, eh? Give the boys a treasure hunt, eh? With clues. What do you say?"

"How, sir? I mean, where would you leave the clues? Who for exactly?"

"Ah! You're thinking of young Edmond, eh? You always mind him, don't you?"

"He'd certainly enjoy a treasure hunt, sir. 'Specially one planned by you."

"Well, why not?" he chuckled. "Let's see what we can devise. He certainly deserves something, poor little bugger. He'll get nothing when I kick the bucket, less I make some provision. He'll appreciate it. Yes, good notion! Let's think up some Lewis Carroll type doggerel as clues."

"Not much cop at poetry, me, sir."

"Her Ladyship's good at that sort of thing. I'll ask her. Where shall we hide it?"

"In the summerhouse, sir?"

"Too risky. Some gardener fellow might spot it. Should really conceal it with old King Khufu. Like to like, y' 'know. Cut him open and pop it in!"

"But we couldn't do that, sir!"

His eyebrows shot up. "Why not? He's a goner. He'll never know."

"I mean, how, sir? Where would you cut him open?"

"I always thought the space above his toes was roomy. What do you suppose those Egyptian fellas used to stuff in there?" His eyes flashed wickedly. "Why don't we slice him open and find out?"

Which is exactly what we did. Sliced open the feet of the mummy with his cut-throat razor, he did. Late one night after everyone had gone to bed. That was before he got sick, of course, before he took to his bed. We had to help him write the clues, and her Ladyship put one in her hat box. "Let him discover it for himself," he said. "If he struggles, help him, but cleverly, don't let him know you're in on it." Ah! my dear old General.

George got into his bed and contemplated each course of action: *Shall I face the girl? Take the treasure back? Or just watch her? She's a smart one, I'll say that much for her. The boy was right. 'Smart filly', as the General used to say. Maybe I should just watch her. Write to the boy, though, let him know what's happened.*

Chapter Eleven

The timetable at Kingsford Hall was more relaxed than it had ever been at the orphanage, there, Annie had insisted everything be done as and when her rigid timetable demanded. At Kingsford Hall the tempo of life was easier. Miss Vines kept Sarah pretty busy, but her tasks weren't nearly so exhausting or taxing as Annie had warned – there were even some afternoons when she had time to herself. Possibly, this was because most of the rooms in the castle were closed, or possibly because there were twenty-four other servants to wait on Lady Isabel, or more likely, because the Lady around whom all their lives revolved was frequently absent. This was when George would drive her to one of her Women's Organisations or charity meetings, to call on estate workers, or visit local farmers, or go to Southampton on business – though what that business was, exactly, was a mystery. These almost daily expeditions, the Lady referred to as "my war work".

On these occasions, after Sarah had attended to the Lady's wardrobe, she worked in the garden or explored the grounds, frequently the north field where the sheep grazed. On rainy days she'd read a book. The previous occupant of her room had left some novelette romances in the bookcase, but among them was a copy of 'The Woman in White' by Wilkie Collins, which, at the moment, was enthralling her. Such was the case on the afternoon following the night she'd found the treasure. She finished a chapter and lay on her bed in the attic wondering what Edmond was doing at Eton. After deliberating, and spending a considerable time trying to improve her hand, in particular, by holding her pen in the way she'd lately witnessed Lady Isabel achieve her flourishing style, she wrote him a letter.

Dear Edmond Kingsford ('Sir' she'd thought too formal, 'Edmond' too familiar)

Hoping this finds you well and enjoying your schooling. I thought I should write to tell you I have found your treasure. It was in the feet of the mummy in the hall. I found it in the middle of the night, so nobody knows. I will keep it safe. It is in a small bag (I think it might be one of your Papa's socks) with bracelets and what looks like bands of silver, and gemstones. I am enjoying working for m 'lady your Mother.

Hoping to see you in your school holidays. Best wishes,

Yours Sarah Smith. Miss.

A week later she received the following reply.

Keate House.
Eton College.
Berkshire
12th May 1916

Dear Sarah,

Thank you for writing with such good news. Congratulations! You are an ace clever girl, brave too, discovering it at night. I never thought of _that_ mummy, but I do know all about him. It's quite a long story so I'll save it till I see you, which will not be until the summer

116

holidays. Meanwhile look after the treasure – and of course yourself.

Yours sincerely, Edmond Kingsford.

Sarah thought having to wait till Edmond's summer holiday was an awfully long time.

The war was changing everything. The Victorian image of womanhood was being shattered. Below stairs in the servants' dining room, over a supper of cod-fish, roast lamb, cutlets and pudding, the assembled staff were discussing this altered condition and the changing times in which they were living. Their conversation had been precipitated by a 'Working for Victory' poster, which had mysteriously appeared below stairs. The talk was of the new opportunities opening for women, of joining the newly-formed Women's Royal Navy Service, the Army Auxiliary Corps or, even more thrillingly, the Women's Royal Air Force.

"I'd rather keep me feet on the ground, thanks very much," commented Cook Walsh, mother to Henry, the boy with the bicycle.

"Be a sight more exciting than this," declared the upper housemaid. "Twenty-five of us lot keepin' this rattling great place clean can't be right, not when the country needs nurses, munition workers and all."

"My Dad says as how they're employing women welders down the shipyards in Southampton," said the first laundry-maid. "Riveting and labouring, they are, just like the menfolk!"

"Well, good luck to them. Me, I'd rather bake a pie of chitterlings."

"Gettin' out of service gets you more respect," said Mary O'Reilly.

"I hear they're taking women as railway porters and for the Fire Brigade up in London!" said another laundry-maid.

"Fat lot of respect you'd get as a porter!" said George Powell.

"Get the tips, though, wouldn't you?" answered Mary. "And in the Fire Brigade, you get to see all sorts." At this there were bawdy cheers. "Or so I'm told," she added, with raised eyebrows in a comic imitation of an affected lady.

Sarah did not join in the laughter. She thought it disloyal to even think of leaving Lady Isabel. Folding up her napkin, fully aware of the bombshell she was about to drop, she said, "I heard her Ladyship say as she was going to hand The Hall over to the medical authorities. Turn it into a hospital!"

George Powell gave her his fish-eye.

"Don't make me laugh!" scoffed the upper housemaid. "If she's going to be doin' that, I'm goin' to be off like greased lightning! This place as an 'ospital! It just ain't suitable."

This latter critique Lady Isabel had voiced herself. However, from her pre-eminent social position, and after lobbying a certain war minister at her husband's funeral, her plan succeeded. Permission from the War Office was granted, and the staff were ordered to open up long-closed rooms and prepare.

As they did so, Sarah received a second letter from Edmond.

Dear Sarah. I hope you are keeping well. I have been thinking it would be a good notion to confide your discovery to George. I told him about us finding the verse and he might still be searching. I am swimming every day from Queen's Eyot, that's the name of the river we're allowed to swim in, and am improving my distance times. Mama tells me Kingsford Hall is to become a Convalescent Hospital. I think it an excellent idea but no doubt it will keep you very busy. I look forward to resuming our friendship when I return in ten weeks. Yours Edmond.

She read the last sentence four times before putting it away in her bedside drawer. But not for one moment did she consider taking his advice. *Sharing the secret with George? Certainly not. This only concerns Edmond and me.*

In the great dining hall the glittering crystal chandelier hung incongruously above forty-eight standard issue iron beds and wooden lockers, and in the gold-embossed ballroom, where once Kings and Queens had waltzed, five rows of twelve made-up beds and their side-cupboards were arranged to await the wounded.

They arrived by ambulance and lorry on a sunny afternoon in June, all one hundred of them, men and boys, accompanied by Voluntary Aid Detachment nurses in starched cotton uniforms, with orderlies and a doctor. Lady Isabel welcomed them on the front steps with Sarah in attendance behind her. The sight of these helpless bandaged young men – some on stretchers, some on crutches without a leg or arm, men unable to see, blinded by mustard gas – made the war suddenly horribly real. Sarah watched the blind men line up, each one placing his hands on his neighbour's shoulders. Her heart filled with compassion, any distrust she'd harboured towards men evaporated. Instinctively she stepped forward. "Can I help at all?" she asked.

"Ta, luv'," said a young soldier. "You sound nice. This the castle, then?"

"Yes. Where have you come from?"

"France. Verdun. Bob's my name. What's yours?"

"Sarah," she said, leading him up the castle steps.

The strain of feeding, watering and tending this influx proved too much for Miss Vines, who promptly gave notice. Sarah heard later she'd joined the Voluntary Women's Police Patrol, where she had to patrol military camps to protect young girls from the advances of the soldiers. *Still enforcing Rule No 4,* she thought. As a result of Miss Vines' departure, Cook Walsh became cook-housekeeper, Mary O'Reilly was promoted to upper housemaid and Sarah became Lady Isabel's personal maid, and, as time went by, her assistant, but always her gardener.

One afternoon when she was planting carrots in the kitchen garden, Mrs Walsh's son, Henry, pedaled by on his bicycle. He stopped on the pathway beside her. "Hallo there, Sally Alley," he called.

She looked up at him in astonishment, for he was completely dressed in khaki. "Henry Walsh!" she exclaimed. "You've not been and joined up?"

"Now don't you start!' he answered cheerily. "I just had all that malarkey from me Ma. Told 'em I was eighteen down at the Recruitment. Well, have to serve me Country, don't I?"

"Oh, Henry!" she exclaimed. 'You big lummox! You mind you take care."

"I intend to," he said, his brown eyes twinkling. "So, going to wish me luck, Sal?"

"Of course I do."

"Give us a kiss, then, or I shan't believe you?"

Sarah regarded his grinning friendly face. Standing astride his bicycle in a uniform far too big for him, he looked just like a lad in a soldier's fancy-dress costume, and absurdly young to be going off to war. The image of his wounded, mangled body returning alongside the other soldiers, popped into her head. She knew they were the same age, and her heart went out to him. She put down her trowel and, stepping between the newly planted carrots, crossed over, holding out her hand. "If you don't mind my muddy paw?"

Henry grasped her hand and shook it, and Sarah leant forward to kiss him on the cheek. "Mind you come home to us safe and sound, now Henry."

"Mind you wait for me," he answered, beaming. "'Cause I always said I'd get you one day, Sal."

Sarah grinned, and regretting the vexation she'd sometimes felt towards him, watched him pedal away wondering if she'd ever see him again.

Chapter Twelve

At last the day arrived! Edmond was due home for the summer holiday. George was to drive to Eton to collect him. It was the second Saturday in July, and the Rolls left early with enough food and drink on board for a family picnic. Sarah suspected that her name and the treasure might be mentioned on their return journey, but she was prepared.

Taking extra care with her appearance that morning, she washed her hair with the shampoo Lady Isabel had given her. "Hair always looks finer after a wash," she'd said, handing her an expensive looking bottle. "And there's no need to wear that Battenburg cap any more. It's too old-fashioned, spoils your lovely hair. We don't want the soldiers mistaking you for a nurse, do we?"

At sixteen, changes beyond her control were happening to her body. "Filling out nicely," Mary O'Reilly giggled. Since their talk after the incident in Edmond's bathroom, they'd grown closer, sharing chats in their bedrooms, and gossiping together in the servants' bathroom. Listening to Mary's hilarious descriptions of the relative attractiveness, or otherwise, of the soldiers downstairs, Sarah's attitude to menfolk mollified. She now gladly sat with the blind soldiers in the garden writing their letters home for them. She'd taken heed of Mary's warning, too. "Don't allow painful memories of Fred to paralyse your relationships with men."

She was determined to show Edmond he was mistaken in his opinion that she was a silly ninny of a servant girl, and that she was really a sensible lass with a head on her shoulders. She'd been on the lookout for his return since lunchtime, but it wasn't until teatime, as she was dusting the alcove by the window on the first-floor landing, that she spotted the Silver Ghost coming up the drive.

George parked the Rolls next to a Red Cross van by the entrance steps and unloaded the bags. Edmond emerged peering about his home like a stranger. Soldiers were strolling on the front lawn wearing dressing gowns and smoking. Others, accompanied by nurses with flowing white head dresses, were exercising their wounded limbs. Two officer types were sitting on deck-chairs taking tea and reading newspapers.

Sarah went to the top of the gallery and waited to see him as he came through the main door. In he walked, followed by George, who put down the bags and went outside again. *Should I go and meet him now or wait till he asks for me?*

Below, Matron bustled past him on her way to raucous male sounds issuing from the ballroom. Curious, he followed her. Sarah moved around the balustrade to observe him more easily. Evidently surprised by what he saw in the ballroom, he returned, stopping by the Mummy. He bent to examine its feet. Reassured, he proceeded up the stairs.

Sarah moved to the top of the staircase. Unable to stop herself grinning, she stood waiting for him to notice her.

"Sarah!" he said, almost laughing as he approached her. "How are you?"

"Very well indeed," she said, beaming back. "It's good to see you."

"You too." With a grin wrapped around to his ears, Edmond arrived at the top of the stairs. "Grand! The ballroom's full of beds and singing soldiers!"

"I know." Standing next to him, she noticed how he'd grown,

they were now almost the same height. The fluff on his face had gone, too. *He must have started shaving.*

Gleefully he demanded, "So... where is it? Sorry, I just can't wait."

"Up in my bedroom. I'll go and fetch it. Excuse me," and she dashed along the corridor to the servants' stairs.

"Bring it to my room," he called after her.

Excitedly returning with the bulging sock she knocked on his bedroom door.

Lady Isabel opened it. "Ah, Smith!" she said. "He's home. Isn't that good news? Bring us up some tea, would you? We'll take it outside on the terrace," and she shut the door.

Later, while Sarah was serving tea and as Lady Isabel was cutting the cake, Edmond gave her a secret wink. For one dreadful moment it reminded her of Fred winking at her. No one had winked at her since Fred. But she caught herself in time, she'd fallen into that trap before. *Forget the vile man.* She smiled back at him – at least, she thought she did – actually the corners of her mouth just twitched.

"Mrs Walsh made this specially," said Lady Isabel handing Edmond a plate with a slice of fruit cake. "Thank you, Smith. That'll be all."

Once again Sarah was dismissed.

That evening, after supper, while Lady Isabel was playing cards with some officers in the drawing room, Sarah noticed Edmond leave, so she left, too. Hurriedly she climbed the stairs to her room to retrieve the treasure. Back outside his bedroom, she knocked again.

This time he opened the door himself. "Quick," he said. "Come in." Once inside, from behind her back, she produced the bulging tartan sock.

Somewhat deflated, he stared at it. "Is that it!?"

"Wait!" Sarah lifted her eyebrow, which gave her face a rare beguiling expression. In her idle moments she'd polished the bracelets and bands of metal, so that now, as she walked to the center of the room with a certain panache and proudly poured the contents onto Edmond's bed, they gleamed and dazzled as they must have done when they were originally created. The deep blue and green jade scarabs, aeons old, like succulent translucent jewels, nestled with the glittering silver cartouches and golden amulets on Edmond's blue quilt.

"Wow!" he gasped. "They must be worth a fortune!" He turned to Sarah. "You beauty!" Exuberantly he grabbed and hugged her. "You little beauty. You're brilliant, you know that! Brilliant!" He kissed her on the cheek and for a moment they held each other's eyes. He leant forward and kissed her tenderly on the lips.

"I've been wanting to do that all term," he said.

Me too, she thought. *My first proper kiss.*

They both grinned.

"And all in Papa's old sock!"

They laughed and Sarah stammered, "But what... what, exactly, are they?"

"Ah now, I know all about these things," he said perching on the bed. "I've seen pictures. Papa was fascinated by Egyptology. There are heaps of books on the subject in the library. These," he said picking up one of the slim bands of silver, "are cartouches. See the Egyptian hieroglyphs here, that's someone's name. And these bracelets and scarabs are all magically empowered objects, charms and talismen to protect Pharaohs and their Queens. You see, the Mummy in the hall, well, actually it's not a Mummy, it's called a cartonage, it's the inside of a Mummy. The original Mummy case is lost, no one knows where it is. Anyway, he was once a great and powerful pharaoh, King Khufu, sometimes called King Cheops, the builder of The Great Pyramid of Giza. Have you heard of that?"

Sarah shook her head, fascinated by Edmond's glistening blue eyes.

"It's one of the seven wonders of the world. It's the largest pyramid ever built."

"Golly! Why? I mean, I thought a pyramid was a sort of tomb."

"Absolutely, yes, it is. They were built as transportation devices to the afterlife. All the material possessions the Pharaoh had cherished in his life were placed alongside his mummified body, ensuring he would be as happy in the afterlife as he had been in this. Anyway old King Khufu there, was a gift to Papa from Sir Flinders Petrie, who was his great friend and a very distinguished Egyptologist. It was his way of thanking him for financing his expedition to Eygpt in 1880. That was ages before I was born, of course, but I remember he stayed with us once when I was little. At breakfast he told us that, before the expedition, everyone told him ancient robbers had plundered the sarcophagus centuries ago, and when he eventually entered the 'King's Chamber' he'd thought they were right, because there was nothing inside but a huge granite sarcophagus without a lid."

"So where was it? How did he find it?"

"He told us that King Khufu and his architects had become so adept at designing decoy passageways and chambers, they'd outsmarted both the grave-robbers and the archaeologists. But he'd always been convinced that, somewhere in or below the pyramid, the old Pharaoh and his sacred gold still existed. He said it took him three years of studying every layer and shovelful of earth but, eventually, he discovered a secret door and cut through the stone till he found a passageway that led right under the heart of The Great Pyramid, and there they found him in all his glory."

"How thrilling!"

"I don't know where the treasure got to. In collections over the world, I suppose, and in the museum at Cairo. But he gave the prize to Papa. Egyptologists still claim King Khufu's Mummy and cartonage were never found, but there he stands, outside the library door! All thanks to old Flinders Petrie. And these," with his palms he gathered up the glistening scarabs, bracelets and amulets, caressing them like so much soft ripe fruit, "these, I suppose, were the bonuses," and he let them run through his fingers onto the quilt.

"And now, your Papa has left them to you."

"By hiding these things away for me, Papa was ensuring my future."

"Surely, sir, your future is secure enough."

"Sarah! Don't call me 'sir', please. Edmond. Call me Edmond."

"Edmond," she repeated, smiling.

"That's better. Sarah." For a moment they grinned at each other. "No, my future's not at all secure," he said soberly. "Nobody's is, you must know that. Leastways, not for the third son of a baronet. I didn't inherit anything from Papa. No property, no title, nothing. But by this gift, he was ensuring I'd at least be financially set-up. Because, of course, I'll have to sell it all."

Just then there was a knock on the door. Edmond quickly flipped the corner of the eiderdown over to cover the jewels. "Come in."

But it was too late, George had already entered heaving a big wooden box. "Thought you'd want your tuck box in here, Master Edmond."

"Thanks." Edmond smiled reassuringly at Sarah, then glanced back, waiting for George to close the door. When he'd done so, he said, "Come and see what Sarah found."

George hoisted the tuck box next to an ottoman, then came

over to the bed holding his side and grimacing. Carrying the box had obviously been an effort for him. Edmond flipped back the quilt to reveal the nest of ancient ornaments.

"Well," said George, staring in wonder. "That looks a bit of alright." He glanced across at Sarah. "I heard you'd been busy, miss. Well! Well done, girl." Nodding, he looked at Edmond, then back at her. For the first time he grinned at her. It was a nice grin, too. "Well done," he repeated and winked.

Another wink. And from George, of all people! A surprise and a very different wink from the sly way Fred had winked – wickedly and condescendingly. George Powell's wink was one of comradeship – conspiratorial and warm. *At last, he's accepted me,* she thought. She tried to wink back, but couldn't.

George laughed, saying to Edmond, "I take it back. She's okay. Can't wink, of course!"

Edmond laughed, too, and Sarah hoped that embarrassing business in the bathroom months ago had been forgotten.

Even as King George V watched the Battle of Pozieres with his Generals in France, and half-a-million soldiers faced their fears and died for their country at the Battle of the Somme, the summer of 1916 at Kingsford Hall was the happiest Sarah had ever known.

The sun shone so continuously it blistered the paintwork on the summer house by the lake. This delightful pavilion, hidden by trees from the castle, was built on a slope. Raised on stilts like a Russian dasha, it had a row of plank-like steps leading up to the decking. It was from here Edmond swam every day, sunning himself surrounded by dogs and studying his holiday homework, Homer's "Iliad". Furnished with a day bed, wicker chairs and tables, Edmond had his books, clothes and phonograph moved down from his room. On the walls hung photographs of his brothers as boys, some taken at Wellington, posing with boating sculls and team mates in old-fashioned swimming costumes, others in P.T. kit doing gymnastics, there was even a picnic scene with Edmond as a baby wrapped in a shawl held by his Nana accompanied by Sir Thomas and Lady Kingsford dressed in Edwardian country style, his laughing brothers lying around in open-necked shirts with servants standing self-consciously behind them.

At the start of the holidays Lady Isabel took her luncheon at the pavilion with Edmond, but often her commitments took her away. Then, it was, that she asked Sarah to ensure Edmond was taken his lunch. Sarah took it down to him herself, and at Edmond's request stayed – with Lady Isabel away she would never be missed. Then, and these were the best times, he told her stories from the 'Iliad', about the wanderings of Ulysses, and one afternoon he told her how he felt about his leg.

"Lord Byron said, 'Deformity is daring. Why hide it?' Take a look at history, at the brilliant people who have achieved so much." Edmond was lounging on the steps in shorts, a sock covering his withered foot. Flourishing a copy of 'The Iliad', he continued, "Homer, who wrote this, was blind, and Alexander Pope, who translated it, was crock-backed. Byron was lame, Beethoven was deaf, Toulouse-Lautrec was a dwarf, Keats consumptive and John Clare was locked up as a lunatic. So I'm sure as hell not going to let this leg hold me back. Like you should never let the fact that you're an orphan hold you back."

"I'll try not to," said Sarah, admiring his honesty and bravery. "But I don't know who any of those people are. What did they all do?"

Enjoying himself enormously, Edmond gave her a potted biography of each one, finishing by saying, "In the library there's a encyclopedia, it's a Chambers' 1908 edition, look at it anytime. It tells you about everything and everyone. Take it up to your room. It's amazing."

Later, after she'd brought him tea, he selected a record from the back of the phonograph. "You have to hear this," he said. "Beethoven wrote it."

The strains of 'The Pastoral Symphony' drifted through the trees and over the lawn. They listened, sitting next to each other on the veranda steps looking across the lake, and Sarah's ears opened to Beethoven's vision, which wasn't so very different from the sylvan landscape before her. Edmond's hand reached out to hers and she allowed him to hold it. He looked into her eyes and slowly leant over to kiss her. His kiss was the sweetest sensation she'd known. Time vanished, everything vanished, except Edmond and the music. The record came to an end... but still they kissed. Eventually, and clearly, reluctantly, Edmond moved away to take the needle off the record. Returning to her side he held her hand again, softly he said, "Come inside."

Sarah knew about the bed in the pavilion, and exactly what was on his mind. Since the bathroom episode, she'd spent a great deal of time thinking about what she might do if the situation arose again... and here it was. But since it was in a very different way from the nightmare experiences with Fred, she wasn't upset. Yet she didn't like sex, of that she was certain. She abominated it, infact. Since this was the case, she instinctively rejected it. She simply wasn't interested. As she'd confided to Mary O'Reilly, "I don't think I'll ever been interested. I never was with lads at the orphanage or at school, and with Fred, well, that was just awful." The memory of the indignities he'd forced her to endure – things she didn't care to think about – had decided her that she would never have sex again, not until it was with someone she could really trust, someone who would marry her, someone who would be the father of her children, and that someone was quite clearly never going to be Edmond. So, very firmly, she told him:

"No." But, smiling, added, "Not because I don't like you. I

do. But I'm your mother's maid, and you are the son of the house. It's an old story, and if we did what you want, I think it would spoil everything."

"Well," said Edmond, grinning, "I'd never want to be the one to do that. Just as long as you allow me to kiss you sometimes, for you are so very pretty, you know. In the meantime, I suppose I'll have to make do with us being friends, is that alright?"

"Very alright."

So it was these two young people pursued their 'friendship', crossing the centuries-old barrier between the sitting room and the servants' hall. Edmond's principles never permitted more than what he called 'soul kisses', so that, in a spiritual sense, though not, of course, in a physical sense – for what Fred had done, no one could undo – Sarah remained complete.

If Lady Isabel noticed what was going on, she didn't comment. George, too, was content to let it slide, as long as Edmond was happy. Mary O'Reilly grinned and was all for it. If any of the rest of the staff noticed or bothered to think about the pair, they may have guessed they were falling in love, but, charmed by both of them, nobody spoke ill, they simply stood passively by, hoping no one would get hurt.

Chapter Thirteen

Shortly after Edmond's return to college the following significant letters were exchanged.

> Keate House, Eton College, Berkshire.
> 12th Sept 1916

Dear Sarah,

As promised, the note to let you know that I arrived back at Eton yesterday without mishap.

It's quite fun being back with my school chums, but at the same time odd waking up in a strange bed with the prospect of having to go through an entire day without seeing you, or the next day, or the next. I feel most sad at the outlook of the long term stretching ahead sans you.

I've had such a splendid holiday and know that a great deal of it is due to the time we spent together. Meeting you seems to have been what my heart needed. Thank you for helping me to enjoy the happiest summer I've known. I never expected to find such a sweet friendship within the walls of Kingsford Hall. I know very well that we are too young ever to be more than just friends, but whatever the future holds for us, I shall long treasure our poetic intimacy, your purity of heart and soul, and your grace.

Your friend, Edmond.

P.S. When you've finished H. Rider Haggard's 'She', you must read 'King Soloman's Mines', which is absolutely super and I'm sure you will enjoy very much.

Kingsford Hall
18th Sept 1916

Dear Friend,

I have finished all my chores, cut the flowers and done the vases. Now it is overcast and has started to rain. So here I am up in my bedroom writing to you.

Your letter of the 12th really cheered me up. You are a romantic fellow! The separation of which you complain, is something I am very familiar with. At the orphanage, when I made friends, they all vanished when they found employment, and I had much heartache at the loss of those friendships.

I finished reading 'She' last night and found it thrilling. Fancy living two thousand years waiting for your reincarnated boyfriend to appear! I would never have the patience. Having to wait three months for you to come back at Christmas is bad enough. Until then, I'll have to make do with the memory of our jolly times and talks we had in the Summer House. You talked of wanting to become a writer, but I think you would make an excellent teacher, for I seem to have absorbed so much of the higher things in life from you, far more than I ever managed to learn at school.

The idea of reincarnation is fascinating. As you know Christianity was the main thing at the orphanage. I never admitted this before, but I never found much comfort in it. Before I came to Kingsford Hall, I experienced such wickedness and prayed and prayed that God would put things right, but he never did. He never even punished the wrong-doer. Now God allows this dreadful war to happen. I cannot believe Our Lord, who, we are taught, preached love and forgiveness, now wants mankind to kill each other. Not that I have lost my faith, I still say my prayers every night, but sometimes I do have wee doubts. Believing in reincarnation might make me a better person. I might meet some people who had once been my parents – that's silly though, because if they had been, they'd be children, and I'm always nice to children anyway. I really wish you were here so we could discuss it. I could never talk to the Rev Ralph about it.

Next Day.

George took me into East Boldre this morning, the little chestnut mare had to be shod, she has only been in the trap twice. Frou seems to be getting fatter. I don't like being a tell-tale, but I suspect the soldiers are feeding her tidbits. I will make sure she gets more exercise. One of the soldiers can play the piano very well, so we are hoping for some good music.

I have been thinking a lot about what you said about us all having free will and there being no such thing as Fate. I don't think I can agree with you about this. I would like to, but free will is not possible when you are in service. Rich people see the world *differently. Sorry, I know talk of this kind irritates you, so I'll stop.*

You must admit though that Fate seems to make us pay for the good things that happen. Like you don't have to go to war, but at such a severe cost, and after my unhappy childhood we have met, and I am happy looking after her Ladyship, your mother.

Must away, it is nearly suppertime and I shall be needed downstairs in the kitchen. Good-bye for a while, my dear friend. May the good Lord keep you and look after you till we meet again.

Sarah.

PART THREE

For King and Country

Chapter Fourteen

The very thing Annie Cox dreaded most, happened.

The postwoman was at her cottage door holding out an official-looking buff envelope. *Oh God! Is it Albert, Fred or, God forbid, one of the twins?* She accepted it with a stony face and closed the door. Alone, she stood staring at it. It could have contained something official to do with the orphanage, with the animals, anything, but Annie just knew it didn't. She ripped it open.

It was from the Records Office, Army Form B104-82B. There was a reference number. It was part-typed and part-handwritten. '*Madam*', she read.

> 'It is my painful duty to inform you that a report has been received from the War Office notifying the death of:
>
> (No) 233827(3124) (Rank) Private
> (Name) Albert Walter Cox
> (Regiment) Royal Hampshire.
> Which occurred in the field
> on the 25th day of July 1916.
> The report is to the effect that he was killed in action.
>
> By His Majesty's command I am to forward the enclosed message of sympathy from Their Gracious Majesties the King and Queen. I am at the same time

to express the regret of the Army Council at the soldier's death in his Country's service.

I am,

Madam,

Your obedient servant. J.T. Taylor Major

Officer in charge of records.'

Annie's knees gave way, she steadied herself and sank to a chair. With her eyes welling up, she read the attached letter with a Royal crest. 'The King commands me to assure you of the true sympathy of His Majesty and The Queen in your sorrow. He, whose loss you mourn, died in the noblest of causes. His Country will be ever grateful to him for the sacrifice he has made for Freedom and Justice.'

A tear dribbled down her cheek and fell on the signature of the Secretary of State for War, causing the black ink to bleed. She leant back and sobbed, praying to God to give her strength, and for Albert's guiltless soul. Not having seen him for two years – she only had his letters – she prayed that he had not suffered. Opening her eyes, her glance fell on Fred's old accordion lying in the corner. She prayed for him, too, and wondered if he'd been with Albert when he'd died.

He had.

Over the years, out of the hellish situation of war, Fred and Albert's lopsided friendship had developed into a fierce loyalty and do-or-die comradeship. Though the official report concerning the battle where Albert's death had occurred was noted as 'Attacks on High Wood', in truth, Albert was shot after gaining only a few yards of greenwood thicket.

Fred had been crouching a few yards behind him when he saw him fall. He ran to him. Blood was pumping from Albert's neck. A bullet had struck his collarbone and ricocheted into his heart.

Fred cradled him in his arms, "Hang on, mate," he'd said. "Hang on. I'll get help."

Albert shook his head, "Don't leave." Gasping he said, "Think I'm a goner."

"Bollocks, mate. Don't you dare."

"Annie..." Albert choked on his blood. "Look after her."

"Don't talk daft, mate...."

"Promise me!"

Fred nodded grimly. "I will, mate. I will."

But even as Albert died in his arms, he doubted he could honour such a promise.

With Albert gone, Fred, battle-hardened and exhausted, decided he'd had enough. He made the decision to shoot himself in the hand to qualify for repatriation. Then he heard the rumour his division might be transferred to Italy, so delayed. The rumour proved true, and in 1917 the Royal Hampshires were relocated to Italy where they took no part in any major action. Fred rested, drank a good deal, and caught a dose of the clap.

Back at Kingsford Hall, Lady Isabel was celebrating her forty-second birthday by giving a tea-party in her private drawing-room. Sarah was serving tea and birthday cake to an assembly of the highest Hampshire society, mostly genteel, middle-aged ladies wearing handsome feathered hats. Among them were Lady Isabel's sister-in-law, Mrs Christiana Ambrose with her husband the Reverend Ralph; Lady Isabel's younger sister, Beatrice, a stout lady with a superior expression, whose chauffeur had driven her over from Brighton for the occasion with her son, a fourteen-year-old youth with severely brushed-back hair, called Bernard; and two exceedingly handsome, tall, convalescing young officers.

Edmond, who was sitting next to his cousin, Bernard, accepted a plate of cake from Sarah with a secret smile. Looking up into her eyes, he murmured confidentially, "Thank you, Sarah."

Attempting to inject a little spice into the somewhat tame proceedings, one of the officers produced the June edition of the popular magazine "Punch" from inside his arm sling. "Did you see this cartoon?" he asked, his eyes twinkling provocatively, "we all thought it rather hit the spot!"

The cartoon was passed around. It portrayed King George V, wearing his crown and ermine sweeping away his 'Made in Germany' royal regalia. The caption read 'A Good Riddance'.

"Well!" said Christiana Ambrose, regarding it with an expression of sincere respect for her sovereign mingled with regret. "There's so much anti-German feeling around, I can well understand His Majesty's feelings."

"Indubitably," said Lady Isabel, regarding the cartoon through her lorgnettes. "The other day, I witnessed one of our soldiers downstairs even kicking Frou Frou!"

At the mention of her name, the dachschund perked up her ears.

"I had to rescue you, didn't I, Frou?" Lady Isabel beamed at her pet.

The dachschund's ears flattened, then, re-aligning her nose across her paws, went back to sleep.

"I do apologise, y' Ladyship," said the officer. "You must point the man out to me."

"I wouldn't dream of doing so. For I confess I've had occasion to kick Frou out of my way myself sometimes, and not because of the 'Made in Germany' tattooed on her tummy."

There was polite laughter.

"How does a King actually do that?" asked young Bernard. "I mean, officially. What about all the documents and things? Does he just say, 'I change my name', and everyone has to obey him?"

"Through an Order-in-Council," answered the officer. "By doing this he's exchanged his German titles and names for English-sounding versions. When Queen Victoria married Prince Albert of Saxe-Coburg and Gotha, the Royal family's surname became Wettin. The other day he renamed them all Windsor.* There's a joke going around that the German Emperor, William II, when he heard that his cousin had changed the name of the British royal house, remarked that he planned to see Shakespeare's play 'The Merry Wives of Saxe-Coburg-Gotha', instead of 'The Merry Wives of Windsor.'"

Early in 1918, Fred Oliphant's division returned from Italy to France. Cured of his venereal disease, he still felt jittery. After a bombing attack, his platoon were taking pot-shots over a parapet, when his rifle somehow managed to fire just as he was lifting it. The bullet passed through his left knee and right ankle. Fred had spent so many hours thinking about harming himself, he wasn't even sure in his own mind that it had been an accident. There was an investigation into the incident and a report from the M.O., but no punishment was dealt out. His evacuation process proceeded. At the Casualty Clearing Hospital he was declared 'A Blighty Case'.

Lying among the wounded and dying, Fred thoughts drifted more and more to home and Annie. He thought he ought to try to write her a letter. With an effort he succeeded. Pleased to have done so, for letter writing was not among his talents, he held up the envelope to the Medical Officer who had just arrived at the

---

*The King's Order-in-Council only referred to descendants in the male line. It was not until 1952, two months after her accession, that Queen Elizabeth II ended the confusion when she declared to the Privy Council that it was her "Will and Pleasure that I and My Children shall be styled and known as the House and Family of Windsor."

bottom of his bed with a clipboard.

"Could you post it for us, sir?"

"Certainly," replied the Medical Officer, collecting the letter. "Royal Hampshires, eh?" he added, noting down details from the information sheet clipped to the bottom of the bed. "Let's see if we can't find you somewhere near home." The officer ran his eye down his list. "There's the West Sussex County Asylum, near Chichester, now known as Grayling War Hospital. Fancy an asylum, Private Oliphant?"

"Fancy I been in one for the last four years, sir. Got anything near Southampton?"

"There's Kingsford Hall, now known as Kingsford Castle Hospital?"

"Kingsford Hall?" Fred frowned. "Not near Lyndhurst?"

"That's the one."

"Blimey! That would be just the job, sir. I mean, it's near me home and I was in service there twenty year back."

"Were you, now? Well, times have changed, Oliphant," said the officer noting down his name. "You'll have the lady of the manor waiting on you now. Bringing you breakfast in bed, I daresay. Good luck."

A crafty grin crept over Fred's weathered face.

Sarah's position at Kingsford Hall had risen over the two years. With the staff shortages, the traditional posts of footman, coachman, groom, gardener, upper and under housemaid, between-maid, upper and under laundry-maid etc, had all become vacant. Whenever Sarah had finished tending to Lady Isabel and her wardrobe, and the hundred and one other tasks the household demanded, she moved into the garden – for she had become a passionate gardener – she fed the dogs, looked after the poultry, even joined the old shepherd up on the pasture field to help him with the sheep. It never occurred to her to ask for a day, or even an evening off for herself. She devoted herself entirely to Lady Isabel and the running of Kingsford Hall and she was happy to do so, for she had no other life.

With the convalescent soldiers, the unpaid VAD nurses – all well-to-do women who could afford to finance themselves – the orderlies and staff now living in the castle numbered 125. Housekeeper/Cook Mrs Walsh, had the task of producing some 375 meals a day. With only inexperienced girls to help her in the kitchen, she had enough worries without the responsibility of being Housekeeper, so she asked to be relieved.

Lady Isabel took the role upon herself. "In a crisis," she said, "one must turn the wheel oneself."

However, with so many other commitments, she was frequently absent. In the evenings she did the accounts, compiled lists, made rosters and organised schedules so every staff member knew what and when their jobs were to be done, but, inevitably, there were hiccups. When these occurred it was her assistant, Sarah, who had to deal with the problem. Having lived with Annie Cox (the ultimate Housekeeper), for sixteen years, doing household accounts (for she'd always enjoyed mathematics at school), and dealing with staff (not so very different from children) held few terrors, she merely asked herself what would Ma Cox do, and the answer usually solved the problem. Annie's lessons had been well learnt.

One slightly tricky dispute, though, is worth reporting because of its subsequent consequences. The nurses and staff required to run the Convalescent Hospital were organised separately from the domestic staff and were overseen by a Matron. When Lady Isabel first put Kingsford Hall at the disposal of the medical authorities, one of her stipulations had been that the sterilisation of hospital bed-linen be overseen by the medical staff.

Recently a new Matron, a forcefull martinet in her forties had arrived. She bustled about in a starched headdress ordering nurses and orderlies around like a little strutting cockerel. She decreed her nurses were far too busy to wash 200 or so sheets and pillowslips every other day, and the work should be either sent out, or be done by the castle staff. The day on which this little scurry became a storm, was, unfortunately, a morning when Lady Isabel was out. Sarah had to deal with a furious and implacable Matron. She explained to her, as politely as possible, that the castle did not have enough staff for such a full-time job, that the orderlies who usually did the work should continue to do so. Matron responded, patronisingly, that she, Sarah, did not have the experience or authority to tell her how to run her Infirmary, and that she, Matron, would inform the War Office directly, which would result in "significant repercussions".

On Lady Isabel's return Sarah related what had happened, asked for, and was granted permission for three young girls from the orphanage to join her staff, and the problem was solved. Though Sarah thereby acquired three new allies, she learnt she had no friend in the new Matron.

Then, Lady Isabel, like Annie and thousands of other mothers in the kingdom, received a letter from the Records Department. Her second son, Arthur, had been killed in a bomb explosion at Beauval in 1917. He'd been just twenty-two years old. The news shook her severely. She continued making her round of calls, to her charities, etc, and to Annie Cox at the orphanage – where the grieving matrons commiserated with each other on the loss of their loved ones – but grief seemed to cast an inconsolable shadow over the Lady. It was from then that she seemed to rely more and more on Sarah, eventually asking her to take over the post of Housekeeper.

"Oh, your ladyship, I couldn't."

"Nonsense!" countered Lady Isabel. "You were Head Girl at

the Orphanage, you're used to giving orders. Well, now you can run the show here. The responsibility will be good for you. You know how I like things done. You can have the Housekeeper's apartment up in the turret wing, it has a nice round bedroom with a bathroom, and I'll pay you an extra ten shillings a week."

So it was, that when rationing came into force in February 1918, it was Sarah and Mrs Walsh who had to ensure there was enough nutritious food provided. Stews were made from chestnuts, bread from potatoes, tripe was served and lentil soup, and herrings for breakfast instead of bacon, fortunately there was no shortage of eggs or fish. The walled kitchen garden flourished, more flower beds were turned over to vegetables, and Sarah became unafraid of ringing a chicken or goose's neck. She did blench, though, when she became aware Mrs Walsh was constantly serving up lamb, then noticed the herd of sheep on the north field diminishing. Mrs Walsh's excuse, reasonably enough, was that it was the only unrationed source of meat available. Sarah immediately set forth to visit the estate workers and local farmers, saying, "They must be encouraged to produce more. In wartime everyone should contribute."

When the time came for the recovered soldiers to return to their families and civvy street, Lady Isabel made a point of wishing each man personally good luck. Likewise, it had become a matter of principal with her to welcome the newcomers. Today was changeover day. A new intake was expected. She'd already made her round of good byes to the departing soldiers, now, despite feeling fragile and against Dr Robert's advice – for she'd recently had a cold which she'd been unable to shake off – she stood wrapped in her fur coat by the front door to welcome the latest intake disembarking from the lorries. George stood close by, holding up a large umbrella to protect her from the April drizzle.

From the rear of an approaching military lorry, Fred glowered out at the receding dripping woodlands. Both his knee and ankle were in plaster, but he was able to hobble around with the help of a pair of crutches. As the lorry turned into the main forecourt of Kingsford Hall he was surprised to recognise trees and shrubs he'd known in his youth. Particularly he noticed a sapling he'd helped to plant when he was a young boy was now a fully-grown tree.

His vehicle came to a standstill at the bottom of the front steps and he looked up to see Lady Isabel waiting under the umbrella.

She still looks as haughty as ever. Her hair's greyer. Wonder if she'll know me? How long has it been? New Year's day, 1900. Eighteen year back...when I was wed to Annie. On this exact spot. She was grateful enough to me that morning.

The back flap of the lorry was unhitched and with the aid of an orderly he was helped down. As he mounted the steps he heard her clear voice greeting the men up ahead. At last he came level with her.

"Welcome to Kingsford Hall," she said looking him straight in the eye and smiling. "There's refreshment waiting for you inside. Do make yourself at home. We are all so glad you're here."

"Thank you, y' ladyship," he mumbled, passing through. *She don't remember me. With this haircut, hardly surprising! Maybe I should write her a letter. Remind her, like.*

It was only two days after Fred's arrival that Lady Isabel had a second letter from the Records Department, Army Form B104-82B. It fell to Sarah to hand it to her.

Collecting the mail from the silver platter in the hall, she glanced through the envelopes hoping to find one addressed to her from Edmond. She found none, but mounting the main stairs to the private dining room where the Lady was having lunch, she spotted the buff envelope. Sensing its importance, she placed it on top.

At the sight of it Lady Isabel blanched. Taking a fruit knife, she slit the envelope open. It was the standard letter of the type being delivered all over Great Britain, it differed only in its form of address.

'Your Ladyship',

'It is my painful duty to inform you that a report has been received from the War Office notifying... First Lieutenant, Sir Henry Thomas Kingsford, of the 20th Royal Fusiliers... in the Arras Offensive... on the 9th day of May, 1918... killed in action. By His Majesty's command I am to forward the enclosed message of sympathy from Their Gracious Majesties...'

The enclosure fluttered to the floor unread.

The Lady's face drained of colour. Clamping her fingers around the carved arms of her chair, she whispered, "He's gone! My boy's gone."

Sarah turned. For one awful moment she thought she meant Edmond.

"Henry's gone!" Despite her rigid self-discipline, Lady Isabel's face crumpled, even as she sat bolt upright attempting to control her grief.

"Oh, your Ladyship," said Sarah rushing to her side.

"Help me to my room." Lady Isabel attempted to raise herself but faltered. Sinking back, her eyes fixed on Sarah. Grasping the girl's wrist, she said, "Promise me...Promise me...'

"What, your ladyship?"

"Promise me you'll look after Edmond." With a frenzied stare and a hectic deadly logic, her words tumbled out. "He'll be alone now... he'll have no one. He'll have to take over and he's not ready. He's not strong like Henry, he doesn't have his courage... not like his father. Oh God!" Out loud she cried, "Henry! Henry! Why is God so cruel?" Sinking into despair, she bowed her head, still holding on to Sarah's wrist. After a while she took in deep breaths. Regaining a semblance of composure, she repeated, "Promise me you'll look after him for me. You like him, don't you? I know you do, I've seen you together. You're a strong girl. I'll see you all right, if you do. I'll make you a rich woman." Her hot eyes pleaded, burning into the girl.

"Of course, y' Ladyship. But you'll be here. You're not going away. You'll be here."

"I won't be always."

Sarah knelt by her side. "Your Ladyship, don't say such things. Please. Anyway, master Edmond is strong. I've seen him swimming in the lake. He's a lot stronger than the wee lads I grew up with."

"But his leg, his leg," Lady Isabel insisted. "He can't walk without his boot. When he was small the doctors all told me. They said ... he wouldn't live long."

"Well, that was very wicked of them to say that, y' Ladyship. He's a magnificent young man, and you should be proud..." she corrected herself. "You are proud of him, I know you are. And if he needs looking after, of course I'll help him. And be glad to do so."

Lady Isabel lifted her chin and closed her eyes. Tears rolled down her cheeks.

"How about a nice nip of brandy, m' lady?"

The Lady nodded.

Sarah poured a dram from the decanter, and passed her the glass.

Lady Isabel downed it in one. Holding the empty glass she looked into Sarah's eyes. "Sarah," she whispered, looking at her for a long moment. It was the first time she'd called her by her Christian name since fetching her from the orphanage. "My dear, steadfast Sarah..." Biting her lips she summoned up her strength. "Help me to my room."

Taking the empty glass, Sarah helped her stand.

Lady Isabel put her arm through hers, and with great care, Sarah led her mistress from the dining room.

Donner and Blitzen followed listlessly, as if they understood what had happened.

Chapter Fifteen

Clouds loured over Kingsford Hall. Despite the heat and it being late May, thunder was in the air.

Wearing only his pyjamas, Fred lay on top of his bed gazing up at the magnificent plastering on the lofty ballroom ceiling. He'd been fortunate enough to be allocated a bed next to the French windows. By consensus these were wide open, though the hoped-for cool breeze was not forthcoming. The air remained still and sultry. Holding a pencil and pad he was attempting to write a letter to Lady Isabel, but as he could barely string a sentence together on paper and his theme was blackmail, he was not having much success. At first he'd tried writing to Annie again, but sympathising with her about Albert's death he found beyond his literary powers. *Besides,* he reasoned, *if she knows I'm here, she might visit me and complicate things.* Hoping for inspiration he sat up and gazed into the garden, but the afternoon light was so poor, the magnificent vista to the lake was dull and overcast. Someone turned on the electrified chandeliers and a chorus of men around him cheered.

"What's that noise?" asked Lady Isabel, stirring from her afternoon nap. Dr Roberts had visited her that morning and prescribed "Plenty of bed rest" following her recent debility.

"It's the soldiers downstairs," answered Sarah, who was sitting sewing. Lady Isabel's bedroom lay directly above the ballroom and the French windows to her balcony were wide open, as they were downstairs, the sound had drifted up. "They're probably playing some game or another."

Lady Isabel smiled faintly. Sitting up, she arranged her greying tresses around her shoulders. "It's good to hear the sound of young men's voices around the house again. Nothing I've done has pleased me more than opening up the castle to these brave men. I'm particularly glad I specified 'all ranks'. My husband would have approved of that. He was a great egalitarian. They're all so grateful, too." She meditated a while, then, pushed her bedclothes away. "It's very oppressive this afternoon. I believe there'll be a storm later. Can you see to do that mending, child? Turn on the electric light. You'll strain your eyes."

Sarah put down her mending, crossed to the door and switched on the ceiling light.

"No, no! Sorry," said Lady Isabel, shielding her eyes. "It hurts my eyes. Light the oil lamp. Lamp light is so much kinder."

Sarah returned, lifted the opaline globe and funnel, struck a match and lit the wick.

"This one, too," requested Lady Isabel, indicating her bedside lamp. "I should try to finish this book," and she picked up her copy of Dornford Yates' 'The Brother Of Daphne'.

As Sarah was lighting the bedside oil lamp, she observed, "These roses look a bit sad. There are some lovely yellow ones blooming in the garden. I'll fetch them." So saying she removed the bowl of roses and took them to the bathroom.

Lady Isabel smiled at her. "Do you have your secateurs?"

"They're upstairs, y' Ladyship. I won't be a minute."

"Take your coat," she called. "I think it may be going to rain."

Downstairs, on his bed by the window, Fred stared at his writing pad. After three attempts he'd finally decided upon, "Unless I have £20 by next Monday, I shall tell about your illegitimate daughter".

He was now considering how to sign off. He lifted his eyes to the garden again. Should he sign his real name or what the French called a 'nom de plume'? He grinned to himself and thought about the French girl who'd taught him that phrase. His mind drifted and he found himself thinking fondly of his other conquests, then, a shade guiltily, of the little girl, Sarah Smith. *How did all that happen? Lust, I suppose. And loneliness. But she was a pippin. Wonder what happened to her? Wonder if she's still with Annie at the orphanage?* On the lawn a girl appeared in his line of vision. He felt in some odd way as if he'd conjured her up, he couldn't quite believe his eyes. The girl was slim and pretty and about the age Sarah might be. She was some forty yards away and walking towards him from the direction of the rose garden. *That's no nurse,* he reasoned, *they're always in uniform.* This girl had her hair coiled up at the nape and wore a plain black dress, like a young lady. She was carrying a bunch of yellow roses. As she came nearer, he raised himself from his bed to get a better look. Although he'd not seen Sarah for four years he became convinced it was she. She was heading straight towards him in the ballroom, then, gracefully, she turned aside and trotted up the curved staircase beside the patio to vanish from his sight. *Could that really have been her?* He reached for his crutches.

"Ah, yes," cooed Lady Isabel from her bed as Sarah came through the balcony doors. "Mary Rose! They're so lovely. Bring them over. Let me smell."

Sarah showed her the roses, absently setting the secateurs down on to the bedside table.

Lady Isabel absorbed the fragrance. "Perfect! They have such lovely bowl-shaped blooms, don't they?"

"Mmn. I'll put them in water," said Sarah moving to the bathroom where she'd left the bowl. "You were right. It's beginning to rain."

Returning a moment later with the bowl filled with roses, she placed them carefully on Lady Isabel's bedside table. After adjusting them a little, she retrieved the secateurs.

A bolt of lightning suddenly flashed. Startled, she turned to the window. Simultaneously an ear-splitting crack of thunder exploded, and there, standing on the terrace, leering at her from under his black caterpillar eyebrows, was Fred Olyphant.

In the split second that followed, a shriek of fright escaped her, she clutched her mouth and the rose secateurs fell. Ice-cold frissons of fear shivered through her whole body. Thought was paralysed, all was emotion. Everything she'd promised herself she would say and do if she saw him again went out of her head. She took in his dressing gown and crutches and realised he was one of the convalescent soldiers. The long ago promise of revenge surfaced. *So you didn't die in the war. You survived. I'm going to make you suffer for what he did to me. I'm strong now. I can deal with you now.*

The rose secateurs dropped onto the opaline globe of the oil lamp, smashing it and knocking it over. Oil glugged out, spilling over the table and down the bedside. Within seconds the oil caught fire and the bed was aflame. In a flash the rose-silk tabernet curtains were on fire, the flames leaping higher and higher, licking the canopy above and engulfing the hangings beside and behind Lady Isabel. The Lady screamed, shielding her face with her arms.

Fred immediately hobbled into the room towards her, striking the burning curtains with his crutches.

Sarah, still frozen with shock, stared at the hateful man.

"My hair, my hair," cried Lady Isabel, scrambling to get out of reach of the flames.

"Come to the other side," ordered Fred, hobbling around the end of the bed. "Here." He dropped his crutch and stretched out his hand. Reaching over he grabbed Lady Isabel's arm and dragged her across the sheet. "It's alright, your Ladyship. I've got you. You're safe, you're safe now. Water, girl. Water!" he called to Sarah. "Get water."

Sarah snapped into action. "M'lady!" She dashed around the bottom of the bed.

Lady Isabel, 'deshabille' but out of danger, stood in bare feet clutching her head.

"You okay, y'Ladyship?" asked Fred. "You okay?"

"Is my hair burning?" she cried. "Is it still burning?"

"Oh m'lady! I'm so sorry," said Sarah, putting her hands over Lady Isabel's singed tresses. "No, it's out. I think it's all right now. I'll get some water."

Fred rescued his wooden crutch and vaulted back to the other side of the bed where the fire was fiercest. He beat at the flames but seemingly to little effect.

From the bathroom Sarah called, "Come in here, m' lady." Grabbing a towel, she ran it under the tap. Returning to the bedroom, she found Lady Isabel standing by the hall door, shouting, "Help! Fire! Fire!" The side of the bed where she'd been lying was now fully ablaze.

"Put this towel over your head, y'Ladyship. Does it still hurt?"

"No, no. Fetch help," said Lady Isabel, breathlessly wrapping the towel round her head.

Sarah tore back to the bathroom to fill a jug with water. She heard Lady Isabel calling for help and Fred's crutches striking the bedposts as she waited for the jug to fill. Running back she flung the water at the bed. But it made no difference. She ran to the balcony to call for help from below. "Fire! Fire!" she yelled. "Help!" Rain was now falling and thunder rumbled.

Lady Isabel was screening herself from the heat by the hall

door, shouting: "Help! Help! For God's sake somebody, quick, help!" But no one came.

Fred, impaired by his limited leg movement, wasn't having much success either. Choking with the fumes, he leant against the bedposts and pulled at the bedclothes to try to stifle the flames with the covers. Burning ashes of material rose into the air. Sarah rushed back to the bathroom for more water. When she returned the room was chaotic, filled with smoke and men shouting. She flung the water at the flames, they seemed to subdue a little. Soldiers in dressing gowns had come up from below and were moving furniture away onto the balcony. Mary and George arrived and dashed to help Lady Isabel. One of the soldiers was tearing down the flaming curtains from the posts with his bare hands, others beat at the fire with pillows, and, guided by Sarah, fetched water from the bathroom.

Soon the fire was under control and was only smouldering. Fred lay exhausted on the floor. Lady Isabel was choking and had collapsed into an armchair by George, who had his hand round her shoulder. Sarah went to her side and held her mistress' hand. "Are you alright, y' Ladyship? Are you sure you're all right? I'm so terribly sorry."

"Let's get you out of here," said George, encouraging Lady Isabel to stand up. "There's too much smoke. Come into his Lordship's room."

"Water," the Lady gasped. "Water!"

Mary appeared with a glass of water. "Here, y' Ladyship."

The half dozen or so soldiers in the room were stamping out the smoldering bed linen and dragging it out onto the balcony. Sarah looked around for Lady Isabel's dressing gown. It lay half burnt on the floor. She hurriedly collected another from the dressing room and put it round the Lady's shoulders just as Mary was leading her to the adjoining bedroom. While George was unlocking the door, the barefoot Lady turned around to face the men. With her normally feminine and graceful exterior now reduced to a long nightgown and towel wrapped turban-like round her head, her beauty and nobility of breeding were, if possible, even more apparent.

"Gentlemen, gentlemen," she articulated, "I thank you all so much. What would I have done without you all? And you, sir," she said, singling out Fred, who was propping himself up against the wall by the marble fireplace. "You're a very brave man. I may well owe you my life. Thank you. Excuse me now. I really must rest. We will talk later. Thank you all so much," and she turned away. One of the soldiers started clapping and the others joined in.

Lady Isabel raised her hand in regal acknowledgement of the applause, and allowed George to lead her into her late husband's bedroom.

As Sarah followed, she glanced sideways at Fred Oliphant. Smirking, he said, "You've growed up pretty, Sal. Didn't mean to give you a fright, lass. 'Ere, you dropped these," and he held up the rose secateurs. "It was them what started the fire."

Sarah took them without a word. Not wishing to draw attention to them by taking them with her into the next room, she was unsure for a moment what to do with them. Her dress pockets were too small to put in such an awkward heavy object. Taking two steps to the bedside cupboard, she slid open the top drawer and deftly dropped them inside. Then, without meeting Fred's eyes, which she knew were on her, she joined her mistress in the next room.

Closing the door behind her she felt extremely relieved. Whether because the fire was out, or because Fred was no longer in her sight, she couldn't swear. Both, probably. Her heart was pounding fast. Fred had obviously thought the whole thing had been her fault... *certainly if I'd not dropped the secateurs the oil lamp wouldn't have spilt...but then if he hadn't been there in the first place...*

Lady Isabel was choking badly as she sat on the monumental four-poster bed. Sarah went to her side and helped her into bed. Mary removed cushions and pulled back the covers. It was the first time Sarah had been in this dark-panelled bedroom. The canopy and hangings around the bed were richly embroidered and had gold-fringed curtains, the massive bedposts were of dark carved oak. A smoke haze cloud hung in the centre of the room. She crossed to the French windows to open them. It was still raining, so she didn't open them fully, just fanned the door to encourage the smoke out.

Mary came to her side. Confidentially she whispered, "Did you see that soldier with the crutches in there? I think it was Fred Oliphant."

"It was," whispered Sarah.

"Holy Mother of Jesus! What are we going do?"

Sarah shrugged.

"M'be we should break his arms too," said Mary. "Really make the sod unfit! Listen, I don't think the old lady should stay in here. This was his Lordship's room. It'll only bring back sad memories. She's not been in this room these past two years, not since he died."

Sarah nodded and whispered, "Leave it to me." Moving to the bed she asked, "How are you feeling y' Ladyship? Would you rather we open up master Edmond's room for you?"

"No, no, I like it here. I'd forgotten what a magnificent bed this is. It feels good. It's right I'm here. Well," she said with a sigh, looking around at their anxious faces, "you can't say we don't see life! George, do go and find out that man's name, will you? The man with the crutches. I'd like to reward him. He really is a hero."

Sarah met Mary's twinkling eyes across the bed. *Some hero*!

Chapter Sixteen

"**F**red Oliphant?" muttered Lady Isabel to herself. *I seem to know that name.*

She was still sitting up in her late husband's elaborate bed, from which, after yesterday's fire, Dr Roberts had ordered her "not to stir" until he'd made another examination later in the week.

George was standing by her bedside. "He said that he used to be in service here!" George's tone left little doubt he considered such a claim dubious.

"Really? It's certainly an unusual name. I should have remembered that."

At this point in the conversation, Sarah re-entered the bedroom from the late General's bathroom. She'd spent the last ten minutes transferring Lady Isabel's wardrobe from the boudoir in her bedroom into the General's dressing room: for the Lady had decided to use this room whilst her own was being redecorated, plans for which were already being put into place.

"Of course!" Lady Isabel exclaimed. "That was Annie's married name. Oliphant. It must be her first husband. How extraordinary! I believe he used to be a groom or something. But that was years ago." Directing her remarks to George, she explained, "Annie left us to marry him, you know. Annie Cox, as she now is, who looks after the orphan..." As the word faltered on her lips, her eyes flicked across to Sarah. *Heavens! She'll know him. And he her. AND ME!* "Tell him..." Her words hung incomplete, as, in her mind, Isabel pictured herself taking leave of him... *On the front steps... eighteen years ago... from his trap... a misty New Year's morning. I tipped him two guineas, and thought it too much. I thought he might think I was bribing him to hold his tongue...which, of course, I was.*

George waited. "Tell him what, your Ladyship?"

Lady Isabel swallowed. "Tell him. . . I should like to see him. Ask him up."

"Certainly, y' Ladyship," said George, making for the door.

"Do you think you should, y' Ladyship?" Sarah interrupted. "I mean, Dr Roberts said you should rest. Wouldn't you prefer to see him when you're up and feeling stronger?"

"Tush!" dismissed Lady Isabel. "Such propriety! The man has seen me with my hair on fire and saved my life. I need hardly be formal with the fellow. I must thank and reward him. However, I grant you have a point. George!"

George stopped by the open door. "Yes, y' Ladyship?"

"Smith, here, thinks it improper of me to receive him while I'm in bed. Tell him I'll see him on the balcony," she said waving her hand in the direction of the French windows, "in an hour. It's a fine day. I'll take my lunch out there too.' Teasingly she faced Sarah, 'There, does that meet with your approval?"

George hid a grin and departed.

"Your Ladyship, I just meant you shouldn't tire yourself."

"Don't fuss, girl. I'm not made of glass! My chest is just tight after all that smoke yesterday. The fresh air will do me good. Look, the sky outside is quite blue. It's a fine day."

"Well. Allow me to dress your hair first, y' Ladyship. Maybe trim the burnt bits out."

"Ah! Yes. My hair. You're right. Help me dress and we'll prepare to greet the er... the hero." With a physical effort quite new to her, she proceeded to rise from the great bed.

An hour later, fully coiffed, armed with her pince-nez on a ribbon and, as it were, chromium plated in an elegant grey day-dress with three rows of pearls, Lady Isabel sat on a wicker armchair on the balcony, awaiting the arrival of her now privately-admitted nemesis. The revelation that 'the hero' on crutches was Annie's divorced first husband, a man who possessed knowledge that could stain her reputation, a reputation guarded and burnished, over eighteen years, had ignited cerebral and emotional fires in her she'd long imagined she had succeeded in dampening. Before her on the wicker table was a jug of lemonade, a glass and some books: among them a leather-bound copy of Aeschylus' Oresteia, some lines of which, disquiet and curiosity had urged her to remind herself. She poured herself a glass of lemonade and sipped. *Well. It seems my reputation could be at stake. I must be careful and behave wisely. What was it Thomas said? Keep friends close, but those that would harm you, closer.*

Donner and Blitzen, who lay at her feet, lifted their noses and growled a warning someone was approaching. As Fred lumbered on his crutches up the exterior mossy brick staircase, their growls grew to full-blown barks.

"Quiet," ordered Lady Isabel, immediately welcoming Fred with a radiant electric light smile. "Good morning, Mr Oliphant." The dogs obeyed her and resumed their positions, nonetheless they scowled warily at the intruder.

"Mornin', y'Ladyship," said Fred cheerfully.

"How are your legs this morning? Not too painful, I hope."

"Gettin' a bit easier, y' Ladyship. Getting the hang of these things anyroad," and he tapped one of his crutches on the flagstones. Blitzen barked once again.

"Behave," Lady Isabel called sharply to her pet. "Good," she cooed to Fred. "You must forgive me, but with all the excitement and 'howdy-do' yesterday, when you so gallantly rescued me, I failed to recognise you. I really must apologise. You behaved most bravely. Annie always used to tell me what a fine fellow she was marrying. Now I have reason to know the truth of it myself. I thank you, most sincerely."

Fred shrugged. "Just instinct, y' Ladyship. When I saw the girl break the oil lamp, I just...."

"Quite, quite. May I ask..." momentarily, she paused, "if you have any plans? Do you have any work to go to? When you are healed, I mean. When the time comes for you to leave?"

"No plans, y' Ladyship. Just get meself mobile, like."

"Of course, of course." Lady Isabel moistened her lips. "Mr Oliphant, I hope you won't think it presumptuous of me, but how would you feel about returning to work here, on the estate?"

"Your Ladyship," Fred bowed his head, "that would be, well... that would be just grand."

"We would be most grateful. I feel it's the least I can offer to reward you for your bravery. As you may know, my youngest son, Sir Edmond, is now head of the family, but I'm sure he will agree with me that we could offer you a position somewhere. Either in the gardens, or as a Groom or Coachman, wherever you felt most comfortable. Powell, I know, would welcome any help, he's so overworked. Of course, the decision is entirely yours. What do you say?"

"You're most gracious, y' Ladyship. That would be grand. But..." with a hard glint in his eye he asked, "would I be allowed to live on the estate, too?"

"Ah! Well, if one of the cottages is available, certainly."

"That would be just the ticket, y' Ladyship. Something to get better for. Take all the worry away, like."

"Good. Well, when you're better, we'll talk further and make the proper arrangements."

The interview apparently concluded, Fred tugged his forelock, said "Y'Ladyship" twice, "thank you" thrice, and backed away. Looking well pleased with himself, he hobbled down the steps, back to his chair in the sun on the terrace outside the ballroom.

Lady Isabel sighed, and glanced over the parapet towards the lake. *Well. That was easily done. Perhaps too easily. Will it suffice? Oh, I never asked him about Annie. I don't believe she knows he's here. She never mentioned anything when I visited her last.*

The sun was at its zenith, glistening on the mirrored lake, the reflection dazzled her. She looked away. Releasing the catch on the marquisette lorgnette hanging around her neck, she picked up 'The Oresteia'. Opening it up at the passage she'd previously marked, she read:-

"Zeux, who leads men into the ways of understanding, had established the rule that we must learn by suffering. His sad cure, with memories of pain, comes dropping upon the heart in sleep, so, even against our wills, does wisdom come upon us."

Indeed, I hope so, she mused, closing the book and letting her lorgnette fall to her bosom. *I surely must have learned something over the years. Yet is seems such wisdom as I have acquired drains from my mind like a water through a sponge. What I have left though, is quite sufficient to lay bare my foolishness.* Gazing back to the lake, the reflection blinded her again. Closing her eyes, she tried to relax, to enjoy the warmth of the sun on her cheeks. But her unsettled emotions provoked memories of another sunny morning, a bright spring morning in 1899, when other sparkling waters had dazzled her eyes.

The glinting waves of the Mediterranean. I was twenty-four. Holidaying with Tom's mother, Lady Emma, on the Riviera – staying at the luxurious Hermitage Hotel in Monte Carlo. Lounging in deck chairs, we were, under palm trees overlooking the beach. Coloured umbrellas, golden sands, beach huts, elegantly dressed Edwardians, and young people wearing those funny old-fashioned swimming costumes splashing in the waves. Emma! She really was the most unconventional, disarming and charming of mother in laws. Tom took after her – in a masculine way. He was always fun, too, ready for jokes and adventures. Heaven help me, I think I rather wanted to be like Emma in those days, I admired her so. I certainly recall trying to emulate her sophistication. She was chattering away in that delightful gossipy manner of hers...she always spoke as if she were confiding intimate and scandalous secrets. She was rattling on about her favourite subject, the Prince of Wales, and in particular Lillie Langtry's daughter, Jeanne-Marie. "Apparently, or so Gladys, the Countess of Grey tells me – and she should know, for Bertie asked her to make the arrangements himself – oh yes, the Prince of Wales is most loyal in matters of that sort – the girl, can you believe, has actually been presented!" Having delivered herself of what, it was plain, she considered to be lese-majeste, she sat back fanning herself with a round fan, basking in the glow of her courtiers' inside knowledge. "They say she's an attractive enough young woman but, of course, no match for her mother's marvellous beauty."

Dear, delightful, warm-hearted, wicked Lady Emma. Such gaiety of spirit, such fun. No doubt it was that combination of charm and wit, along with her noble antecedence and wealth, which ensured her such popularity among the racy Marlborough House set. She used to talk as if she hadn't a brain in her head, but she never fooled me. She possessed exceedingly shrewd wits. I suppose in her milieu she needed them. That elegant wide-brimmed straw hat she wore, protecting her delicate-but-oh-so-carefully-painted complexion... for it would never have done to be tanned. I used to wear my hair down sometimes in those days. Emma called it "Your luxuriant copper knob". I remember I tucked it up inside my hat in same the way she'd done and asked,

"What does Mr Langtry say about all this?"

"Oh, my dear," she answered, *"he died in a Lunatic Asylum eighteen months ago. It wouldn't surprise me, now that the daughter is safely launched, if Lillie doesn't make a bid for respectability herself. Probably marry some ineffectual young aristocrat for a title, for she's quite a wealthy woman, you know. Oh, yes. Owns racehorses, and one supposes she's paid for those plays she acts in. Unhappily, relationships between mother and daughter are not harmonious, though. Oh, no! Apparently Margot Asquith asked the girl what her father had given her for her eighteenth birthday present. Jeanne-Marie protested her father was dead. Margot, plainspeaking as ever, replied that, on the contrary, her father was very much alive, he was the handsome Prince Louis Battenberg. Hadn't her mother told her? Apparently the girl was appalled!"*

Sarah stepped onto the balcony with a tray, jolting Isabel out of her reverie.

A cord of guilt tightened around her heart.

"Here we are, y' Ladyship. Mrs Walsh has made you up a nice chicken salad." Setting the lunch tray on the table before her she asked, "Is there anything else I can get you?"

"No. No, thank you, Smith."

"I'll be in the dressing room if you want me," she said, returning to the bedroom.

Lady Isabel closed her eyes and pressed the pain in her breastbone.

Will this ache never cease? I seem to have had it for weeks... it's like a burning lump of coal in my breast. Time is so strange. Was I really that soignee young woman on the Riviera? I remember that holiday like no other...though, God knows, I've tried to forget it. How could that girl now be me? And Emma. Such a darling, but oh, so Machiavellian. I actually asked her to tell me about him.

"Prince Louis?" she answered, shading herself with her jewel-handled parasol.

"No. Edward, the Prince of Wales."

"You've met him."

"Only once. Thomas presented me after he'd inspected the West Yorkshire Yeomanry. He's their colonel-in-chief."

"Oh, I know. I heard all about it."

"You did?' I glanced at her. Her eyes twinkled in amusement, the corners of her mouth curled up in a mocking secret smile. "From Thomas?" I asked.

"No. From Bertie, of course. He was most taken with you."

I should have known then she had it all planned. Refusing to be drawn, I said lightly, "I've heard the jokes, 'Edward the Caressor' and 'He likes his women either stylishly dressed or naked', but is he really the philanderer everyone says?"

"Like me," Lady Emma laughed, "he is a sybarite. He enjoys the luxuries of life. Also, like me, he has many other remarkable qualities. He's loyal, the most charming man you'll ever meet, warm, witty, he adores practical jokes. He's totally self-assured (except in the presence of his mother), and he's been my very good friend for nearly thirty years. He's also an excellent Bridge partner. I promise you, we'll have a most amusing dinner. Just don't call him 'sir'. Wear your Worth, the ivory satin. It shows off your sylph-like figure to advantage – though how you've kept it after giving birth to my two gorgeous grandsons, I'll never know. We'll be six for dinner: Bertie; and because Alice is delayed in Biarritz with a cold, Colonel Clarke... that's Stanley, his equerry – he's been with him for years and is a darling; Ette and William Desborough, who you know and are staying in the hotel; and you and I."

I knew, as did most of England, and probably his wife, Princess Alexander, that the Prince of Wales's affair with Daisy, Countess of Warwick, was over, and that he'd taken a new mistress in the comely shape of the high-spirited Honourable Mrs George Kepple. "Is he genuinely in love with Alice Kepple?" I asked.

"Devoted," answered Emma. "But then, so he was to Lillie, and to Daisy Warwick, and he was certainly not faithful to either of them. I doubt the habits of a lifetime will change overnight."

Neither did they. From the moment he entered that elegant Belle Epoque reception suite – with us all assembled in our finery – his blue mischievous eyes fastened onto me. Lady Emma curtsied as she greeted him, and so did I. I remember thinking how neatly trimmed his beard and moustache was. His famous tubby figure – which I thought rather endearing – was encased in the most impeccable evening dress I'd ever seen. Oblivious to all the how-do-you-do his Royal presence was causing, his geniality charmed us all. The conversation was quite general, but there was no denying I was the favourite, seated on his left at dinner. I wish I could remember what he said, I seem to remember I laughed a good deal...probably too much.

Gustave Eiffel's wondrous glass dome above us in the shape of an umbrella, and the biggest crystal chandelier in the world. Columns of pink marble everywhere – the most beautiful restaurant in Europe, they called it. They served 'Poularde Edward' (chicken stuffed with foie gras) in his honour. I remember his half-hidden smile accompanied by a Royal incline of the head when our eyes met after I caught him gazing at my dècolletage. And after dinner, walking in the moonlit gardens, the touch of his hand on my shoulder. "A delicate beauty", he called me. My hair, he said, was "the colour of beech leaves in autumn". Oh, he knew how to flatter... practised, I dare say, on sophisticated married women in salons throughout Europe! The smell of cigars about him, and later, the fresh smell of eau de Portugal on his cheek when he came to my room and kissed me. May God forgive me! How could I have refused him? It wasn't as if it was my holy duty, like those mistresses of Louis XIV. I simply couldn't. I don't suppose any woman ever did. The aphrodisiac of being made love to by the future King of England was too strong. And all because his mistress had a cold. He couldn't do without love even for one night. Emma literally gave me to him. My own mother-in-law! And all the while her son, my own dear Tom, was in South Africa fighting the Boers.

Then, the following afternoon, payment arrived. A slim diamond bracelet...which I never dared wear, certainly never before Tom. Lord! This pain in my chest is getting worse! It's excruciating... Call her... "Smith!" Where is the girl?

And weeks later, that memorable day when I discovered the intolerable, that I was pregnant. Tom had been abroad for over a year, there was no earthly way I could pretend it was his. I went straight to Lady Emma's, to her lovely house in Curzon Street. I had no one else to turn to... no one. Darling Mama had died the previous year... even if she'd been alive, my lips could never have told her that. Neither could I have confided in sister Beatrice. No. Emma was the only one. She tried to laugh it off... told me I must be mistaken. "If it's true," she said lightly, "you'll simply have to have it and give it away! Send it to an orphanage. No one will ever know, least of all Thomas. The War in South Africa is going on forever, so they say. It's doubtful he'll be back in England this year. Just keep out of town, stay in the country and dress carefully, you must have a maid or someone you can trust?"

I was trapped. A week later she died. A heart attack, they said. I like to think it was her conscience ... always supposing she ever had one! Then there was the anxiety that Tom would return for her funeral ... changing to hope that, if he did, we would have conjugal relations and I could pass the child off as his. Ludicrous! I was crazy with worry. When he telegraphed saying the war was going on and he couldn't get home, I was actually relieved. But *then, I had no option but to follow Emma's advice. Hide the pregnancy, come home and live quietly down here. Thank God for Annie! Dear Annie.*

Lying to Ralph, 'Ralph the Reverend'. That was before he became my brother-in-law, of course. It was through him visiting me he first met Christiana. Asking him to persuade the Bishop to open an orphanage! An orphanage in which to hide my own daughter! The subterfuge. The expense! Manoeuvring Annie into the position of becoming House Mother. Will all that stand in my favour, Lord, when I stand before you? The orphanage has been a great success ... a triumph ... all those children saved ... I know it was a place to hide my sin, but all these years later she is by my side ... I could never have had her here while Tom was alive... it's been hard enough as it is... Should I tell her? Should she know? Know that blue blood runs in her veins? Know she's the granddaughter of Queen Victoria. What would it achieve? Nothing. Clear my conscience? Oh, dear God! At least Tom never knew of it, of that I'm truly thankful.. When he returned from that war he was so anxious to prove passion had not burnt out in his maturity, he was more erotic than previously, and dear Edmond was born. Darling Edmond, my pride, and my punishment... his poor leg. Oh dear God! All this remembering is too painful, it's making me ill. I'm feeling giddy. Dizzy. Is this conscience my retribution? This...this burning in my chest God's punishment? It won't leave me. It's unendurable. I think ...I may be going to faint.

Passing though the bedroom on her way to Lady Isabel's bathroom, Sarah glanced out to the balcony and noticed the Lady was dozing. Not wishing to disturb her, she continued what she was doing, for there were still fresh towels and personal items to transfer to the new bathroom. When she passed by later, with her hands full, she noticed that the chicken salad on the table was untouched and that her Ladyship's head was slumped onto her chest.

It was only after taking a sun-hat out to her and feeling Lady Isabel's icy hand, that she realised something was terribly wrong.

Chapter Seventeen

"Help!" yelled Sarah over the balcony, for the second time in as many days. "Is there a nurse down there? Someone, please! Help! Quick!" Dashing back to Lady Isabel she tried to rouse her again. Gently lifting her head she looked into her open staring eyes. They were no longer their usual startling blue, the same clear blue eyes that Edmond had inherited, but deep black pools. Looking into them, Sarah was unsure if the Lady was seeing her or not, she smiled and whispered, "Your Ladyship?" For a flickering second she thought the Lady focused and smiled back, but it may have been wishful thinking, for a moment later it was clear Lady Isabel was quite unconscious.

It was Fred that answered Sarah's call. Labouring once again up the mossy staircase, he stopped halfway up and called, "What's up? Sarah! What's the matter?"

Donner and Blitzen flattened their ears and growled.

"Could you come up?" called Sarah, unwillingly, for he, she felt, was better than no one. "It's Lady Isabel. She's unconscious. Could you call a nurse?"

As Fred turned on the stairs, Sarah caught the dogs by their collars and shooed them away into the bedroom, closing the French windows behind them. Fred called down 'Matron! Can you come up? Lady Isabel's not well."

Almost immediately, Matron, her starched white headdress quivering, bristled and bustled up the steps. Without a word she took in the situation, immediately feeling Lady Isabel's pulse and placing two fingers on her throat. "She's not breathing," she said. "Help me get her on her back."

Sarah pulled the table away and grasped Lady Isabel's ankles. Together they laid the Lady on the balcony flagstones. "Prop up her legs," said Matron, "the blood must flow to the heart. I think it's cardiac arrest."

"You mean a heart attack?" asked Sarah, fetching a cushion from the chair.

Matron nodded and placed the palm of her hand on Lady Isabel's chest, just over the lower part of the sternum. She pressed in a pumping motion using both hands.

Sarah padded the cushion under Lady Isabel's ankles.

"No, no. Lift her feet onto the chair," instructed Matron.

Sarah did so, pulling the Lady's skirt down to cover her calves.

Fred watched. Awkwardly he lowered himself to the floor. Sitting beside Lady Isabel he tilted back her head. "Ambulance driver taught me this," he said, pinching the Lady's nostrils. Taking a deep breath he sealed her mouth with his, and breathed into her.

The sight of Fred kissing Lady Isabel was too much for Sarah, she pushed him away. "Get off her! Leave her be."

Matron interposed. "Leave him, child. He's trying the kiss of life. Try again," she ordered, "in rhythm with me. Again!"

He repeated the process twice, then again.

Sarah, shocked and bewildered, watched as Matron and Fred worked in unison. "Why are you allowing him to do that?"

"He's trying to get her lungs to function," said Matron.

Comprehending immediately, Sarah flinched at her naivety. *Of course! I can hardly believe the ghastly man is trying to do something good. Please, God, let her breathe. Please, God, let her breathe.* Sarah's eyes never left Lady Isabel's face.

But Lady Isabel lay motionless.

"Time is of the essence in these cases," said Matron, still working. "Was she unconscious long before you called?"

"I don't know," said Sarah. "About five minutes, I suppose. I thought she was asleep. She'd had a bad night and I thought she needed the rest."

Fred and Matron continued working.

Suddenly Lady Isabel gulped, choked, and took in air.

"Yes!" gasped Fred.

"Good man," said Matron, leaning back on her heels. "I thought we'd lost her."

"Blimey! Back from the dead," said Fred, removing his hands from Lady Isabel's body.

She did seem to be breathing, but her eyelids remained closed.

"Are you with us, dear?" shouted Matron, feeling her pulse. "Lady Isabel!"

But the Lady still seemed unconscious.

"Her pulse is faint," said Matron. "Get her on her side. Fetch a blanket!"

Sarah opened the French windows to fetch one. "Could we put her on the bed? She'd be more comfortable." The dogs bounded out onto the balcony and went to their mistress.

"Certainly," said Matron. "Quick. Lift her like before."

Together they carried Lady Isabel into the bedroom and onto the huge four-poster bed, placing her on her side. Sarah removed the Lady's shoes and covered her with the eiderdown. Matron checked her pulse once more.

"What can I do?" asked Sarah, as the dogs came to her side.

"Pray," said Matron. "She seems to be in a coma. Talk to her. Try to get her to come round. I'll fetch Doctor." Briskly she left the room the way she'd entered, passing Fred on the terrace.

He peered into the great bedroom, watching Sarah as she sat

on the bed beside Lady Isabel holding her hand. He lifted his crutches and levered himself forward.

Donner and Blitzen growled. Sarah looked up at him. If she could have growled too, she would have done so, instead, she gave him a look that said plainer than words that he was unwelcome. Turning back to Lady Isabel, she called, "Y' Ladyship, can you hear me?"

Fred did not take the hint. He came in further ...nearer...closer.

Sarah looked up. "What is it?"

"Seems I saved her life," he said. "Twice in two days! Must be a record."

Sarah turned away from him.

"When you pushed me, you thought I was kissin' her, didn't you?" he smirked.

Fury surged within her. *Smug brute!* Tightly holding onto Lady Isabel's hand, she said, "Would you please leave. I have to try and bring her round."

"Don't I get no thanks?"

Sarah ignored him, then, after breathing deeply to control her anger, replied, "Of course. We're most grateful, but do please leave us now."

"She thanked me, she did. Earlier, before she passed out. Gave me a job for life, she did. On the estate."

Sarah, surprised, but furiously thinking, kept her eyes on Lady Isabel. "Did she sign anything?"

"No, but...."

"Well, if you've nothing in writing, you'll be wanting her to recover, then. Close the French windows on your way out. You're making the dogs uneasy."

"Yeah. OK," he said, but remained. "Pity you didn't call us earlier. 'Cause if we'd got to her before, she'd most likely be fine.

I heard of people staying like that, in a coma, for weeks on end. Like vegetables, they get."

Disregarding him, Sarah caressed Lady Isabel's cheek. "Lady Isabel!" she murmured, "Lady Isabel!"

"Close, are you..." Insidiously he leaned forward. "You two? You and. . .milady?"

"Of course."

"Well... It's only natural, I suppose..." He stepped in closer. "Seeing as how..."

Both dogs started barking again. Sarah put out a restraining hand. "There, boy." Looking Fred straight in the eye, and in her best Housekeeper manner, she ordered: "You may leave now."

"Don't fret, gel," he said backing away. "I'll still be around. Job for life, she gave me. Be seein' you. Job for life," he repeated as he reached the terrace. "Guaranteed it, she did."

Sarah shut her eyes with relief that the beastly man had gone. "Lady Isabel!" she called, smacking the back of the Lady's hand. "Lady Isabel! It's me, Smith. Can you hear me?" *Oh, dear Lady Isabel, please, please open your eyes. Don't take any notice of him. Saving your life twice, indeed! He's trying to make out I nearly killed you, that's what he's doing. He's rubbish... talking poppycock! Whatever should I do without you? If you were to go, we'd all be sunk. Oh, I wish Edmond was here. He'd know what to do. I should let him know. Write to him? Wait now, there's a letter from his Headmaster in her Ladyship's escritoire desk over there... there was a telephone number on it too... it came with a bill... from a boot maker, the price of a larger boot they had to have made. Yes, I'll telephone the Headmaster. That's what I'll do. Speak to him. After the doctor comes. Oh, please, God, don't let her die. Whatever would we do? We'd carry on, I suppose, till Edmond comes home. I'd have to arrange a funeral! George would help. Yes, we'd have do it the same way as the General's. Oh, please,*

God, make her open her eyes.

God must have heard Sarah's prayer, for Lady Isabel did open her eyes. For a long moment she looked at the girl. Her lips moved, but no sound came.

Sarah took the glass of water from the bedside table and wet a corner of the Lady's lace handkerchief. Gently, she moistened the parched lips. "There, is that better?"

Lady Isabel's eyes crinkled into a smile. Barely audibly she whispered, "Forgive me."

"Forgive you, y' Ladyship? Whatever would I have to do that for?"

The Lady's lips moved. Her throat made a rasping sound as she took in air. Distinctly she pronounced the word, "Princess."

Perplexed, Sarah smiled. "How do you mean? You mean, you're a princess?"

Lady Isabel shook her head. With her forefinger she tapped the back of Sarah's hand.

"You mean me?" Almost laughing, she said, "Oh yes!"

The Lady's pale polished fingernail tapped again.

"I don't understand."

"Your father. . ."

Sarah stiffened. "My Father? What about him?"

The Lady's eyes wandered absently, glazing over, they appeared to rest but without focus on the hangings above the bed.

"What about my father? Did. . ." she faltered, "did you ever know him?"

But Lady Isabel appeared to be in another world.

"Your Ladyship!" called Sarah softly.

Without taking her eyes from the point above the bed, Lady Isabel's head slowly nodded. Then she closed her eyes, either to shut this world out or see more clearly in her own.

Sarah stared at her hard trying to divine her thoughts, but

only recognised the change that had taken place in the Lady's face – she now seemed to have the shrunken look of a frail old woman, a dying woman. "Who was he?" Sarah persisted.

But the Lady remained silent.

"Tell me. Please..." With every fibre of her being now alert, trying to control an urge to shake the Lady into answering, she commanded, in a trembling voice, "Tell me!"

Lady Isabel's eyes opened and rested on the girl. "Forgive me," she murmured again.

"I don't understand... you mean, you knew my father? How? Who was he?"

Lady Isabel beckoned with her finger.

Sarah leaned in nearer.

She beckoned, closer.

Sarah put her ear to the Lady's mouth.

"King," breathed Lady Isabel. "Your father was King."

Sarah looked at her in astonishment.

The Lady held her eyes and nodded.

Bewildered, not knowing what to make of such an absurd, yet, to Lady Isabel, obviously important secret, Sarah stared at her blankly. *She's delirious, she must be. Why else say such a thing?* The pupils of Lady Isabel's eyes moved, seeming to stare at something behind Sarah. "Jewel case," she murmured.

Sarah followed her gaze. It seemed to rest on the dressing table. "You want me to fetch your jewel case?" she asked. The Lady nodded. Sarah crossed the room to the dressing table and opened the top drawer where she knew the case was kept. Taking out a large cream leather jewel box, she brought it to the bed. The Lady moved her forefinger indicating she wanted it open. Sarah opened it. The Lady repeated the gesture, signing that she wanted the top tray removed. Sarah obeyed, placing the purple velvet tray, laden with glittering rings and brooches onto the bed.

Lady Isabel's wrinkled, but beautifully-manicured hand, reached inside the box. Her watery eyes peered among the pearls and necklaces, with one finger she moved them aside till she found what she was looking for. Withdrawing a slim diamond bracelet, she held it by the clasp so the fall of jewels sparkled. Carefully she lowered them into Sarah's palm, closing the girl's fingers around them. "For you," she whispered, clasping her hand round Sarah's. "Your father gave it to me."

Sarah looked at the bracelet, then at Lady Isabel.

The crow's feet round the Lady's eyes crinkled into a smile.

"You really knew my Father?"

Lady Isabel gave a drowsy nod.

Joy, and some mysterious elation seemed to flow into Sarah. *My father touched this bracelet! What was he like? Who was he? When did he give this to you? Why? How did you know him? Did you know my mother?* But this was a very special moment, almost holy, it seemed the wrong time to ask such mundane questions. Lady Isabel's expression was so full of love, yet full of sadness, too. They just carried on looking at each other, smiling.

There was a knock on the door.

Locked into Lady Isabel's eyes, wanting to hold their precious moment of connection, Sarah didn't move. Another louder knock. Reluctantly she stood up, and put the diamond bracelet into her dress pocket. "Come in," she called.

George entered, followed by the efficient, but bantam sized, Matron. Accompanying them was a man dressed in khaki. Sarah recognised him as the Doctor who sometimes attended the soldiers downstairs. "A moment," she said, returning the velvet tray of jewels on the bed into the case. She closed the lid, placed it on the bedside, and stepped aside. Businesslike, the Doctor strode across the room to Lady Isabel. He felt her pulse, lifted her eyelid and put his ear to her chest. Finally he raised himself and said,

"The lady is dead."

"No!" gasped Sarah. *She can't be!* Clasping her mouth, she searched for life in Lady Isabel's open staring eyes. The Doctor bent forward and closed them.

The Matron glanced oddly and somewhat suspiciously at Sarah. "Did she regain consciousness at all after I left?"

Sarah remained frozen.

"Well, did she?"

Sarah nodded, unable to speak.

"Well, how was she? Did she say anything?" persisted the Matron.

"Yes. Yes, she did." Aware that George, the Doctor, and Matron were all examining her waiting for an answer, she managed, "It was private." Turning away, she reached for her handkerchief.

"Take the girl away, will you," ordered the Matron dismissively to George. Rolling up her sleeves, she added. "You get back downstairs, Doctor. I'll lay Lady Kingsford out and wash her."

"No!" exclaimed Sarah firmly, turning round. "That is my job. I will attend to her Ladyship. You will all please leave now. Doctor, would you be good enough to prepare the death certificate and give it to Mr Powell here. George, I'll be down when I've finished, and we'll talk. Unless you'd like to stay, that is?"

George was standing to attention with his head bowed. Deeply moved, he shook his head and made for the door.

In complete control, Sarah stood straight with her hands clasped. "Thank you, Doctor. Matron." She met the older woman's eyes and waited for her to leave.

Matron glared back. Unused to being dismissed by a servant, let alone a girl as young as Sarah, the Matron's umbrage was most apparent. For a moment Sarah thought she might have a fight on her hands, but then, the doctor offered his condolence.

"I'm so very sorry. She was a fine lady. Would you like me to contact a Funeral Director for you?"

Matron turned to him abruptly, a mixture of astonishment and disapproval on her face.

"Thank you," said Sarah, "but I believe Sir Edmond would wish the same arrangements followed as were made for his father."

"I understand," said the doctor, taking his leave. He held the door open for Matron, thereby obliging her to leave, which, after a preening gesture and a tremble of her headdress she did. The doctor's eyes twinkled at Sarah as he closed the door.

Turning to the dead body, Sarah summoned her strength. *Right. First things first.* She leant forward to unclip the pearl necklace nestling in the hollow of Lady's Isabel's wrinkled throat. She pulled off her rings and placed the pieces of jewellery in the leather box by the bedside, returning it to the dressing table drawer. Then, with great tenderness, she removed the Lady's dress and under garments, washing and sponging down the body. She dressed it in the prettiest nightgown she could find, finally crossing the arms over the chest. After covering the body with a clean sheet, she knelt down by the bedside to pray for Lady's Isabel's soul.

Rather than return to the servants' quarters in the basement, where she knew she'd see everyone and have to explain what had happened, she left by the balcony doors and went to the garden to be by herself and think.

Absently, she drifted towards the north field where the sheep were grazing. Leaning against the gate she watched them, wondering what could have been going on in Lady Isabel's mind to make her say something so astonishing. *Princess? Me? Well, that's just crazy. Lies, really...yet why should she lie? Why would her last words on earth be a lie? She knew my father!* She took the

181

diamond bracelet from her pocket and studied it. *My father a King! She must have been rambling, poor lady, she must have been. What King? Queen Victoria was on the throne when I was born. The next King was Edward VII. Now there's George V. George V, my Dad! She's crazy! Yet ... this bracelet must have been very expensive.* The bleating sounds of a black-faced lamb distracted her. It looked just like Polly, it could almost have been Polly. Reminded of her favourite pet, the one she'd had to sacrifice so long ago to come here, she climbed the gate and went to it, absently dropping the bracelet. She picked up the lamb and soothed the little creature. *It needs some milk.* Unable to find its mother, or any sheep that appeared interested, she returned to open the gate. Noticing the bracelet she'd dropped in the grass, she rescued it and impulsively fastened it round the lamb's neck. *It looks so sweet with its sparkly collar.* She closed the gate after her as she'd been taught, and, nestling the lamb in her arms, smelling the half-forgotten earthy meadow smell in its soft fleece, took it back up to her bedroom at the top of the castle.

The enchantress was dead.

Prince Edmond rode by on his white horse. "Rapunzel, Rapunzel, let down your hair," he called up to the turret window.

The Princess unwound her braids, twisted them around one of the hooks of the window, and let her hair fall down to him.

Up and up he climbed . . . over the sill and into the room. Suddenly he altered.

He became Fred. "You've grow'd up pretty, m'dear," he leered, unfastening his belt. His trousers fell to his ankles.

The old paralysing fear returned.

*Then, magically, as happens in dreams, **the rose secateurs** appeared in her hand. Swiftly, with a snip, snap, snip, she cut off the thing between his legs.*

182

Waking in a sweat, Sarah looked about her in the dark. The black-faced lamb with the diamond bracelet around its neck lay sleeping next to her on the eiderdown. She cuddled it as she brooded on her dream, then worried about what Lady Isabel had told her. "What could she have meant?" she whispered to the lamb.

PART FOUR

Transformation

Chapter Eighteen

Lady Isabel's polished oak and brass-handled coffin stood before the altar in St Edward's Chapel.

Annie Cox made her way up the central aisle towards it, looking for a place to sit. Conscious of the grand, well-dressed congregation looking at her wondering who she was, she wished she'd bought herself a new hat, for she was wearing the same one she'd worn to the General's funeral two years ago, and since then it had become rather squashed. A surge of affection engulfed her as she passed Sarah sitting with her head bowed in the elevated back pew, in the seat traditionally reserved for the Housekeeper. Sarah lifted her head at that moment and smiled briefly in acknowledgement. Annie took in her tired looks and drawn expression with concern. *The strain of the last weeks are telling*, and she couldn't help but wonder if Lady Isabel had told her something she shouldn't before she'd died. Finding a seat in the rear pew of the central section, she knelt to pray for Lady Isabel, for Albert, for Fred, for the safe return of her sons, for all her charges at the orphanage, and for Sarah.

Sitting up, she looked about her and watched young Sir Edmond taking his place in the family pew, followed by a heavy, rather over-dressed lady she thought she recognised. Peering at the woman's middle-aged self-indulgent features, she slowly discerned within it the spoilt young face of the girl she'd once known as 'Miss Beatrice'. *Lady Isabel's younger sister. Good heavens! It must be twenty-five years since I last saw her.*

Beatrice was followed into the pew by a thin ascetic-looking gentleman, Annie correctly took to be her husband, Professor, Sir Robert Bragington Curram. They both knelt to say their prayers. *Edmond has altered, too. He's no longer the pretty boy he was at his father's funeral. He's grown rather gawky, what with wearing those specs. He looks the image of the swotty young English gent – unlike my poor wee pinch-faced lads at the orphanage.*

The Reverend Ralph stood up and began. "'I am the resurrection and the life,' saith the Lord; 'he that believeth in me, though he were dead, yet shall he live.'"

After the service, outside in the quadrangle, Annie sought out Sarah. Greeting her with a kiss and an emotional hug, they both fought back tears. Tears of grief at the loss of Lady Isabel, mixed with tears of sadness at the loss of their former attachment. "My!" said Annie, holding Sarah at arm's length, "you're all grown up! And you're Housekeeper now, I hear."

Sarah grinned. "Only because there was no one else."

Too moved to say anything more, Annie rummaged in her bag. "I've had a letter from Lady Isabel's solicitor in Southampton. He says, can I ... 'attend the reading of her Will?'"

"Ah yes," said Sarah. "It's happening in the library after the internment in the crypt. The family will be a little time yet, but I've arranged for a buffet in the marquee. Shall we go?"

Annie nodded, and as they strolled over to the west lawn, she put her arm affectionately through Sarah's. "It's a sad, sad day, indeed it is." Sighing, she went on, "I've known Lady Isabel since we were both wee lasses."

"I didn't know that."

"Well," said Annie, aware suddenly she'd revealed more than she intended, "how could you? How are you? All this must have been a strain. How long was she ill? How did it happen?"

Sarah shrugged and frowned. "I still can't believe it. She'd not been well for a few days, she complained of chest pains, but I never realised it was that serious. Then, after the fire..."

"Ah, yes, I heard about that."

"She had a stroke or a heart attack, it must have been."

Annie nodded. Testing the ground, she asked, "Did she say anything..." Immediately regretting her choice of words, she changed them to: "I mean, were you with her, at the end?"

"Yes," said Sarah, and then, almost breaking... "Oh, Ma! It was awful. So sad. She was always so kind to me...she never behaved like a grand distant lady to me, at all. She..."

"I know." Annie patted her arm, unable to ask the question uppermost in her mind. "I know," she repeated softly.

"Tell me," said Sarah, attempting normality, "how are Reggie and Stan?"

Recognising the depth of feeling the girl was covering up, Annie gripped her arm affectionately. She was about to answer her, when Sarah said:

"Oh, Lady Isabel told me about Mr Albert. I was so sorry to hear about that. And you know Mr Fred's here, I expect?"

"What?" said Annie, suddenly halting in her tracks. "No, I didn't know. I heard he'd been wounded but I never knew he was hospitalised here." She clutched her handbag a little closer to her side, for it held Fred's letter. Dated two months ago, from the Casualty Clearing Hospital in France, it said:

Dear Annie. I expect you have heard from War office by now about Bert. I was with him when he got shot. He was a truly good man with a big heart, and I'm proud to say we became very good mates. His last words were about you. I keep hoping to see our boys, but I never do. I pray they are well. I am wounded a bit, but not too bad. I expect to be sent home soon. Hope you are keeping well and all the kids too. Love Fred.

Annie had been profoundly moved to receive this simple letter, for not only was it the only letter she'd ever received from him in twenty-one years, but it proved to her that she was still in his thoughts. "Where is he wounded?" she asked.

"In the leg," said Sarah.

"Badly?"

"I've no idea. But he's able to get around with crutches, so it couldn't be too bad."

"Good Heavens! Maybe..." she looked back to the castle, "I should go and see him."

"He'll probably be in the tent here with the others."

They moved into the marquee. The mourners, relieved to be done with their surrogate encounter with death, were merrily chatting away as if attending a jolly garden party. Annie searched the faces of the fine ladies and gentlemen as they ate and drank beside tables of cold cuts and sandwiches. Frowning disapprovingly, she said, "I don't seem to see him."

"No. None of the soldiers seem to be here," said Sarah. "I'll take you to him afterwards."

"Please do," said Annie.

Half an hour later, in the book-lined library, amid leather-bound volumes behind fine gilt grilles, and ancient tomes of gilded-spine Roman and Napoleonic histories, the family solicitor, Mr Garner-Stevens, a stocky gentleman with iron-grey hair, steel spectacles, and a serious manner appropriate to his calling, sat at the late General's immense writing desk waiting for the mourners – and the hopefuls – to assemble.

Edmond came in talking with Sir Robert and Lady Beatrice, who flung her black fox-fur over the arm of a throne-like leather armchair and sank into it – discombobulated to discover its high padded back knocked askew her goose-plumed hat.

The Reverend Ralph followed them with his wife Christiana, who sat in a similar chair. After having an amiable word with George Powell and old John, who were standing by the bookcases, Ralph posted himself beside his wife. Apart from Edmond, none of the men seemed keen to sit, preferring to assume a more detached, disinterested air while listening to the deadly serious business of who was to inherit what. Mrs Walsh put her nose round the door nervously (for she'd not been in this room but once in five years), and Edmond said, "Come in, Mrs Walsh. Do take a seat." She was followed by Mary O'Reilly, to whom Edmond also offered a chair. With the ladies all seated, everyone waited .

Sarah and Annie Cox were the last to arrive. As there was now only one armchair left, Sarah insisted Annie take it. Edmond gallantly offered Sarah his chair next to Lady Beatrice, to whom Sarah nodded politely (for she'd served her tea on several occasions, but, of course, had never been introduced to). Lady Beatrice returned the nod graciously, and civilly continued nodding to Annie Cox, totally failing to recognise her.

Mr Garner-Stevens coughed, adjusted his spectacles, and began.

"'This is the last Will and Testament of me, Isabella Mary Catriona Kingsford of Kingsford Hall, Bagshot Moor, in the county of Hampshire. One. I hereby revoke all previous Wills Codicils and testamentary dispositions made by me. Two. I appoint Mr Henry Garner-Stevens of The Chambers, St Andrews Road, Southampton, to be the Executor and Trustee of this my Will. Three. In the subsequent clauses of this, my last Will...'" On and on the legal jargon continued, revealing nothing of particular interest. Edmond was left a letter, in which his mother acknowledged – and trusted he would understand, that, because he had inherited his father's property and vast fortune on the death of his elder brother – she was leaving him only her paintings, her books and her love.

It was not until clause six, when details of the various legacies were announced, that the assembly leant forward with a little more attention. "I give to my cook, Mrs Gertrude Walsh the sum of twenty pounds." Mrs Walsh simpered and smiled shyly to those around her. (She had every reason to be pleased, for in today's money it would be worth about £612.00)

"To my maid, Miss Mary O'Reilly the sum of twenty pounds." Mary's eyes popped.

"To my trusted butler for many years, Mr John Fitt, the sum of fifty pounds." John's impassive face showed absolutely nothing.

"To George Ashdown, my late husband's batman and in recent years my estate manager, the sum of fifty pounds." George nodded to himself and brushed non-existent dust from off his trousers.

"To The Lymington Church of England Home for Waifs and Strays, the sum of fifty pounds. To the inestimable Annie Cox, who manages the said Home, the sum of fifty pounds. Annie exchanged a look with Sarah and raised her eyebrows.

"To my brother-in-law, the Reverend Ralph Ambrose, the sum of fifty pounds." The Rev. Ralph inclined his head to Christiana, and muttered something indistinct.

At the unexpected and, to some, shocking news contained in the final paragraph, "For her great kindness and the comfort she has given me, the residue of my estate to go solely and in its entirety to my Companion and Housekeeper, Miss Sarah Smith," there was total silence.

Annie smiled discreetly to herself and cast her eyes down.

Apart from Annie and the solicitor, Lady Beatrice was the only one present who fully understood what this meant. Her black-gloved hand clenched, and her mouth took on a hard line as she shot a glance at her husband, thinking of what she had lost. For the aforementioned 'residue' was considerable. It consisted of the ownership and income from twelve houses in Petticoat Lane, East London; three large villas in Dulwich; 'The Imperial Hotel', Pelham Crescent, Hastings, and a hunting lodge in Ayrshire. Properties Lady Isabel had inherited from their father. Considering this to be rather more than a Lady's maid, or even a Housekeeper of two years' standing, warranted, Lady Beatrice rose, swiftly followed by Sir Robert. She bid an icy farewell to Edmond, and, with her nose held high, walked past Sarah, strongly suspecting her of coercion, and, once outside the room, of foul play.

In time, others would come to similar conclusions.

Edmond shook Sarah warmly by the hand and said, "I'm so glad for you, Sarah. But I do hope you'll carry on as Housekeeper for a while. At least till the end of this term. You know it's my last, and I'd like everything to remain the same till I finish my education."

"Of course," she assured him, "of course." On the point of asking him what the residue was exactly, and why it should make him think she would want to leave – she reconsidered. *That might seem discourteous.* So she remained silent.

Mr Garner-Stevens came to her side with his briefcase tucked under his arm. In a confidential tone he said, "I'll be in touch when we have probate. Thank you, thank you." After shaking hands with Edmond and smiling genially to no one in particular, he left the room.

Sarah looked bewilderingly at Annie and whispered, "What does all that mean?"

"I think, perhaps," said Annie, knowing exactly what it meant, but deciding to answer obliquely, "Lady Isabel wanted to show how fond of you she was."

Sarah frowned and was about to ask another question, when Mary came up.

"Hallo, Ma Cox. Remember me?"

"You're hardly one to forget, Mary O'Reilly," said Annie. "And it seems her Ladyship didn't either."

"I know, twenty pounds!" Raising her eyebrows and nudging Sarah, she said, "We're in the money!" Looking around to make sure she was not overheard, she added, "Can't wait to get down the shops!"

Sarah smiled and they drifted into the hall. It had been her custom of late to invite Mary up to her turret room for cocoa and chats of an evening, but she'd not done this for the past week. Seeking to make amends, she answered over-brightly with: "We'll have to plan a shopping spree to Southampton!"

"I've some glam mags in my room," said Mary. "I'll bring them up to you tonight and we'll choose what we fancy."

"Not this evening, Mary," said Sarah, a trifle hastily. "I'll be tired. Another time. I'm just taking Ma along to see Mr Fred."

Mary's eyes popped wider, indicating 'rather you than me', but she said, "I'll be leavin' you to it, then. It's grand seein' you again, Ma Cox. How are Reggie and Stan? Did you hear from them at all?"

"Not for weeks. But these days, no news is good news. At least that's what I tell myself."

"M' prayers are always with them. Indeed they are. 'Bye to yous, now," and she went on her way.

Annie turned to Sarah as they continued down the hall. "I never thought that girl would amount to much, but she seems nice."

"Oh, she is, she is," said Sarah. "She's helped me a lot."

Annie gave her a curious old-fashioned look, but Sarah didn't notice. She was absorbed with trying to find a way of discussing what Lady Isabel had told her about her father. But the whole 'Princess' and 'King' thing seemed even more far-fetched now, than it had done then – besides, they'd arrived by the open doors of the ballroom. "There he is," she said, indicating Fred on the far side of the room. He was lighting up a cigarette and chatting to a soldier.

"Where?" asked Annie.

"Sitting on the bed next to the French windows."

Annie spotted him. She sighed and thoughtfully bit her lip. Turning to Sarah, she said, "Come and see me soon, won't you? You'll be a fine example to my girls. And now you've got a bit of cash, you give yourself a treat, you deserve it." Kissing her on the cheek, she added, "You take care, now."

Unexpectedly Sarah felt a catch in her throat. She wanted Annie to stay and talk. Watching her weave her way through the lines of beds towards Fred, she wondered what her genuine feelings towards her ex-husband were, and she waited by the door to see them greet each other. Annie reached his bed and said something. Fred looked up and stood. Annie embraced him warmly. Too warmly, it seemed to Sarah. Not at all comfortable with witnessing that, she turned away and went to the marquee to check on the refreshment situation.

Passing one of her girls, she said, "See the leftovers are packed up in tins. They should be distributed to the poor, but make sure the dogs are fed first." She was quite unaware she was repeating something Lady Isabel had once told her.

It was dark by the time things were cleared away and she was able to return to her turret suite. Relieved the funeral arrangements had gone well, and, in particular, that Edmond had appreciated her work and had thanked her, she climbed the familiar worn servants' staircase. The day had been an exhausting one. Of course she was grateful to Lady Isabel for remembering her in her Will, but, being unaware of the great change this was going to bring to her life, she was, at this precise moment, more deeply happy to have been reunited with Ma Cox. *And why not,* she told herself, *she is the closest to a mother I have.* Though tired, she felt more relaxed and clear-headed than she had for a week. *Ma Cox has that effect on people. She's so straight, so reassuring. It's not so easy, after all, to break the bonds of childhood formed by so many shared experiences.*

The smell of urine and sheep dung hit her forcibly as she opened her door. She turned on the light. The black-faced lamb was lying on the damp straw and newspaper, panting. For the past week Sarah had been suckling it with milk from a baby's bottle, now she was almost shocked to see it lying there. She knelt down to it. There was a new chocolate-coloured scour on its side and its mouth was dribbling. *That's Watery Mouth,* she said to herself. *It must be infected. I must have been crazy bringing it up here. I'm surprised the dogs didn't smell it out. Whatever was the matter with me?* Deciding she'd better return it to the field before it stank the place out, she wrapped it in a towel and took it down the stairs and out into the back vegetable garden. There was a full moon, it appeared like a large dirty white globe hanging in the sky. Trying to stay in the shadows of the trees, she hurried up to the north field. Once there she unwrapped the towel and lay the lamb on the grass. It lay still. Too still. It was dead! Aghast, she didn't know what to do. Hiding it under a bush, she made her way back to the outbuildings where she found a spade. She returned to the field, and after digging for five minutes, buried the lamb in a corner, replacing the sods of grass on top and marking the grave with a stone on which she scratched a cross. Feeling guilty and a bit ashamed, hoping no one had seen her, she crept back to wash herself and clean up her bedroom.

It was not until nearly two months later, when Sarah received the Notice of Probate from the solicitor, with a bill for his services and an even larger bill for Death Duties, that she began to comprehend the size of 'the residue' that Lady Isabel had left her.

It was only during her meeting with Mr Garner-Stevens, at his request, at his office in Southampton – at which she signed various documents, was explained her new land-owning position, advised to sell one of her Petticoat Lane houses to pay for Death Duties, and was given a cheque book of her very own – that she completely grasped what had happened to her. Wondering why Lady Isabel had left her such a fortune, she remembered her words when Henry had died. "Take care of Edmond for me, and I'll see you all right. I'll make you a rich woman." Lady Isabel had been true to her word. Sarah was now an exceedingly wealthy young lady.

Mr Garner-Stevens assured her of his continued service, for, as he pointed out, he'd successfully advised Lady Isabel for many years, and, as he was showing her to the door asked pleasantly, "May I enquire if you've thought of what you might like to do? I take it you will no longer remain in service."

"No," she answered. "No I haven't. It's all rather bewildering."

"Go for a holiday, that's my advice. Think things over."

"I've never been on a holiday."

"All the more reason to take one now. The Lake District is very fine at this time of the year. I know of a little hotel there, if you're at all interested. It must be an exciting time for you. Please don't hesitate to contact me if there's anything I can help you with. Anything at all."

"Thank you," she said, and thoughtfully went down the stairs.

In the street, George was waiting for her in the Silver Ghost Rolls. He'd insisted on taking her, telling her not to deny him the pleasure of driving to Southampton as he had so many times with her Ladyship.

Sarah stepped up onto the running board and sat next to him – she didn't think it right to sit in the back seat. "George,' she said, stopping him as he was about to jump down to turn the handle. 'Do you know of a shop called 'Madame Ziniah', where Lady Isabel bought her dresses?"

"Indeed, I do. Hungarian woman, she is. Passes herself off as French. It's just round the corner in Brunswick Place."

"Would you take me there, please?"

"Why?" he asked, with a faint grin. "All that money her Ladyship left you burning a hole in y'pocket?"

She smiled. 'I think it must be. Well, I've only ever worn dark work clothes and yes, I admit it, I should like some pretty dresses, and it seems now I can afford them.' Looking at the threadbare cuffs of her old overcoat, she panicked. "They would serve me, wouldn't they?'

"Course they will. Your money's as good as anyone's, ain't it? I'll take you there.' So saying he jumped down to rotate the turning handle below the front bonnet. The engine started up, and he returned to his seat. "Don't ask for my advice, though,' he said, 'I'm not up to any of that. Ask for the Madame herself. Her ladyship always dealt with her, said as how she was most helpful, but she's a caution, I warn you.'

'Madame Ziniah. Haute Courturier' was an exclusive ladies' dress shop, with three pink painted plaster models in the window displaying three expensive, spring suits.

Sarah opened the door. A bell tinkled over her head and a

haughty woman in black looked her up and down. 'May I help?' she enquired.

"Madame Ziniah, please," answered Sarah, feeling a twinge of wariness.

"Name?"

"Smith. Miss Smith. I was Lady Kingsford's maid."

Making no attempt to hide her opinion that Sarah was a person of insignificance, the woman dismissed her with, "a moment", and disappeared.

Sarah looked about her. The room appeared to be more of a showroom than a shop, small gilt wooden chairs stood against the walls, and lying on a table was a 'Vogue' magazine with an Erte design on the cover, just like the magazine she and Mary had studied the other week up in her bedroom. Next to it was a jewelled evening handbag, draped artistically with a pair of long white gloves and a rose. Her eyes feasted on the beautifully-tailored suits in the window. *Could I ever wear something as elegant as that?* An outrè plaster-cast advertising 'Gossard Foundation Garments' peered scornfully down at her. There was a noise of beads rattling. From behind a peacock beaded curtain, a lady with blue hair, a long row of pearls and an imposing manner appeared – apparently Madame Ziniah.

"Oh, quelle tragedie!" she announced, speaking in what Sarah took to be a French-Hungarian accent. "Ma cher Lady Isabel. A great lady! So chic, so distingue. My most favourite client." Focusing on Sarah 's plain black coat, she froze. "And you are?"

"Her maid."

"Ah! What is it?"

Immediately regretting coming into the shop at all, and not knowing quite how to leave, Sarah said, "Well, it's um... rather difficult."

"Pourquoi? Speak!"

"My circumstances have changed, you see, and I, well...."

Madame Ziniah was staring at her with either incomprehension, or an unnaturally frozen listening face. Sarah swallowed. Calling upon some grit within herself, she started again.

"Her Ladyship left me some money, you see, and I should like to buy some of your fine dresses. I would like a pale-coloured one for the day and a dark one for the evening, and some shoes to match, please, but I would like them to be simple and ladylike, please...the dresses, I mean. Well, the shoes too, of course."

Madame Ziniah's eyebrows shot up as she leant back clasping her hands.

"And I would like a new overcoat, if you have one, please," continued Sarah, determined not to be put down, but just in case, added tactfully, "But I will need your advice, please."

Apparently overcome by emotion, Madame Ziniah combined her condolence with an ecstacy of bountiful condescension. "Ma petite!" she exclaimed, her eyebrows sweeping so high, her eyelids appeared practically shut. "But of course! Enchantee!" Extending an arm sheathed in maroon silk-jersey, she ushered Sarah to a distant changing room. "You are so charmant, it will be a pleasure. Clair!" she called fiercely, in contrast to the sugared tones she was using to Sarah. "Come! We have work to do."

To transform a lady's maid into a lady requires more than just clothes, a fact that Sarah was only too aware of, but, according to the Chambers Encyclopedia in the library that Edmond had recommended to her, there was an ancient Chinese proverb that said, 'A journey of a thousand miles must begin with a single step'. Sarah had decided to take that step.

Madame Ziniah and Clair, her vendeuse, were both delighted by the challenge.

Chapter Nineteen

On the balcony at Buckingham Palace, Sarah's unknown and unknowing half-brother, King George V, stood with his Queen by his side, acknowledging the cheers of the multitude. Throughout his kingdom newsboys shouted out the news, "World War Over! The War is Over!"

The Armistice signed at Compeigne in northern France came into effect on the eleventh day of the eleventh month, 1918. Celebrations and mass euphoria took place everywhere, across Europe and beyond, expressions of profound thankfulness, mixed with grief at the loss of so many loved ones.

At Kingsford Hall, Matron came into the ballroom with a telegram. The news that the Armistice had been signed raised few cheers – from Fred, for he was now able to walk and had been working as an Orderly – but, for the others, the news had come too late. It mattered little to the maimed and blinded lying there, they were out of it forever.

At Eton, Edmond, attempting to disguise his limp (for he'd grown so tall that now he had to wear a six-inch-high boot on his withered right foot), marched into the schoolyard with the other boys whooping, carrying torches and joyously singing blasphemous and seditious words to the tune of 'Rule Britannia' and other jingoistic songs. Having enjoyed a good deal of eccentrics in its history, Eton prided itself on tolerance and individuality in training its principally landowning aristocracy. On the death of his elder brother, when he'd come into his unexpected inheritance, his grief had been tempered by relief and even excitement that the acquisition of Kingsford Hall would allow him the financial and personal freedom he'd feared he would never have. As a King's Scholar in College, and now a Classical Specialist, he had ambitions to write; being both a romantic and common-sensical young man, this translated into travelling, for, only then, he thought, would he have something to write about. Accordingly, he made his plans.

Having money was not bringing Sarah happiness. Still wearing her plain black housekeeper's dress with the fawn lace collar, with the addition of Lady Isabel's cameo brooch at her throat as a modest concession to her new wealth, she was making her way along the arcaded corridor on the first floor of Kingsford Hall to Edmond's bedroom. In her hand she carried a pink cyclamen in a silver pot. On entering his room she placed the plant on his desk. Looking around, she checked all was in readiness for his arrival. Preparing for his return from school for the last time, she'd made up his bed with fresh linen, put clean towels in his bathroom and ordered his fire to be lit. *Yes,* she thought as she bent to stoke the coals, *everything is as he would wish.* Yet her brow was furrowed – anxious thoughts were buzzing in her head.

After her visit to Mr Garner-Stevens and her initial excitement at becoming a landowner, she'd become full of doubt. Several events had contributed to her uneasy feeling, not the least of which was the constant looming presence of Fred Oliphant.

No longer confined to the Wards, Fred was now free and able to walk -- though still with a pronounced limp – about the estate and castle as he wished. With the cessation of casualties of war arriving and some soldiers having returned to their homes, he considered his status as a Hospital Orderly superfluous. The time had now come, he thought, to make his move to improve his position and ensure his future. Consequently, and unbeknown to

Sarah, he'd had a man-to-man conversation with George explaining and justifying Lady Isabel's wish that he should be found a permanent position on the estate. George, only too relieved to have more help, had obliged him, and offered him the post of groundsman, on a wage of one pound, ten shillings and sixpence a week (this, when a loaf of bread cost almost a shilling – 5p). The 'promised' cottage on the estate, however, was not forthcoming; his sleeping quarters were to be one of the bedrooms off the top floor servants' corridor.

As Housekeeper, Sarah had always been punctilious about keeping household accounts and presenting them to Lady Isabel. Since the Lady's death four months ago, she'd conscientiously taken upon herself the role of paymaster. With the aid of George, who actually handed out the cash, she'd sat behind her office desk off the kitchen overseeing her staff as they filtered in to collect their weekly wages. On hearing George's casual, and very reasonable account of why he'd hired Fred, she'd baulked, but not wishing to put herself in opposition to George, or undermine his authority, she'd disguised her feelings and kept silent. Fred had, after all, as George had commented, fought for his country and was trying to adjust to a new life.

The day that Fred first walked into her office to collect his wage, she'd nodded to him in a diffident manner, and with a reserved smile passed over the receipt book for his signature. Aligning herself with George, she said, "We're glad you're fit enough to take up this position and wish you well."

At first her words had made her feel better and magnanimous, it appeared wiser to seem to allow him this employment than otherwise. But her feeling of superiority did not last. His dark menacing presence depressed her. He seemed, to her, to be everywhere; in the garden that she loved, up in the sheep field, around every servants' corridor, and inevitably, at every meal, sitting with the staff at the table being charming and making himself popular. She would have liked nothing better than to see the back of him and give him his marching orders, and was empowered so to do, but she didn't. The result was that she mentally flayed herself for allowing him to invade her territory, for permitting him to stay, for consenting to take him into service and for being so weak as to not speak up. But that would have meant giving George her reasons, and that, she never could have admitted. The momentary spark of fire that had been in her belly when she'd ordered Fred to leave her alone with Lady Isabel was doused. Besides, there was something else... although she didn't dare admit it to herself, Fred still exerted something of his old paralysing power over her and she feared him. *This is the penalty Fate has devised for my new wealth*, she reasoned, *that I should endure the presence of this man I hate above all others.*

It seemed to her that people's behaviour toward her was changing. She'd noticed Mrs Walsh guiltily stop talking once when she'd come into the kitchen as if she'd been talking about her. There were other significant looks she intercepted. The servants appeared to regard her with awe, even servility, there was a new deference shown her that she had never experienced before, and she did not like it.

Torn between aspiring to make something of herself, and people's critical reaction to her stepping out of her class, Sarah had become more cautious and reticent – not even admitting to Mary that she'd visited Madame Ziniah's. Her new dresses were, in fact, still hanging up unworn, wrapped in tissue paper in her wardrobe. Shy at confessing such extravagance, and sensing something hostile in the air (for Mary had hardly spoken to her since Fred had been hired), she'd become withdrawn and cautious with her staff. Mostly these were girls drawn from the orphanage who, mistaking her behaviour as 'toffee-nosed', had taken to calling her

'Ma'am" instead of "Miss Sarah", which previously they'd always done.

Gazing into the fire she pondered once more on Mr Garner-Stevens' idea of giving up service. It seemed obvious and the sensible thing to do. *Yet, if I leave Kingsford Hall, where would I go? What should I do? I suppose I could advertise for a post like Jane Eyre, but I couldn't possibly leave Edmond. Lady Isabel left me her fortune on condition that I look after him.* Part of her longed to go to the hotel in the Lake District that Mr Garner-Stevens had recommended and show off her new dresses, but with each bank statement that arrived, proving to her that the income derived from her properties was making her richer and richer with every month that passed, she became more uncomfortable. *All this money changes things with Edmond, and he is the dearest person in the world.* In her early days at Kingsford Hall, after she'd found Edmond's treasure, as he'd gone back and forth to boarding school, her emotions had see-sawed between joy at each of his of arrivals and pinpricks of heartache at each parting, just as, she recalled, Jane Eyre's emotions had when Mr Rochester had gone to and fro from Thornfield Hall. Now that Edmond was *Sir* Edmond and returning as master of Kingsford Hall, and she was a lady of property with expectations of a new life, their relationship was bound to change. Inevitably, they were going to have to sit down and discuss the future. Sighing, she put the poker back in its brass holder and left his bedroom.

On the first morning of Edmond's return, George, with the help of Fred and a couple of soldiers, hauled a fir tree in from the woods and raised it up in the Great Hall. With Mary O'Reilly's help, Sarah was decorating it when Edmond came down the stairs with a letter in his hand.

"Capital! A Christmas tree!" he exclaimed with new baritone

notes in his voice. "Can I help at all?"

"Of course," answered Sarah, deliberately gaily, from the top of a ladder where she was attaching a beautiful gilded star to the highest point. "The trimmings are in the box there." At the bottom of the ladder was a cardboard box full of well-loved decorations, glass bead garlands, old ribbons, glitter balls and silver tinsel. "You can hand them up to me, if you like. Have you had breakfast?" Immediately she regretted her question, for the letter in his hand confirmed he'd found it where she'd placed it earlier, by his place in the upstairs dining room.

"Thank you, yes. Good morning, Mary. How are you?"

"Well, sir, well. T'is grand, so it is, to see you back home for good."

"Well..." answered Edmond cautiously. "Thank you, Mary."

"Would you mind holding the ladder, sir, while I fetch t'other box?"

"Not at all," he said, murmuring "at all" again under his breath, in imitation of her Irish accent.

Mary grinned at him good-naturedly and left by the servants' door under the stairs, leaving them alone.

"Now which of these do you want first?" said Edmond, lifting out a once-beautiful angel with golden hair. "Oh, I remember this one. She looks rather bashed now, poor dear with her bent halo. Still, straighten it out and no one will notice. Here!" and he handed it up.

"Ah, she's lovely," said Sarah, adjusting the angel's halo and wiring it to the tree.

"Maybe this year we should pin a Union Jack below the star."

"Of course! What a grand idea."

"Sarah," he said, a serious note in his voice. "I've had a letter from the War Office. They say they're planning to disband the hospital in January."

"Oh! I suppose it was bound to happen. Matron says that most of the soldiers are going home to their families for Christmas, anyway. It'll be nice to get the place back to normal. There! How does that look?"

"Very fetching," he said, looking up at her.

Glancing down at him she caught his grin. He'd not been referring to the angel. As he returned to his letter his smile faded. "I'd been anticipating this," he said. "There's something I have to tell you Sarah."

"What's that?" she answered, smiling, though conscious of a warning in his voice hinting this was the introduction to the conversation she'd been dreading.

"When the convalescent soldiers have all left," he continued, "I've decided to close up the castle."

"Oh?"

"For a while. You see, I'm planning to go abroad."

"Oh!" Sarah's jaw dropped.

"I'm going to Egypt to see the great pyramid at Giza."

"Oh!" *Stop saying oh.* With her hand she steadied herself on the ladder.

"See the Sphinx and sail up the Nile."

Feeling she should say something intelligent, she muttered unconvincingly, "How exciting."

"And I'd like you to come with me."

For a moment Sarah was quite still. A shiver of excitement ran through her soul.

"This one's got candles in wooden hoops in," called Mary, bursting into the hall from the servants' door carrying another box of decorations, "and sort of featherlike snowflakes." She put the box down by the tree and glanced at Edmond, whose focus was totally on Sarah. Following his gaze, she saw that Sarah, too, appeared transfixed, she was looking down at him with a frozen expression not easy to interpret. Frowning, Mary said, "You look a bit wobbly, Sal. Are you all right?"

"I'm fine," she answered. "Fine." Nevertheless, she stepped very carefully down from the ladder.

"Yes, she's fine," murmured Edmond, extending his hand to help her. "Would you mind leaving us for a moment, Mary? I need to talk with Sarah privately."

Mary looked from one to the other. Both were locked into each other's eyes and seemed barely aware of her. Retreating, she said, "Not at all." There's a wee job I have to finish anyroad," and she backed away through the swing door, relishing the fact that something was definitely up!

Smiling and still holding onto Sarah's hand, Edmond said, "Well, say something... even if it's only 'get knotted!' It'll be a terrific adventure, you must admit."

Sarah's emotions were tingling. "What an idea!" she said in a small voice, thinking *I'll remember this moment for the rest of my life. I'll remember his hand holding mine and this Christmas tree for the rest of my life.* The twin thrill of travelling to exotic places and seeing them with Edmond seemed an impossible fantasy come true. "But, but what about The Hall?"

"What about it?"

"Well, there are a lot of people on the estate depending on you?"

Withdrawing his hand, he said, "They've managed perfectly well without me since Mama died. They can carry on."

"But the situation's different now."

"Sarah," he said seriously, "I've thought it all out most carefully. The way I see it is, I'm the only one left now, and I'm not going to permit my ancestors to dictate the way I live my life. Military glory is never going be mine 'cause of my leg. And I'm damned if I'm going to be a boring old country squire looking after Kingsford for the rest of my days – not till I'm much older, anyway. So I want to travel around for a while. All that's needed here is a skeleton staff to keep the place ticking over. What do you say? Come and see a bit of the world with me. We could visit old King Khufu's pyramid. It'll be fun."

"But..." Myriad thoughts crashed about her head, she didn't know where to begin. "But who'll manage the estate?"

"I discussed all that with George while he was driving me home yesterday. He's agreed to take on the management of the place. He's virtually been doing it for ages, anyway. He tells me he's been collecting rents and paying bills in conjunction with mother for years. So there's nothing to worry about there. More importantly, you haven't answered my question yet?"

Sarah swallowed, trying to rid herself of the emotional lump in her throat. Looking into his pale blue eyes she felt almost tongue-tied. Stumbling she said, "It wouldn't be seemly. What would people say?"

"To hell with being seemly," he said crossly. "People will say what they want to. Anyway, you're a rich young lady, by all accounts. You're an independent woman, you can do as you wish."

"We couldn't tell anyone."

"You are funny! They're all going to find out sooner or later. Look, you can pay your own way if you like. It'll all be quite proper, if that's what you're worried about. You surely realise your life is going to be different from now on. It's bound to be. You're hardly going to be a servant anymore, are you?"

"I suppose not," she said glumly.

"Of course you're not!" he grinned. "Aunt Beatrice is livid, by the way. Well put out at not inheriting Mama's loot. Come on now, what do you say? Hey! Cheer up! Why so serious?"

"It's just that... everything's altered, and I'm not sure I like it."

Edmond laughed and put his arms round her. "Sarah!"

Feeling the warmth of his body, she relaxed, all the worrying, grieving, and troubled thoughts about Lady Isabel and Fred that seemed always to be hovering around her evaporated. She closed her eyes and, for a moment, felt utterly safe, confident and at peace.

"I've just thought what people are going to say," said Edmond laughing. "Probably that I'm after you for your money!"

A good deal more than that was said by the County when they learnt that Sir Edmond Kingsford had left The Hall to go abroad with his Housekeeper. But all that came later – much later – after Edmond's plans had come to fruition.

Earlier, a Canadian friend of his from Eton, Cunard – scion of the Cunard shipping line family – had told him of a transatlantic liner that had survived the war moored at a pier in the Elbe River in Hamburg, which had been handed over to his father, i.e. The United States Shipping Board. Apparently, it was now docked at Southampton in the process of being repaired in preparation for being used as a 'trouper ship' for returning American soldiers home. But first, so young master Cunard informed him, there would be a short goodwill tour around the western Mediterranean. "Come with us," Cunard suggested. "I'm taking that shit-hot American chorus girl I told you about. She's bringing a friend who'd be a pushover for an English lord like you."

"I'm not a lord," said Edmond. "I'm a baronet."

"Same thing," said Cunard, "at least, to her. Do come. It's the perfect jaunt for us to celebrate graduation. Gibraltar, South of France, Rome, Naples. Combines adventure with romance!" and the young blade fluttered his eyebrows wickedly. "What d'you say?"

"Could I bring my girlfriend?" Edmond asked.

"Sure," his friend answered cheerfully.

"Then I'll come. Put me down for two cabins."

Cunard's invitation, Edmond considered, was an opportunity he could not let pass. For while he'd been dreaming romantically of 'soul kisses' with Sarah at Kingsford, at Eton, or, more precisely, at nearby Windsor, he'd become rather more carnally involved with a young war widow. Meeting this warm-blooded, well-dressed lady at Lyon's teashop one afternoon, he'd accepted an invitation to her home, where, though they'd shared minimal chemistry, it had, apparently, been sufficient for her to relieve him of his virginity. This happy episode, far from decreasing his affection for Sarah, had the effect of increasing his desire to 'do the business' with her, whom he'd come to regard as his true friend and, very possibly, his true love. For her image would sometimes rise in his mind and a surge of yearning would flood his being. He longed to be near her, longed to touch her, longed for the sweet smell of her. Surely, he thought, in her present situation, she'll jump at the opportunity of seeing the world. And, once aboard a ship, who knows? The details of how exactly he was going to combine the cruise with a visit to Giza, would all come later.

After he'd persuaded Sarah to join him, he called his friend on the telephone to confirm their arrangement, and inform him that they would be leaving the tour at Naples.

Christmas that year, his first without his Mama and his two brothers, was, as he wrote in his Christmas card to his aunt Beatrice, "going to be weird and unbelievably sad".

During the war years, George had dressed as Father Christmas and distributed gifts from under the Christmas tree: "This year," he suggested to Edmond, "it would be more appropriate if you were to do it." So, after chapel on Christmas morning, Edmond, eschewing the full white beard and Santa Clause outfit, donned a red felt hat with a white fur bobble on top, and prepared to do the honours before the assembled household under the glittering tree in the Great Hall.

At the unfamiliar sight of their host, the tall gammy-legged young baronet, there was a spontaneous surge of applause from the twenty or so soldiers who remained in residence – the ones who'd been unable to join their families. They stood or sat about in wheelchairs with their nurses, Matron and Fred among them, alongside the castle staff and dogs, genially delighting in the festive occasion.

Edmond collected up the presents from under the tree and good-humouredly handed out paper baskets of sugared almonds, candied angels, glass ornaments and toys.

Suddenly he tripped and fell.

The whole company flinched – though nearly all had secretly been worrying that something of the sort might occur.

Sarah rushed to his side.

"Damn boot!" he muttered under his breath as Sarah helped him up. "Bet that never happened to Santa!" he joked out loud.

Nobody laughed, but his quip raised sympathetic smiles and enormous affection.

"Help me out here, will you, Sal?" he whispered.

Swiftly she gathered up the offerings and helped him hand them around. Though the incident was a minor one, it was sufficient for her to realise just how vulnerable he had become.

By the beginning of February, both the Ballroom and Dining room Wards were deserted. The soldiers, nurses, orderlies, beds and lockers had all vanished. In their place, dustsheets covered the grand piano and musician's chairs, even the chandeliers were looped up in muslin. In the dining hall, sheets hid the re-assembled dining table and great oak sideboards. Of the staff, only Mrs Walsh, George, and, to Sarah's irritation, Fred, remained. Mary, too, had left, telling Sarah she intended to go to London to see what the big city had to offer, but both had made promises to write and keep in touch.

Trunks were brought up from the cellar, Edmond purchased Baedeker guide books, and Sarah made another trip to see Mr Garner-Stevens, who, in turn, instructed her bank – Coutts – to furnish her with the necessary letters of credit. From there she returned to Madame Ziniah's to purchase travelling clothes, suitable cruise wear, and light summer dresses for touring Egypt.

George drove Edmond and Sarah to Southampton Docks, appropriately enough, on Valentines' Day. It was a chilly, damp morning and Sarah stepped from the rear seat of the Silver Ghost Rolls, transformed. Wearing a becoming brown velvet suit trimmed with fur, her radiant blue eyes looked out from under her matching fur hat with awe at the sight of the freshly painted, three-funnelled 'S.S. Imperator' berthed alongside the dock.

With a laughing face, relishing the wondrous sights and whooping sounds of tugboats and cheers around her, she stood on deck beside Edmond, waving farewell to George standing far below on the dockside. The great ship moved slowly out of port – *Whoever would have thought?* she said to herself, foreseeing even more thrilling adventures to come.

Chapter Twenty

Annie was becoming increasingly worried about the malicious rumours she was hearing concerning Sarah.

When she'd spoken with Fred at Lady Isabel's funeral, apart from him telling her of his 'job for life' offer – which had caused her pinpricks of pique that he wasn't returning to her at the orphanage – he'd also told her it was common knowledge among the staff at Kingsford Hall that Sarah and Sir Edmond were lovers. Annie dismissed this as gossip, but when two of the five maids Sarah had discharged before going abroad visited her – hoping for work, which she was unable to offer them – they confirmed it. One even went as far as saying – spitefully, in Annie's opinion – that Sarah had been secretly pregnant and was seen late at night burying a dead baby!

"What utter rubbish!" Annie exclaimed, appalled. "Whoever said such a wicked thing?"

"One of the nurses," answered the vindictive little fifteen-year-old. "She said she saw her from her bedroom window in the middle of the night carrying a bundle in swaddling clothes. Said as how she saw her dig a hole with a spade and bury it in the top field. Marked it with a crucifix, she did. I saw it."

Annie shook her head in disbelief, sweat breaking out on her top lip at the very thought. "Well," she said, "when I see her, I'll ask her about it. Meanwhile, I want you two to promise me not to repeat that story to a living soul. Now get yourselves off. I hear tell there's a new linoleum factory starting up in Swanage, m'be they'll be needing workers."

Nothing had been heard from either Sarah or Edmond for two months. Then, on the eighteenth of March, Annie received a picture postcard of Mount Vesuvius. On the back, in Sarah's neat hand, was written:

> *Dear Ma Cox, Naples. 29th February, 1919.*
> *Sorry not to visit before I left, but decided to take your advice and have some fun. Arrived here on a liner two days ago after visiting Marseilles and Rome – magnificent architecture but very dirty. Yesterday went to Pompeii which was interesting. Tomorrow we go to the Palazzo Real, where Nelson met Lady Hamilton. Sailing to Alexandria soon to see the Great Pyramid at Giza. Be happy for me. Arrivederci. Love Sarah.*

Humph, thought Annie, pursing her lips. *So it's true! Though she doesn't say it, it's pretty clear she's with Sir Edmond. I just hope she... Dear God! It doesn't bear thinking about. When she returns, I'll just have to tell her, that's all.*

George was the next one to receive a picture postcard, but this time sealed in an envelope. It was a tinted daguerreotype of the Great Pyramid of Cheops. It said:-

> *19th March, 1919*
> *Continental Hotel, Cairo.*
>
> *Dear George,*
> *Hope you are A1 and all is O.K. This adventure is proving most stimulating. After many difficulties we visited King Khufu's tomb yesterday. (It felt most odd). Had*

photograph taken to prove it! Good wishes to you and all at home.
Yours, Edmond.
    P.S. There's a bit of a revolution going on here.
Demonstrations, railways and telegraph offices suspended.
Hope this reaches you.

Mary O'Reilly had managed to get a job as a dresser to an actress on the London stage. She'd written of this to Mrs Walsh, who, in turn, had forwarded an envelope enclosing a picture postcard of the Sphinx.

> *Dear Mary,*   *2nd April, 1919.*
>   *Have been on a cruise ship with lots of toffs. Now in Egypt. Am boiling hot but having terrific time. Can hardly believe what's happening to me. Palm trees, boat trips on Nile, falcons soar and all the men in turbans. Egyptians seeking independence, so British not popular. Life is so very different. Meeting very interesting people. Hoping you are keeping well.*   *Best wishes.*
>   *Your friend, Sarah.*

By the same post Mrs Walsh received a colour postcard of the Temple at Karnak.

> *Dear Mrs. Walsh,*   *2nd April 1919*
>   *This place is fascinating. The Nile is beautiful. Children follow us everywhere. Don't think they've seen Europeans before. It's so hot! Riding horses and camels! Return to Alexandria and back to Italy soon. Hope you are well.*
>   *Yours Sarah.*

On the 12th May, Annie received another picture postcard,

but sealed in an envelope. It was delivered by the same post-woman who'd handed her the fateful letter about Albert. The postmark on the envelope said 'Florence', but the picture on the postcard inside was of Capri – a composite photograph of a mass of pink bougainvillaea and two high rocks jutting out of a blue sea called the Faraglioni.

> *Dear Ma Cox.*   *21st April 1919*
>
> *Forgive wobbly writing, am writing this on a train to Florence. Edmond and I were married this morning in Sorrento Registry office. Wish you could have been there, He proposed in the Blue Grotto on Capri. It was very romantic. We sailed back through the arch of these rocks and he kissed me. The man on the boat told us the legend that if you are kissed under the arch of the Faraglioni you will have eternal love. He said he wasn't making it up. I am so very happy. I never thought I could love a man so much, He is so kind, gentle and loving, He is sitting opposite me now, (looking very handsome), and says he is looking forward to meeting you when we come home. Lots of love, Sarah. XX*

Annie sat down horrified by the alarming state of mortal sin Sarah was in.

The honeymoon suite in the Annalena Pensione in Florence was not what it once was. Once upon a time it may have been considered grand and ornate, but not having seen a lick of paint for many years, it was not only shabby but downright dilapidated. The double bed boasted a brass bedstead, but stuck on the wall above it, a pair of chipped rococo angels tipped a cornucopia of plaster fruit worryingly down the wall onto the bed. Opposite it, hung a dismal tapestry depicting Paris choosing to whom to award his 'Golden Apple of Beauty', whether to Aphrodite, Athena or Hera, but time and sunlight had faded the goddesses, and, indeed his choice, to an indecipherable brown rag drooping on the wall. There was a balcony with a lonely and empty terra-cotta pot on it, a garden view, and even a bathroom, but the overall impression was of past glories and faded grandeur. The Signora boasted it had once been part of a Medici Palace, but, as Edmond remarked when they walked in last night, "Not many improvements seem to have been made since!"

The night was starry and warm. Moonlight streamed through the open window bathing the room in a cool silver. Edmond's muscular back gleamed as the young lovers coupled. Finally he lay back, spent, on his lips a moist seraphic smile. Sarah opened her eyes and gazed at him. With her hand she reached out to touch his hair ... her lip trembled ... despite herself, her emotions brimmed over... silently she sobbed.

"What is it?" said Edmond, dismayed. "Tears? Did I hurt you?"

Sarah shook her head.

"What, then?"

Stifling her sobs she murmured, "Nothing."

Yet plainly something was deeply wrong.

"Tell me," he said, turning to wrap her in his arms again. "Sarah, I love you. You can tell me anything. Ti amo."

Smiling at his Italian, she whispered, "I feel such a fool... crying at what I'm happy about. Yet... It's just that..."

"What?"

Even now, after five years, she still found it hard to talk about. Although the last eight weeks had been the most thrilling she'd known, an adventure like no other, underlying everything had been the fearful inevitability of where her quasi-platonic friend-ship with Edmond was leading. The thought of having to repeat those horrific experiences with Fred had made her cut short every advance Edmond had made. Fending him off had become a joke. Not for one moment had she done this with the ulterior motive of propelling him to propose, she didn't possess that guile, it had been her genuine fear and abhorrence of the sex act. If marriage to Edmond had occurred to her, as in her deepest fantasies, how could it not ... she'd dismissed it as a foolish nonsense. *He's my best friend and sex would spoil everything.* His proposal that afternoon in the Blue Grotto on Capri had taken her by complete surprise.

The day had started off as another of their larky tourist adventures, boarding a ferryboat in Sorrento harbour with other hotel guests, for the short trip across to Capri. Strolling along the island's Marina Grande, the pretty fishing-boat waterfront, Edmond had asked a gnarled nut of a fisherman if he'd take them to the Blue Grotto. Giovanni was the man's name – Edmond frequently asked the names of people he was doing business with, charmingly introducing both Sarah and himself – Giovanni rowed his little boat to the Grotto, nodding and grinning to them like some wise old ferryman who knew all the secrets of life. Reaching the narrow entrance, as the boat bobbed on the waves a few yards from the cliff face, he explained, in mime, that the tide was too high for the boat to go through, that to get inside they were going to have to dive in and swim underwater. He joked that he wouldn't wait for them long, "Voi giutani," he grinned. (You young people) "Sappiamo benissimo quello che fate li nella grotto azzurra," (I know what larks you get up to in the Blue Grotto) and he grinned.

"Come on, then." Edmond immediately started stripping off his shirt.

Sarah hadn't understood what Giovanni had said, so didn't take offence at his bawdy innuendo, anyway, the man was wreathed in smiles, so, laughing, she undid her belt and unbuttoned her blouse. Knowing that whenever Edmond got the chance he would always go swimming, she had had the foresight to put on a swimming costume under her outfit. Edmond swiftly unbuckled his boot and took off his flannels, revealing his navy costume. Expertly balancing on his good leg he dove into the whirling foamy sea, followed by Sarah.

Swimming underwater through the sunlit aquamarine deep, the pair surfaced, breathless, up inside the flooded cavern. The sudden calm and ghostly illuminated walls of the cave cast its spell. The extraordinary lighting effect of the sun shimmering from beneath them, reflecting up from the pale sand beneath and bathing the chamber in a spectacular blue, bewitched and exhilarated them beyond any expectation. Clambering onto a flat rock, their glistening bodies were bathed in luminous blue, their laughs and splashings echoed around the rocks. Edmond pushed his wet hair back from his forehead and turned to her. The magical grotto was just the setting he'd been waiting for. He stopped laughing and took her hand in his.

"Sal, I want to ask you something, something immensely serious."

"Golly! What?"

"You must know I adore you. Make me the happiest man alive? Say you'll marry me?"

Astonished, yet at the same time, somehow not, her heart flooded with joy. There was only one possible answer. "Yes. Yes, of course I will."

"Really?"

Grinning, she nodded, "Mmn."

"Yes!" he yelped, joyously. "Yippee!" his shouts echoed high and round and round. "You do want children, don't you?"

"Heaps!" she answered.

"Yippee!" He shouted again, grasping her. He kissed her

tenderly, holding her so tight he overbalanced and fell backwards into the water. He went on kissing her underwater till Sarah nearly lost her breath.

Now that their platonic friendship – at least, from Sarah's point of view – had ripened into the physical and passionate love she'd fought so hard to deny, now that the pleasure she took in pleasing him had allowed her to relax sufficiently to give of herself, and finally, she'd overcome her fear of 'the act', her relief was palpable. The terrible thing that she'd been dreading, wasn't the end of the world after all. Nestling in his arms, gazing into his cornflower-blue eyes, those eyes that had fascinated her from the moment they'd first met, she felt she could at last tell him... "Ti amo," she said, softly, repeating his phrase. "It's just that ...all this... before..."

"Before? Before what?"

"I've never told this to a living soul. Well, no, that's not quite true, I did tell Mary."

"Mary?"

"Mary O'Reilly. She was with me at the orphanage, you see, and the same thing happened to her."

"The same thing? What?"

"When we were little... I was eight, I was ... forced to ... a man... raped me."

Edmond frowned and his expression clouded.

"It was the man who was supposed to be looking after us... at the orphanage... and he went on ... week, after week, ... for years... six years, it was... till he left for the war."

Edmond silently gasped. Filled with compassion, he whispered, "My God! Oh, my poor angel." Hugging her tenderly he murmured, "No wonder you never wanted to... My poor darling. I knew there was something. I just knew it. But it's over now...all over. You have me now."

"But the thing is... he's still around. He's working on the estate."

"What? Who is it?"

"His name's Fred Oliphant. He's one of the soldiers. He was posted there when he was wounded. When he got better Lady Isabel gave him a job. A job for life, he told me."

"Well, I'll tell him he's got to go. I'll get rid of him."

"You would?"

"Of course. I'll kill the swine!" With his middle finger he wiped a tear from her cheek. "My poor darling." Tenderly he kissed her on both eyes, then her lips. Their bodies entwined. Closing his eyes, he said softly, "Kiss me."

Sarah kissed his long dark eyelashes, then his cheek, then his lips. Resting her head on the pillow, she gazed at him, running her fingers through his glossy black forelock. "Do you mind, terribly?"

Edmond shook his head.

"You're frowning," she whispered, smoothing the furrow from his brow.

In a steely undertone, he muttered, "Wait till we get home. I'll kill that bastard!"

"Well!" said Fred Oliphant, as he slid the 'The Hampshire Chronicle' across the kitchen table to Mrs Walsh. "What d'you make of that?"

Mrs Walsh looked at him curiously and put on her reading glasses.

'BARONET WEDS HOUSEKEEPER', she read.

'Sir Edmond Kingsford, 18, married his former housekeeper, Miss Sarah Smith, at a civil ceremony last week in Sorrento, Italy. Sir Edmond, the 8th baronet, inherited the title when his brother, the late Sir Henry Kingsford, was killed in action during the Arras

Offensive last year. The couple, who are still abroad on their honeymoon, are expected to return to Kingsford Hall shortly. No member of the family was available for comment.'

"Well, I'll be jiggered!" declared Mrs Walsh. "Well," she added, after a moment, "that'll depress my Henry. Always had an eye for our Sarah, he did. Still, she's beyond us all now. She's away! Can't say I'm surprised, though, young Edmond always was potty about her. Good luck to them, I say. It'll certainly give us something to celebrate when they get home, eh?"

"Mm," muttered Fred, smirking, chewing a piece of nail off his ring finger.

With Europe exhausted after four years of war, arranging any itinerary was difficult. Train timetables existed, but were, at best, erratic. Yet Edmond knew how to charm the world. Faced with him – his wealth and title – few requests were denied the couple. At nineteen, Sarah was now in the flower of her youth, happiness and confidence had intensified her blue-eyed prettiness into a glowing auburn-haired beauty. With her combination of grace and strength, her unaffected manner, and the irresistible quality of not knowing how captivating she had become, she delighted everyone she met.

Unable to drive himself, Edmond insisted on buying them a smart new French Citroen as a wedding present – though Sarah was going to have to drive it. With much laughter and a few minor ditchings, she learned on the deserted stradinos and stradas of Tuscany and Umbia, visiting Assisi (where they visited the home of St Francis), Siena (where they joined the roaring crowds in the Piazza del Campo to watch the thrilling Palio horse race), and Pisa, climbing the leaning tower. They practised their Italian on waiters, garage attendants and hoteliers. Sarah even becoming so sure, she would stop to happily chat with the street children in whichever village they were exploring.

Garaging the car, they stayed for two weeks in Venice, where they were shown around the Doge's Palace; visiting endless churches and galleries in the mornings and crossing to the Lido beach every afternoon to swim and sunbathe. Their evenings were spent over candle-lit suppers and taking late-night rides in gondolas, sharing the beauty and dazzlement of the city by night.

From Venice, Sarah drove to Milan and on through the Alps to Geneva – where Edmond acquired a sturdy knobbly walking stick – and finally across France, to Paris.

The postcard of the Eiffel Tower they sent to George, written on the 6th June, read:-

> *Dear George, Prepare Mother's old bedroom. Plan to return Blighty, 15th June. We will make our own way home.*
>
> *Looking forward to seeing you. Best wishes, E.*

It was, in fact, not until late afternoon on the 16th of June, that Edmond, with his new bride, Sarah, Lady Kingsford seated at the wheel of their cream open Citroen, her hair flying behind her in the wind, drove up the long approach to Kingsford Hall.

Chapter Twenty-One

Should I carry her over the threshold? Edmond considered as he gripped his new Swiss walking stick. *Maybe not. Damned leg's feeling weedy again. Wouldn't do to drop her!* Instead, holding Sarah's hand and grinning at her broadly, he pushed the heavy front door open.

The Great Hall was deserted. "Hallo!" His voice echoed round the cavernous space.

Dogs started barking. The Great Danes, Donner and Blitzen, were the first on the scene, bounding and wagging their tails. Leaping up, they nearly knocked Sarah over. She crouched down, ruffling their velvety grey ears and kissing their heads. In return, as they always did, they licked her laughing face. The four King Charles spaniels followed, yapping their welcome. Last of all came a rather stouter Frou Frou, waddling across the hall, positively beaming hallo to his young master.

"What's all this racket?" bawled Mrs Walsh from the servants' door under the stairs. "Oh! They're back!" she called out excitedly. "Oh, bless you both, sir," she exclaimed, hurrying across the hall to greet them. "Oh, Miss Sarah! Or y'Ladyship now, I have to call you. Congratulations. Congratulations to you both, and welcome home. Welcome home, indeed." Impulsively she grasped Sarah by the shoulders and kissed her cheek.

"Mrs Walsh!" Sarah grinned, returning her kiss. "Bless you. It's grand to be back."

"Mrs Walsh," repeated Edmond grasping her hand. "Thank

you. I trust all is well?"

"Yes, yes, everything's fine, sir."

"George!" shouted Edmond in delight, seeing his old retainer arriving by the staircase. "How are you? It's really good to see you. How have you been?"

George, wreathed in a rare grin, but still gruff and military, walked over, nodding. "Struggling on, struggling on, y'know. Well, congratulations to you both. We read the news. Yes, indeed. May you enjoy many years of happiness." To Sarah he inclined his head and said deliberately, "Your Ladyship."

"George!" answered Sarah, half in reprimand at him addressing her so formally, half delighted that he'd done so. "Thank you." Grasping his hand, she shook it firmly. "It's good to be home." Glancing up, she noticed the black browed figure of Fred Oliphant emerging from the servants' door. Her smile faded and her excitement suddenly ebbed. She squeezed Edmond's arm in a secret signal.

Fred stepped forward, limping. "Your Lordship. Welcome home, sir." His eyes locked onto Sarah's as he crossed the hall. "Your Ladyship. Well, it seems congratulations are in order."

"Fred," she said, politely, gripping Edmond's arm, "thank you."

Edmond examined him closely. *So this is the fellow.* "I don't believe we've met."

"Oliphant, y'Lordship," he answered, bowing his head. "Groundsman, driver and handyman, sir. I was here at Christmas when you...er.."

"Ah, yes," Edmond stopped him, dimly recalling handing him a gift after tripping up under the tree. Sarah's was still applying pressure to his arm. "Yes, of course. I rather wanted to have a word with you, Mr Oliphant."

"Certainly, sir. Whenever you wish." Turning to Sarah, Fred smiled charmingly. "I'll fetch your bags in for you, your Ladyship."

Sarah gave him a tight smile.

"Ten o'clock, tomorrow," called Edmond firmly, as Fred moved to the front door. "In the study."

"Certainly, sir," replied Fred, barely breaking step.

"We've prepared your Mama's old room, like you said," said Mrs Walsh, picking up Edmond's leather travelling bag and heading for the stairs. "Now it's been redecorated it looks just fine. Everything's been cleaned, carpets, curtains and upholstery, and, of course, the bed's all brand new."

As they climbed the staircase, Fred re-entered below with the suitcases. Sarah glanced down back at him. Edmond took her hand and whispered, "Stop worrying. Tomorrow he'll be gone."

Entering the bedroom where she'd spent so many hours with Lady Isabel, Sarah breathed a sigh of contentment. She felt more at home here, than in any other room in the house. Edmond had wanted his father's old room with the magnificent bed to be theirs, but Sarah had said, "No. That's the bed I saw your mother die in. I couldn't possibly sleep there." Edmond had given way and they'd settled upon this one. Now, she was sure they'd made the right choice. There was no trace or tell tale sign of the fire in sight, no reminder of that horrific afternoon when Fred had surprised her on the balcony. With the new brighter pink hangings of rose silk tabernet surrounding the four-poster, the room looked even fresher and more opulent than it had on the first morning she'd walked in and found Edmond hanging from the dressing room wardrobe. The bedside oil lamps had been replaced by modern pink-shaded electric lights. Sarah turned one on by the switch below the bulb – yes, it worked. She snapped it off. Her fingers strayed along the cool marble surface of the bedside cabinet. The top drawer slid open smoothly. *Is it still there?* Her hand crept inside. She felt Lady Isabel's soft delicate handkerchiefs – no one had bothered to empty the drawer before the cupboard was stored away. *Yes, there it is* ... nestling among the soft linen and silk, she felt the hard steel of the rose secateurs.

That night, after changing into her nightdress, she sat at Lady Isabel's old dressing table to brush her hair. Only then it was, as she thought of the times she'd stood behind the stool and brushed Lady Isabel's hair, that the full realization of how far she'd come impinged on her. Edmond came to her side. She looked up at him in the mirror, and he bent to kiss her neck.

"Happy?" he asked.

"Very," she answered.

Together they got into their sumptuous new bed.

The flowing full-length net curtains billowed lightly by the open windows in the cool night air as Edmond made love to her. Having to submit to her marital obligation in so lavish a setting, she overcame her aversion to sex more easily, it seemed a small price to pay for such luxury, such position and prestige, such security.

The following morning Edmond sat behind his father's old desk in the study feeling distinctly apprehensive. He'd never had to sack a servant before. There was a knock on the door. "Come in," he called.

Fred Oliphant entered. "You said you wanted to see me, y'Lordship."

"Yes. Sit down, please," said Edmond, indicating the chair opposite.

Fred crossed the room limping (it was still quite pronounced), and sat down.

Edmond was curious about the limp, but refused to allow it to divert him. "I'll come straight to the point," he said. "My wife," – secretly he savoured those grown-up words – "tells me she is not happy with you working here. I think you are aware of the reason, and we wish you to leave our employment."

"I see," said Fred, nodding. "Thought this might be on the cards. So..." His mouth puckered in an attempted smile. "But what you don't know, sir, with all respect, is that your mother promised me a job for life. I saved her life, see, and young Sarah, your ... um, wife, knows it."

"I appreciate that," replied Edmond firmly. "I know the story of the fire and how you helped her. But I am the head of the house now, and I am discharging you. I don't want any excuses or any further discussion. You're leaving here, and that is the end of the matter."

"Oh no, sir. Oh no, it ain't. I know things."

Edmond blinked. "And what would that be, now?"

"Things about your mother she was ashamed of. Things she tried to cover up. Things about your so-called wife, too."

"I think," said Edmond, standing up, "that you'd better leave."

"Oh, high and mighty, are we?" answered Fred, confidently leaning back in his chair. "Well, if I'm going, I'm going to make bloody sure everyone hereabouts knows why. You're breaking the law, you are. Breaking the law of the land, and offending Christian decency."

Edmond gave a wincing frown.

"That's taken the wind outta your sails, ain't it? You're wed to your sister, you are! I was there. Downstairs in the parlour, I was, when she was born, see, and I know. Illegitimate, she is. Your mother gave birth to Sal when I was wed to the midwife, see, and I know all about it."

Edmond's withered foot started to shake. Seething, he clenched his jaw and gripped the desktop. "How dare you! I know all about you, sir. You abused my wife when she was a girl. And if I were to tell that to the County Sheriff, you, sir, would go to prison."

Fred stared at him. "I see. Goin' t' tell the Sheriff you're wed to y' sister, too, are you? Tell him y' poor dead mother was a tart? I don't think so. What about the old family name, eh? That news would shake the County up a bit, wouldn't it? No." Still wearing his sickly grin, he went on. "I'm a reasonable man, sir. Times is hard, see, for my kind, and I need a good regular job. I'm hoping you'll be keepin' me on 'ere. 'Cause if I go, then I'm going to tell everyone, ain't I? I can prove it, too. Prove everything, I can. Just you ask Annie Cox. She knows it. She used to be your Ma's maid, see, knows all about it, she does. So I think I'll be keeping my job here, don't you, sir? I'll be as quiet as a mouse, then. Good as gold, I'll be. Not a word to no one. What do you say, sir?"

Edmond stared at the man speechless.

"I thought so." Rising from his chair, Fred's grimace assumed that of the obsequious menial. "I'll be leaving you now, sir. And don't you fret, sir. Y'secret's quite safe with me." At the door, he turned and nodded respectfully. "Thank you, sir," and left.

Edmond's face hardened. In an effort to stop the nerve in his foot from trembling, he suddenly vented his fury with a heavy punch on his thigh.

The cream and black Citroen – now somewhat muddy from its European travels – sped across Hackett's Heath. Sarah was experiencing something of an epiphany as she drove through the New Forest, returning to her foster roots. Of all the beauties of nature she'd witnessed in the last five months, in Egypt and Italy, in Switzerland and France, there were few sights, she thought, to rival the green, soothing and pleasant sight of the English countryside. It seemed so right to her, that it should be a wondrous sunny morning. Life was indeed a wondrous marvel. Driving her own car, dressed in one of her new cream pleated summer dresses and married to her own personal Apollo – the statue she'd seen in Florence looked just like Edmond – everything seemed at last to have come right in her life. Edmond was getting rid of Fred; those frightening re-occurring 'secateur nightmares' had stopped; she'd long ago banished Lady Isabel's haunting dying words from her mind telling herself the poor lady had been delusional. And after wearing the diamond bracelet for the first time – on board the 'SS Imperator', where it had been so admired by Cunard's girl friend – she'd made up her mind to sell it, after all, there were many other lovely jewels in the box, and why bother keeping something with such unhappy associations.

In short, she was at peace. Her transformation from abused, illegitimate orphan girl, into the rich and beautiful, happily married first Lady of the County, was complete.

On she drove, finally reaching the familiar Lymington lanes she'd known in her childhood. Apart from the excitement and joy of seeing Annie again, of relating to her all the heady adventures and interesting people she'd met, she was also on a mission – and the irony had not escaped her – to hire servants. Annie's girls, she knew well enough, always knew how to behave and had clean fingernails. Earlier that morning, she'd telephoned Annie to tell her to expect her, but to her surprise, Reggie, Annie's son, had answered the telephone. The two had been friends as children, never all that close, nevertheless, she was delighted to learn that he was back from the war unscathed, and they'd chatted pleasantly. He'd asked about Mary O'Reilly and her whereabouts, and Sarah was reminded of Mary's story about him beating up Fred.

She parked the car in the lane outside Annie's cottage. Next door was the barn, still with OPEN ALL NIGHT written across the door, but now the letters were scuffed and faded. She collected up her parcels of food and small gifts, and, unable to stop herself grinning with happy anticipation, opened the picket gate and walked up the path. She lifted the brass knocker she'd polished so many times as a girl, and knocked.

Annie opened the door with a set, heavy expression. "Come in," she said, "come on in, lass."

Sarah's beaming face melted, instantly aware that something was wrong. "Whatever is it?"

Annie shook her head. "Give me a moment, lass. Come on in." Noticing the Citroen in the lane, she nodded to it. "Did you drive over in that?"

"Yes. It's mine. Pretty, isn't it?" said Sarah, stepping over the threshold. "It's Edmond's wedding present." She'd intended telling her all about buying it and learning how to drive, but immediately she entered the room, she was distracted by the ghost of memories that came tumbling back.

"Well," declared Annie, closing the door and taking in Sarah's new clothes, her tanned face and arms. "It's mighty grand you're looking." Examining her, her chin quivered as if a pang of sadness had overwhelmed her. "Oh, my dear!" she said, embracing her. Though Sarah was still carrying her parcels, Annie hugged her for a long moment, then, embarrassed that she'd expressed too much, flapped her hand at the sofa. "Sit down, sit down. You must be thirsty. I've made you up some lemonade, you always used to like that. Or I'll make you a cuppa' tea, if you'd prefer?"

"No, no. Lemonade will be fine. These are all for the children," said Sarah, setting down her packages on the table. "Now, why so serious? What's the matter? Has something happened? Is Reggie all right?"

"Oh, yes, he'll be fine," dismissed Annie, shaking her head and waving her hand as if trying to brush something away. Pouring a glass of lemonade, she said distractedly, "Of course, he's still heartbroken. 'Cause his twin died, y'know."

"Stan? Oh no!"

"Last week of the war it happened. Reggie's still finding it very hard," and as she bit her cheek, she handed over the glass of lemonade.

"And for you, too," said Sarah, regarding Annie's stoic expression. "Thank you," she added, accepting the glass. "Oh, I am sorry. He didn't say anything on the telephone this morning."

"Well," said Annie, "he wouldn't, would he?" Tapping the table absently with her fingers, she murmured, "Still..." Clasping her hands, she added more forcibly, "I've sent him off 'cause I wanted to talk to you. I was planning to come over and see you anyway when you got back, but...well..."

Recognising Annie's distress, Sarah decided to wait. She sipped her drink.

Watching her, Annie said, "I've waited so long to say. Now, I'm not sure I can."

Sarah frowned. "Say what?"

Annie sat down on the sofa and reached up to her. "Come, sit by me." Sarah set down her glass and obeyed. Annie leaned over to clasp her hands. "I have something to tell you that isn't easy, and will come as a shock."

"Fire away," said Sarah, trying to make light of whatever it was. "I'm strong."

"Yes. I think perhaps you are now. I used to think you weren't when you were wee, but you've grow'd up so fine. A proper young lady." Taking in a deep breath she closed her eyes and bit her lip. Hesitantly, she started. "I always told you, you were an orphan."

"Yes," said Sarah warily.

"That you were left on the doorstep there."

"Yes."

"Well, that wasn't true."

Sarah frowned. "Oh. So ...?"

Annie stopped her speaking by gripping her hand. "Do you

remember," nervously she wiped the corners of her mouth, "at Lady Isabel's funeral, me saying that we'd been lasses together?"

"Yes. Yes, I do. I thought it was funny. You'd never said anything about that before."

"I had a reason. You see, my Ma was Housekeeper to her family – to Lady Isabel's mother and father. The Honourable Mr and Mrs Angus Farquharson were their names. They're both dead now, but they used to have a fine estate up in Ayrshire in Scotland. My Dadda was their groundsman, and that's where I was born and grew up, on their estate. Miss Isabel was born on my fourth birthday, and Mrs Farquharson allowed my Ma to take me up into the nursery to see the new baby as a treat. I always used to think of Isabel as my own birthday present doll after that. All through our childhood I used to look after her, watch over her, like. Even after she came back from boarding school – some ladylike convent in Switzerland, it was – I still cared for her. I'd been out in the world a bit meself by then, of course, learnt dress-making and even been nursemaid to a titled lady's children. Isabel said she wanted me back to be her personal maid. So I gave notice, and went back, so I did. Well, it was nice being at home again, working alongside me Ma and all. Anyway, when Miss Isabel got married to Sir Thomas in, oh, '93, it was, what a party we had! A whole ox was roasted in the Old Cattle Market in Ayr, and my lady asked me if I'd like to go with her to her new home. I said 'yes', and Mr Farquharson released me, as a wedding present to his daughter, like, and together we went to Kingsford Hall. That's where I met Fred. He was working there as a stable hand and odd man. Funny name. Funny man!"

At the mention of Fred, Sarah recalled the anger she'd felt towards Ma Cox when she'd thrashed her after telling her what had been going on, but she controlled her face, showing no sign of her feelings.

"When young master Henry was born," Annie continued, "I nursed him. Then, when Master Arthur came along, the same. Then the General went off to fight the Boers in South Africa, and Lady Isabel got into trouble. She had some affair and got pregnant. And I looked after her... as I always had." Annie wiped the corners of her mouth again, as if unsure how to continue. "She had the bairn upstairs in Reggie and Stan's old room. That bairn ... was you."

Sarah stared at her for a long moment. "Me?"

Annie nodded. The pupils of Sarah's eyes quivered unsteadily. *This can't be happening to me. This isn't happening.* "Lady Isabel was my mother!!"

"Yes," Annie said softly.

Annie's whisper struck her like a thunderbolt splitting an oak. Deep, deep inside her, something cracked. "No! NO!" she gasped. "Not true!"

Annie reached across to hold her. "Oh, my dear, I'm so sorry. So terribly sorry."

"That's not possible! That means... Edmond is my..."

"That's why I had to say. I had to. I'm so sorry, lass. I never could have before. But... You're breaking God's holy law, child. I know you didn't know it, but that's why you must never have his children. Never, never. The boy has that crippled leg and you both share the same blood. You must never have his children. God will punish you. It's a sin. The child would be... well, it would be...deformed. A freak! You must promise me that you'll never, never have his children. Promise me."

Breathing very heavily, Sarah stood up. "I'm not listening to this. I must go." With her mind reeling and in a blind effort to escape, to stop everything in her life from draining away, she moved unsteadily to the door.

"Listen to me!" cried Annie. "You have to."

"NO!" cried Sarah. "I can't." Angrily she turned back. "Why are you saying this? Not to have children? Edmond is my husband! No! Oh God! No, no. Please, this isn't possible. Never have ... that's one of the reasons we married. He wants an heir and I love him. I love him with all my heart and soul. I never thought I could feel this way about anyone, that such a wonderful thing could ever happen to me, that it could be possible, and now you're telling me..." Sarah grabbed the table to steady herself. "Lady Isabel was my mother! Oh please, God, no! Ma," she pleaded, her features distorted in misery. "Don't! Don't. Please. It's not so. It can't be. Not possible. How can such a thing be? Why are you saying this?"

"Because Edmond is your half-brother, that's why!" Annie said firmly. Equally emotional, but trying to stay strong, she went on. "'T'is true. I brought you into this world, lass. I was there. I attended Lady Isabel, and she was indeed your Ma. God forgive me for hurting you, but you have to know the truth. You must. You must never, never have his child. Listen to me well, now. I'm willing to hold my tongue about Lady Isabel, God knows I have all these years. No one will ever know from me. The scandal would ruin you both, there's enough talk as it is..."

"Talk? What talk?"

"Oh, in the newspapers, some class nonsense about him marrying his mother's maid. But you listen to me, you must. You have to promise me. I know enough of the heartbreak those kind of children bring to folk, believe me. You get him to use protection, anything. Tell him you're too weak to give birth, anything. Why am I saying this? You shouldn't be married to him! It's a sin!"

"Don't!" Sarah cried, clasping her hands over her ears. "Don't say that." Anger and confusion flooded her. "He's the bestest thing that has ever happened to me. Stop!" she shouted. "Just stop! Let me think."

Getting up from the sofa Annie clasped her by the shoulders and tried to sooth her.

Sarah looked at her incredulously. "Lady Isabel was truly my Ma?"

Annie nodded. "Mmn. That's how I came to look after you."

Wrenching herself free, Sarah wrapped her arms around herself and paced the room.

Annie watched her, helpless.

Breathlessly Sarah muttered "That's why she left me all that property. That money. Those jewels, and the bracelet!" Suddenly she stopped. "The bracelet!"

"Of course," Annie murmured.

Covering her face with her hands as the fearful thought struck, she slowly slid them down from her ashen face, until, palm to palm, as if in prayer, they were at her lips. When Sarah spoke, her voice was low. "When she was dying, she whispered something. She tried to tell me..."

"What?"

"I thought she was delirious. She said... she said... my father was 'King'."

The two looked at each other. Annie silently put her hand to her mouth.

"She said 'Princess', and tapped my hand."

"Oh, my dear," said Annie, going to her and taking her in her arms. "Don't think about that. Please, you mustn't dwell on that. You can't. You'll make yourself wretched if you do. Oh, my dear." Closing her eyes, she muttered, "What have I done? What have I done?" Soothing and petting Sarah, she went on. "I had to tell you, child. You know I did. Try to understand. You do, don't you? You do understand?"

"I understand she was guilty!" hissed Sarah. "I understand she was selfish and ashamed of me." Squeezing her eyes shut and fighting to control herself, she rambled on. "I always thought my mother would be someone poor, someone who couldn't have afforded to look after me. But she was rich! And she gave me away. Just like all the others in the orphanage. And I was her servant! And my father was a ..."

Annie stopped her mouth with her fingers. "Stop! Don't say that. That way madness lies. You mustn't think that way, lass. Try and be sensible. Don't make things worse."

Sarah grabbed Annie's wrist. Taking it firmly away from her face, she said, "Worse? Worse than this?" She turned away from her and went to the window, beating her breast. "I feel a knife is sticking in my heart. However could she have done that? That was wicked! So wicked. To give me away!"

"You know well why," Annie answered. "She had a position in society to uphold. I know it was wrong what she did, but her world was different. So different. Try to understand her."

Sarah stared about her like a lost child. *I'm trapped. This can't be happening.* But remembered incidents crept into her mind. *Brushing Lady Isabel's hair... her eyes watching me in the mirror... the gift of the rose secateurs... her smile when I came into a room... the look on her face when she lay dying... possibly, yes, perhaps she did repent, but...* Sarah shivered. Drained, numbly aware that an earthquake had destroyed her wonderful new world, she sank back onto the sofa. *Everything is broken... it's over... gone, finished. How can I go on? My darling Edmond is my brother!* Panic-stricken, she suddenly looked up at Annie. "I can't see him! How can I see him?" Shaking her head, she said, "Oh Ma! I can't see him!"

"No." Annie lowered herself down next to her, patting and soothing her. "No. Maybe it's best not to. Just for a day or two. Give yourself time to think. You stay here."

"Can I?"

"Of course. You can sleep up in the supervisor's cub, up in your old bed."

It was later that evening, after struggling to eat some supper with the children round the familiar dining-table in the orphanage, that she felt her first pang of sickness.

The following morning, she felt it again.

Chapter Twenty-Two

On the stage of 'The Alhambra Music Hall' (the site of the present day Odeon cinema, Leicester Square), George Robey and Violet Lorraine were reprising their duet, "If You Were The Only Girl In The World". The song had made the show famous, for "The Bing Boys Are Here" had been running for almost three years. Sarah sat in the packed dress circle. She'd seen many wonders on her European tour, and on board the S.S. 'Imperator' had even met an actress – the one who'd admired her diamond bracelet – but this was her first visit to a Music Hall. The reflected pink light from the stage gave her face a glowing radiance totally at odds with her emotions. A tear glistened on her cheek as she listened to Clifford Grey and Nat Ayer's poignant song:

"Nothing else would matter in the world today
We could go on loving in the same old way
A garden of Eden just made for two
With nothing to mar our joy
I would say such wonderful things to you
There would be such wonderful things to do
If you were the only girl in the world
And I were the only boy."

Brushing the tear away, she added her own bitter lyric. *And if he weren't my own half-brother!*

After the curtain calls, she made her way through the crowds to the Stage Door and asked for "Miss Mary O'Reilly". In the cramped backstage vestibule, with waiting stage-door-johnnies, electricians and scene-shifters passing, actors and musicians calling out "Good night" to the stage-door keeper, Mary eventually appeared, and the girls gleefully greeted each other. It was a warm night and they walked arm in arm from the theatre with Mary bombarding her with questions and excitedly admiring her engagement and wedding rings – both bought, as Sarah related, on the same morning in the glass-domed Galleria Umberto in Naples. Reaching Lyons Corner House, on the corner of Coventry street and Rupert street, they went upstairs for a late-night supper. Over their meal, Mary gaily reported – but in hushed tones – that Reggie Oliphant had turned up at the theatre last night and had stayed with her. "So I can't stay long. He's waiting for me at home, right now!"

Sarah was glad, and reckoned she was partly responsible, for it was she who'd told Reggie on the telephone where Mary was working, but she merely said, "How is he? Is he all right?"

"Bit shell-shocked, bless him, but I'm working on him! But tell me about you? When did all this happen? Tell me all about it. How did Edmond propose?"

"You go first," said Sarah, trying to delay the moment of telling her the purpose of her visit. "What's it like working in the theatre? What's Violet Lorraine like?"

"Oh, she's so ladylike, you wouldn't credit," said Mary. "Posh! You'd never believe the carry on. I think she only employed me 'cause I'd worked for a real titled lady. Like you now, y' Ladyship!" She hooted her familiar laugh and Sarah smiled wanly. "And Mr Robey, well, he's the proper card! He's posh, too, mind. But more like a schoolmaster, he is, than a comedian."

Sarah was studying Mary's hair, it looked redder than she

remembered. Her face, too, was more heavily made-up. "Well, you're obviously enjoying yourself," she said, toying with a sprout on her plate. "You look happy enough, anyway."

Mary looked at her friend shrewdly. "Which is more than I can say for you, y' Ladyship."

For an instant Sarah met her eye, then put down her fork and stared at the table.

"You've not been yourself since we left the theatre," considered Mary, her head on one side. "When I got your note this evening, I was expecting to find you over the moon. Yet... What is it, luv?"

Having rehearsed over the last two sleepless nights what she might say to her friend, Sarah came out with it. "I need your advice."

"Advice?" said Mary, half laughing. "From me?"

"You're the only one I know that might help. The only one I'd trust to keep it secret." Checking that the couple at the next table couldn't overhear, she leant across the table and, under her breath, but looking Mary straight in the eye, said, "I need an abortion."

Mary's mouth gaped in astonishment. "What? Why? I thought everything was rosy."

"No, it isn't." Sarah's nostrils dilated as she checked herself from saying anything more. "Do you know of anyone," she insisted, "who could do it?"

"Sal!" Mary reached across the table to cover her friend's hand.

"Do you?"

Frowning, Mary said carefully, "I might." The two held each other's eyes. "He'd cost, though."

"I'm prepared for that." Sarah retrieved her hand and sat back, but her body remained rigid. "How soon could you get in touch with him?"

Still frowning, Mary shrugged. "That depends. Tomorrow, maybe. Where are you staying?"

"The Strand Palace Hotel. But under another name. I signed in as Miss Annie Walsh."

Mary gave a crooked smile.

Sarah finished her drink and put her glass down. "Would I..." she faltered, "have to go to him, or would he come to me?"

"Probably," answered Mary slowly, "he'd come to you. But, luv'... Why? Does Edmond know about this? Or... isn't it his?"

"Oh, it's his, right enough. Don't ask, Mary, please. He just knows that I've come up to London to see you, and that's all." Ashamed and angry with herself that she'd lied, she bit her lip, but continued as calmly as she could. "I've done all my thinking and it has to be done. Just be my friend and arrange it for me if you can. I'm going nearly crazy." Delving into her handbag, she withdrew a card. "I'll wait in the hotel to hear from you. This is their telephone number. My room number's on the back."

"Oh, luvvy'!" said Mary, taking the card. "Are you quite certain this is what you want?"

Sarah nodded gravely.

"Well!" Mary sighed. "I'll try... but I can't promise anything."

"Do your best." Not wanting to prolong the painful topic, Sarah cut the conversation short. "Let's get the bill," she said, looking up for the waiter and opening her purse. "I can't eat anything more."

The bill was put on the table and Sarah paid it, adding two sixpeny pieces, being the 10% tip that Edmond had advised her was the thing to do. In the street, they embraced fondly and hurriedly parted.

Edmond lay alone in his new marital bed with his eyes wide open.

He'd been unable to sleep properly for two days. He was missing Sarah terribly and Fred's words were still painfully hurtling around his brain. Since their talk in the study on Sunday morning, he'd wandered about, lost and shaken to the very root of his being. Unable to believe any ill of his mother, or even to discuss matters with Sarah, he'd decided he needed to confide in a man of God. So on Sunday afternoon he'd visited his uncle, the Reverend Ralph, and told him all. The Reverend had reacted remarkably coolly. Commenting that Fred had always been a problem, was probably lying, but, if not, a dispensation to dissolve the marriage would be required, which he promised to look into, he concluded their interview by telling him not to worry.

Returning home to find a message that Sarah was staying the night with Annie Cox, he'd become even more distraught, angry even. *Hardly the action of a new bride. Well, two can play at that game!* On Monday morning he'd set off with George to visit his aunt and uncle in Sussex. Lady Beatrice and Sir Robert had both been welcoming, affectionate and had persuaded him to stay the night, though he'd checked himself from confiding his troubles to them. Arriving back home this afternoon and finding Sarah was still away – Mrs Walsh reported that she'd been home, but then left again – he thought it about time he spoke to the lady herself. The lady he'd heard about all his life, from his brothers, his mother, his wife, and now, Fred Oliphant; this Mrs Annie Cox. *She has to tell me the truth. For, please God, that fellow Fred Oliphant must be lying.*

He'd telephoned the orphanage.

A female voice answered. "Mrs Cox is just putting the children to bed, sir. Can I help at all?"

"I should like to make an appointment with her for tomorrow, Wednesday, at midday, please, if that is convenient?"

"Certainly, Sir Edmond," said the voice. "I'm putting it in the book right now. Mrs Cox will be expecting you."

Edmond turned over in the great bed and tried to stop worrying. *Concentrate on making my mind a blank, then I might be able to sleep.*

Chapter Twenty-Three

*T*errified that she wasn't going to get the abortion, but terrified of what the man might do if he arrived, Sarah waited anxiously in her hotel bedroom all Wednesday morning. The telephone didn't ring till after lunch.

A female voice asked, "Miss Annie Walsh?"

Instantly, Sarah recognised Mary's Irish lilt. "Mary!" she exclaimed. "Thank heavens! Were you able to speak to your friend?'

"A Mr Jones will call at four o'clock. It's not his real name, of course. He'll want thirty pounds – cash – and there's not to be anyone else there." Her tone warmed. "I couldn't be with you anyway, luvvy', I've got a matinee. But are you really sure this is what you want?"

"Oh, Mary. I have to. I'm sorry I can't tell you everything. But it just has to be."

"I'll come and see you after my show, okay? See how you're doing."

"Bless you. I was planning on going home afterwards, but I'll wait."

"I think it'll take longer than a day, luv'."

Silence. Sarah chewed her lip.

"Anyway, see you later. Hope it... Hope everything works out okay. 'Bye, luvvy. Must dash."

"'Bye," said Sarah, putting down the phone feeling distinctly queasy.

For two-and-a-half long hours she waited. At last the telephone rang again.

A man's voice asked, "Miss Walsh?"

Hardly daring to speak, she answered, "Yes."

"Jones, here. You alone?"

"Yes."

"I'm down in the lobby. I'll come up."

Two minutes later there was a knock at the door. Sarah took a deep breath and opened it. A thin man, about thirty years old, wearing a trilby hat and raincoat, stood in the corridor. He had a wispy brown moustache and carried a doctor's black leather bag. He removed his hat and she saw that his straw-coloured hair was a different colour to his moustache. "How do?" he nodded.

Sarah nodded back. "Mr Jones?"

Assuring himself that no one was watching in the corridor, Mr Jones slipped past her.

She caught the reek of drink on him. It was the same stench Fred had smelt of sometimes.

Once inside the room he looked about nervously. "Is that a bathroom?"

"Yes," she said, tensely gripping the back of a chair.

He opened the bathroom door and looked inside. "Get good hot water do you?"

"Yes."

"Usually do in these places." Satisfied they were alone, he turned to her. "How far gone are you?"

"Twelve weeks, I think."

He nodded. "Got the cash?"

"Yes," said Sarah.

"Let's have it."

"Now?" said Sarah. "Before?"

"Now," repeated Mr Jones.

Sarah fetched her handbag from the bed. "Thirty pounds, I believe."

Mr Jones took the notes and counted them. "Ta. Now then, lock that door and get on the bed." Pocketing the money he took off his raincoat and jacket. Sarah locked the door. "Just wash me hands," he said, rolling up his sleeves and heading for the bathroom. "Like to be hygienic." He reached for his bag, winked at her and disappeared.

Sarah went cold. *Am I really going through with this?* Her heart pounded. Clenching her jaw, she took off her shoes, then her stockings and knickers and lay on the double bed. Breathing deeply to try to keep herself calm, she waited for him to return. She could hear the tap running next door. Back he came carrying a bowl of hot water. "You an actress?"

"No," she answered.

"Thought not. Don't be scared. Used to be a medico." Placing the bowl by the bed, he said, "Don't use knitting needles no more. Just this," and he held up a long piece of elm bark. "Just wet it, see, like this. To make it slippery," and he dropped it in the water. "Works a treat!" He took a towel from his bag and laid it out at the bottom of the bed by her feet. On it he placed some lanolin oil, a roll of gauze, a bottle of spirit, and a menstrual pad. "Raise your knees," he instructed.

Paralysed by humiliation and shame, she lay still.

He tapped her leg. "Come on."

She lifted her knees... there was a strange cold sensation. "Just antiseptic," he said, "to keep it all clean."

She felt his hand probing.

"This'll hurt. But don't you make a sound, not one. Bite the pillow."

She grabbed the spare pillow and stuffed it into her mouth.

His fingers moved into her and the torture began. *Oh, God, this is like Fred all over again! When will it be over? Please, God, let it be over. Why am I putting myself through this? Annie's voice echoed in her head. 'You share the same blood... You must never have his children. You're breaking God's holy law... God will punish you... The child will be deformed... a freak, a monster! It would be a sin. Wicked...Wicked! No, I could never be a mother to a creature like that. I just couldn't.*

Mr Jones inserted the slippery elm bark, then packed it with pads of gauze soaked in lanolin. He handed her the menstrual pad. "Keep it in place with that. Replace it after you've been to the toilet. But the elm bark must be in the cervix. Right, that's it. All over. Well, not quite, eh?" he said with a grin as he started packing up his bag. "Rest is up to you."

Covering herself, Sarah asked, "What will happen now?"

"Wait a day or two, maybe a week, and it'll go. But if anything goes wrong, don't you dare tell anyone. Not a doctor, nor the police, no one. 'Cause you've just broken the law and you can go to prison." He disappeared into the bathroom again saying, "I'll just wash up, and be off."

Sarah lay stiff, her arms wrapped round her stomach.

Mr Jones returned from the bathroom rolling down his shirt-sleeves. As he put on his leather-patched sports jacket, she made to rise to see him out, but the pain stilled her.

"You rest awhile, eh?" he said, putting on his raincoat and making for the door. He unlocked it and looked out. "Coast clear." Turning back, he nonchalantly put on his trilby, tipped it to her, and said, almost comically, "Thank you, Miss. Good day!" and was gone.

She looked at the clock. It was twenty-five minutes past four. He'd been with her barely twenty minutes. Shakily she picked up the telephone to ask for a pot of tea to be sent up.

Sipping the hot sweet tea waiting for Mary to arrive, she prayed she'd done the right thing and that all would go well, but her thoughts kept drawing her back, as if sucked into a whirlpool, to her conversation with Annie. *Lady Isabel was my mother! And the man who gave her the diamond bracelet was my father! Edmond! Oh Edmond.*

It had now been three days since she'd seen him. Not since the morning she'd left to visit Annie. He'd not been home on the morning she returned from the orphanage. Mrs Walsh had given her a message that George had driven him to visit Sir Robert and Lady Beatrice in Sussex. Relieved, in a curious way, not to have to see him and talk, she'd gone to her room to change, but, from the balcony, to her horror, she'd noticed Fred working in the garden. At that precise moment he happened to glance up and see her. He nodded to her and smiled. Sarah thought he even winked. Hurriedly hiding behind the curtains she wondered why he was still there, why Edmond hadn't got rid of him, as he'd promised. Now, as she lay on the hotel bed, she worried about it all over again. *Whatever could have happened? Oh, Edmond! I wish... I don't know what I wish. I just wish all this was over and we were together like before in Venice and in Florence. I just wish all this had never happened. I wish I was with you... and not here.*

Edmond was loading his rifle in the taproom beside the stables, having returned a few hours earlier from a painfully frank interview with Annie, where he'd learned that, not only were Fred's allegations quite true, but that Sarah also now knew whom her mother was. In the taxi returning home – for he'd not wished George to drive him to the orphanage – he'd become even more worried at her disappearance. He'd come to realise that, to survive this ordeal, he had to be more than just resilient. *The qualities most required,* he told himself as he snapped the shaft of the rifle in place, *are mental strength – my own and Sarah's – and, crucially, containment. Just so long as she doesn't do anything stupid. Where the hell could she be? Is she so upset that she's left me? She'll have get in touch soon, she must do. So, she's my half-sister, but I still love her, I'm certain of that. I can't just stop loving her. I suppose our marriage will have to be annulled, well obviously, as uncle Ralph said, but that doesn't mean we can't still be together. We can live together as brother and sister. Ensuring the family's reputation is going to be the tough thing. If we've already made headlines, then this becomes known... the scandal will attract a whole new hoard of publicity. Yes, containment is the thing.*

Not knowing quite what he was going to shoot, but sure that if Fred Olyphant walked into his sights, it might well be him, Edmond set forth.

Two further days passed before he had any news. Bottling up his emotions, Edmond had forced himself to attend to matters on the estate, not even confiding in George, though he and Mrs Walsh were both in a high state of curiosity about Sarah's whereabouts. Fraught with heartache, which was giving him strange pangs of stomach pains, Edmond was at a loss. *Please, please,* he prayed, *bring Sarah back to me.*

Then, on Friday evening, at about seven o'clock, the telephone rang. It was Mrs Cox.

"Pardon me for calling you, sir,' said Annie, 'but I was wondered if you'd heard anything from Sarah?"

"No, not a word. Have you?"

"Yes. I just had a telephone call from my son, Reggie. He's up in London staying with a friend. He told me his friend had dinner with Sarah three days ago. I thought you would want to know. She's staying at the Strand Palace Hotel under the name of Annie Walsh."

"Mrs Cox!" said Edmond, his heart lifting. "Thank Heavens! Thank you so much. Maybe it's a bit too late to go up to London at this hour, but I'll leave first thing tomorrow morning. Thank you. You've relieved my mind no end. And Mrs Cox..."

"Yes," she answered.

"About our talk on Wednesday. I just wanted to say... I appreciate your confidence, and everything you told me. I'm deeply conscious of how painful it must have been for you, as indeed, it was for me, but if we 're to help and support the person we both love, we must know everything."

"Of course, sir, I agree," said Annie, in a quavering voice. Then, more firmly, she added, "Let's hope she comes home soon. You will let me know, won't you, sir."

"Of course, and thank you, Mrs Cox."

"Goodbye and thank you, sir."

At the Strand Palace, Sarah lay curled up in a ball on her bed. After two miserable nights and days – Mary had visited her twice, but had only stayed for a while – the interference was at last producing contractions. She got up and staggered into the bathroom.

The contractions were excruciatingly painful and were followed by a great deal of bleeding. Not daring to call for help, all she could do was sit on the toilet and keep flushing the blood away. Eventually, after five hours, she expelled something. Wanting to see it, but hardly daring to, she looked down at the fairly-formed foetus. *That tiny thing... almost perfect... it doesn't look deformed at all! That's what Edmond and I have made... and I've killed it. Killed our baby! Oh God! Please, please forgive me.* She stood up and flushed it down the toilet.

Trying not to think, trying not to feel guilty, she lay on the bed to rest. *It's over! No guilt. No guilt. It had to be done. It's over.* Numb, cold and empty, unable to focus her mind on the future or any of the consequences of what she'd done, the only thought that came to her was, *I need a bath.*

After it, she rested again, and a vague feeling of having done something monumentally wicked filtered through the mist of her relief. *Was it a boy or a girl? I couldn't see properly... I think it was a boy. But what else could I have done? What have I lost?* An overwhelming sense of sadness loomed over her like a heavy aching cloud. Her tears welled up. She brushed them away and blew her nose. *I can't stay here. I suppose I'd better go home.*

She dressed, paid the hotel bill – without bothering to check on the many room service extras she'd had – the commissionaire hailed her a taxi, and she asked the driver to take her to Waterloo Railway Station.

Edmond arrived breathlessly at the Strand Palace Hotel and made for the Reception desk.

The receptionist told him, "Sorry, sir. Miss Walsh checked out half an hour ago. No forwarding address."

Disheartened and overwrought, he didn't know what to do. Guessing and hoping that she might be on her way back home, he accepted the commissionaire's offer to hail him a taxi, which he instructed to take him back to Waterloo Station. Perching on the edge of the back seat, he examined every face along the way.

Sarah had found an empty carriage and was sitting in a corner, her reflection staring out of the window, appearing to faintly watch the aching cloud of sadness that had now become an unbearable pain in her breast. Visions of the foetus flickered past in the window, of Edmond, of Lady Isabel. Wretched and weak from the loss of so much blood, she tried to shake the emotional pictures from her mind. She became aware she was sweating, that she had an abnormally high temperature. Fearing it was a fever, she dabbed some eau de Cologne from her handbag onto her forehead.

At last the train arrived at Southampton. It was nearly dark when she alighted. The cool evening air was a relief after the stuffy train, but nevertheless, she requested a glass of water from the porter. In the station car park she found her Citroen where she'd left it, but had to concentrate exceedingly hard to drive it home. Night had fallen by the time she reached Kingsford Hall. As she feebly mounted the wide front steps, a gust of wind blew her coat and hair awry, nearly making her lose her balance. *A storm is brewing*, she thought.

The night-light was on in the hall, but apart from the eerie sounds of the wind hooting and whistling, the castle was still. Everyone was asleep. No dogs greeted her, for Mrs Walsh had decided months ago they should bed down in one of the kitchen anterooms. With an effort, and a certain amount of dread at seeing Edmond and having to explain everything, she dragged herself up the stairs to their bedroom. Relieved to find he wasn't there, she went straight to the bathroom. From the medicine cabinet she took a small bottle of sleeping draught. Measuring out ten drops of the drug into a glass – which was the amount Lady Isabel always used to take when she felt poorly – she poured in a dribble more, and drank it. She undressed, put on her nightgown, and, taking care to lock the bedroom door, went to bed.

Princess Briar-rose sank onto her luxurious great bed embroidered with gold and silver... the wind fell, and on the trees before the castle, not a leaf moved. Silence. Utter silence. Only the throb of her heart beating in her ears, and the lonely sound of the ticking clock. Slowly, the black velvet blanket of Morpheus enveloped her, for she had pricked her finger on the spindle of Knowledge and she would sleep for a hundred years. Ghosts and nightmares swirled around her fevered brain. A sea, an ocean of blood stretched before her. Lady Isabel's dying face whispered, "Princess." Dead, half-formed children sang nursery rhymes in the distant castle corridors.

The black-faced lamb wearing the diamond necklace bleated. A tiny foetus floated by crying, "Mama! Mama!" Edmond's distant voice shouted, "Let me in. Sarah! Let me in, it's me!" Prince Valiant was fighting through the briars to reach her. Annie shook her finger, "The only way you will ever make anything of yourself is to be a good servant." Mary O'Reilly sang, "If you were the only girl in the world." Edmond, sitting naked on a rock, asked, "You do you want children, don't you? Yippee!" and splashed into a pool of blue blood. Mr Jones looked down and winked. His face turned into Fred's, grinning and nodding to her from the garden over the terrace parapet. 'You've grow'd up pretty m'dear.'

Knocking!

Is that someone at the French windows? Is this part of my dream? Open my eyes! I can't, I can't. Try...

The great curtains to the balcony billow open. For a moment, silhouetted in the moonlight, he stands as he did before when she'd dropped the secateurs. In he steps.

It's him! This isn't a dream. I think this is real. Real! He's limping. It's Fred! Oh God, help me. What shall I do? I can't think straight. Everything's woozy. He's coming closer ...nearer.... Shut your eyes. Pretend to be asleep.

He's at the bed.
Don't move.
He's breathing heavily.
He kissed me.
He smells of liquor.
He's moved away.

Where's he gone? Don't look, keep your eyes shut. That's the sound of water running in the bathroom. He's washing, preparing.

Her small slim hand slipped out from under the bedclothes and reached over to the bedside drawer next to the bed. Slowly she slid it open... so smoothly it opened, so silently. Feeling inside she freed the hard steel from the soft linen handkerchiefs and gripped the buckram handles. Furtively, she sneaked it under the sheet beside her. She loosened the spring. Holding it fast by her leg, she waited. *Revenge, revenge!*

He came back to the bed, lifted the covers and lay down beside her.

Keep your eyes closed. He's moving over! Closer, closer. His body! That's it, pressing on my side. He's never going to do that to me again. Never. Ever. Wait. Don't move. Wait till he's asleep. Wait. Yes, he's moving away. He's dozing... dozing. His breathing is getting heavier. Heavier, yes, he's almost asleep. Wait now, wait till you're quite sure.

Slowly, inch-by-inch, she stealthily reached over. Her fingers touched his thigh. His flesh. She stretched further... there it was in her hand. With her other hand she leant over, with a quick squeeze of the secateurs, she cut.

An ear-splitting screech of pain snapped her out of her drugged semi-consciousness. Fighting the bedclothes, she scrambled away from him, but, barely conscious, she stumbled, falling down by the bedside.

Howling and screaming in agony, Edmond struggled from the bed as best he could. "What...what have you done?" he shrieked, trying to stem the bleeding. "Why? Why?" he gasped.

Sarah clambered up the bedside table to turn on the light-switch. Recognising her beloved, her Prince Valiant, she wailed a horrified, soul shattering, "NOOOOOOOOOOOOO!!"

Bleeding profusely and yowling in pain, Edmond limped to the bathroom.

Far, far away in the servants' quarters upstairs; George Powell stirred in his sleep.

Chapter Twenty-Four

"She's home!" announced George, returning to the kitchen where Fred was sitting with his tea and Mrs Walsh was pouring boiling water into a Wedgwood teapot. "That Citroen of hers is parked by the front steps. She must have come back late last night!"

"So's Master Edmond," said Mrs Walsh, placing the lid onto the teapot. "I spotted that funny new walking stick of his on the refectory table. I was just going to take him up this tea." She fetched another cup and saucer. "Well, thank heaven for that, anyway! Now we might get to the bottom of her disappearing act!" After fussing with the tray, and covering the teapot with a woollen tea cosy she'd knitted last month, she picked it up and made for the servants' staircase.

On the first floor landing, she placed the tray on the mosaic table outside the bedroom, and knocked. Silence. She turned the doorknob. It was locked. Frowning, she knocked again. "Your Lordship! Sarah! Y'Ladyship!" Still nothing. After a moment of indecision, she went back downstairs, leaving the tray of tea things on the hall table.

Fred made his way up to the north field, preparing to start work. The cockerel crowed and the morning birds chirped merrily. He glanced up at the red clouds in the eastern sky and knew a gloomy day lay ahead. Approaching the sheep pen, an odd sight met his eyes. Alongside the sheep, lying in a foetal position on the straw, was Sarah, fast asleep in her nightgown.

Leaning over the pen, he shook her by the shoulder. "Hey!" he cried.

Awaking, Sarah looked about disorientated.

"What on earth are you doing here?" he asked.

Seeing him, she screamed. Cowering away from him like a mad woman, she covered her head with her arms.

Scowling at her and not knowing what to do, Fred went for help.

No one was in the kitchen, so he passed through into the Great Hall. George and Mrs Walsh were talking at the bottom of the stairs. "I just seen her," he called. "She's curled up in the sheep pen! She's in her nightie!"

"What?" exclaimed Mrs Walsh. "I don't believe it."

"Go see for yourself," said Fred.

"I will," she said, looking at George in astonishment. "Whatever can be the matter with her?" she bustled past Fred making her way to the servants' door.

The two men looked at each other. George frowned and chewed his lip. Beckoning Fred, he said, "Come with me," and he led him out of the front door.

In the garden, beside the ballroom patio, they mounted the mossy brick steps up to the bedroom terrace. One of the French doors was half open, part of the curtain was flapping in the wind. They could see nothing of the room inside, for the curtains were still drawn across the windows. George knocked on a glass pane of the French window. "Edmond!" he called. Stepping through the open door, he parted the curtains and moved inside. Fred followed him.

At first, the watery, filtered daylight revealed little out of the ordinary. The bed was unmade and open, then, they noticed that the pink bedside lamp was still on.

Moving in closer, Fred noticed dark stains on the bedsheets. "That's blood," he said.

George pointed to the floor. "Look!" On the carpet were blooded footprints. Cautiously stepping by them, he bent to examine them closer. "Open the curtains," he said. "The cord's by the side over there."

Fred drew back the curtains and daylight flooded in.

Silently, they followed the footprints into the dressing room and through to the bathroom. Seeping from under the door they saw a congealed pool of blood. George pushed the door, but it moved only slightly. Fred put his shoulder to it, and it slowly gave way. On the other side of the door, clasping blood-soaked towels to his stomach, lay Edmond's tanned, naked body.

He was quite dead.

George first telephoned the police, then Dr Roberts. Waiting for them to arrive, he unlocked the bedroom door from the inside to allow in Mrs Walsh.

"The girl won't budge!" she said. "I don't know what's the matter with her. She doesn't take any notice of me. Nothing!" Noticing George's ashen face, she said, "What's happened? Where's Master Edmond?"

Unable to speak, he nodded to the bathroom.

Hesitantly, Mrs Walsh went in and saw for herself.

Dr Roberts was the first to arrive. He examined Edmond's body, then sat down and telephoned for an ambulance. Shortly afterwards, a heavy, plain-clothed Police Inspector arrived with his sergeant. They examined the scene, asked questions and took notes. Mrs Walsh and Fred told them Lady Sarah was outside and seemed to be in a confused state of mind. The Inspector and Dr Roberts both frowned, and followed them up to the sheep pen.

Nothing the Inspector said could persuade Sarah into the house. Eventually, Dr Roberts, with his unfailing courtesy and sympathetic manner, was the one who succeeded. He stepped into the muddy sheep pen beside her, and took her arm. As she stood up, they all saw that the front of her nightgown was splattered with blood.

The Inspector's face remained impassive. "Dress her in some warm clothes," he said quietly to Mrs Walsh. "I shall want that nightgown as evidence."

They took her to the Housekeeper's office off the kitchen, and Dr Roberts stayed with her while Mrs Walsh collected some clothes from her dressing room. Oddly, Sarah submitted to being changed quite passively, like a mute doll. When she was dressed, the sergeant led her and Mrs Walsh into the Great Hall, where Dr Roberts was now waiting with the Inspector.

"I'd like you to accompany me to the station," said the Inspector, "for questioning."

Sarah frowned at him, then looked at Dr Roberts and Mrs Walsh, who both nodded. Submissively, she allowed the sergeant to lead her out.

George was standing on the front steps, his features as tense as granite as he watched his dead young master being lifted on a stretcher into the back of the ambulance.

Behind him, on the other side of the portico, stood Fred, his heavy brows scowling.

The Inspector came through the door. Turning back, he allowed his sergeant and Sarah to proceed first, then, followed them down the steps.

Mrs Walsh appeared and waited on the top step between George and Fred. The three of them watched as Sarah was led down into the rear seat of the police car. The vehicle started up, and, passing the dusty cream Citroen, slowly disappeared down the drive out of sight.

Fred remained for a while, his dark eyes filled with sadness. Shaking his head with incomprehension, he turned back into the hall.

Mrs Walsh's lip trembled. Her heart full, she glanced over to George, but his back was turned away from her. Profoundly moved, she, too turned away and went back into the hall.

George was left alone, staring out over the grounds of the great castle, pondering on the mystery of what could have caused such a tragedy.

Chapter Twenty-Five

Following her questioning, Sarah was taken into custody and formerly arrested. At a hearing at the Magistrate's Court in Lyndhurst, she was remanded to the county gaol in Southampton, to await trial.

Because of the notoriety of the case, immense crowds gathered outside The Old Bailey on the morning of the 6th November – there was even some question as to whether women would be admitted. In today's terminology, the trial caused a media frenzy.

Mr Garner-Stevens had obtained the services of one of the country's leading defence lawyers, Sir Edward Marshall Hall, KC. Council for the Crown Prosecution was another renowned advocate of the time, Mr Curtis Bennett, KC. Both appeared before the distinguished Justice Horace Avory, who enjoyed a fearsome reputation. He had once – or so his colleagues humorously related – objected to opposing council, quoting from the Book of Job. "That evidence is quite inadmissible," he had declared, "seeing you are unable to put Job in the witness box to prove it."

In the courtroom, the accused, Sarah, Lady Kingsford, was led into the dock.

The crowd in the public gallery leant forward eagerly to get their first glimpse of the murderous young bride. Among them sat a frowning Henry Walsh. No longer an adolescent, he looked tense and haggard. He had survived the war and come to court to support his mother and wonder at the girl who had once been part of his youthful dreams. He alone in the public gallery knew of Sarah's true gentleness of character, remembering the lure of her golden brown hair as she sat in front of his desk at school, and her tomboy petulance when he teased her. The others, the curious, the sensation seekers who'd come to gawp and jeer, saw only the vindictive, ambitious maidservant that the newspapers described.

Unusually, her hair was drawn back from her face, showing her clear forehead and emphasising her fine cheekbones. Her eye sockets had become sooty dark, and her eyes were strangely dead. She appeared to have lost a good deal of weight, for her brown velvet suit with the fur at the throat – which Mrs Walsh had supplied at Marshall Hall's request – hung on her like some damp washing-up cloth. Her demeanour was enigmatic, bland and expressionless, distracted, even. It soon became apparent that she seemed not to be aware of what was happening in the court.

Citing the sheer volume of blood at the crime scene and a coroner's report that singled out the severing of the penis – photographs of which were among the exhibits – Curtis Bennett announced that investigations made the victim's wife the only suspect. Another chief concern, he reported, was the discovery of the murder weapon, the blooded garden secateurs – another of the exhibits – which were found in the marital bed.

The evidence of the gentleman receptionist from the Strand Palace Hotel solved the mystery of Lady Sarah's disappearance for a week prior to the murder. Despite the Hotel Register having no record of a Lady Kingsford's stay, he recognised the accused.

"Yes," he answered, looking across the courtroom and studying Sarah sitting in the dock. "She's the lady who stayed up in her room during her stay. She told us she had the influenza." Likewise, when he was shown a photograph of Sir Edmond, he identified him as "the gentleman with the club foot who'd been so upset that he'd missed the lady."

The ticket attendant at Southampton Railway Station confirmed that he'd collected the ticket from the accused on the night of the 24th July. He said he remembered her, because it was the first time he'd seen the new Lady Kingsford, and that she'd asked him for a glass of water. "Said as how she wasn't feeling too well. And later, I took his Lordship's ticket, too. After he arrived on the last train from London. He asked me to call him a taxi, which I was honoured to do for the gentleman."

Lady Beatrice Bragington Curram, appearing for the Prosecution, was given the opportunity to express her view that the motive for the murder of her late nephew was profit. "In the end," she said, refusing to look at Sarah, but addressing Justice Avory and the jury, "it all boils down to money with someone of her sort. She is typical of the grasping mentality of the sycophantic servant who uses a subtle form of coercion to advance herself. She persuaded my frail and impressionable sister to alter her Will, just as she preyed upon the physical disability of my dear nephew to persuade him to marry her. With his death she has succeeded in gaining control of one of the finest estates in Hampshire."

The Prosecution then called a previous staff member of 'Kingsford Castle Convalescent Hospital'. The bantam sized Matron related how worried and suspicious she'd become when, having left the unwell Lady Isabel in the accused's charge for a moment, she'd been astonished to discover, on her return, that not only was the Lady dead, but the girl was rummaging through the Lady's jewel case.

Marshall Hall interposed to remark that, as Lady Isabel had willed her estate, including all her jewellery, to Lady Sarah, Matron need not have worried.

These stories, as irrelevant and inadmissible as Marshall Hall asserted them to be, did, however, succeed in darkening the jury's perception of Sarah's character. As she continued her impassive behaviour in the dock, showing no sign of grief or remorse, the general feeling of the court towards her, and indeed of the jury, was hostile.

Both Mrs Walsh and George Powell, appearing for the Defence, bore witness to how they had found the body. Both were insistent that Lady Sarah was innocent and had loved her husband, and, indeed, Lady Isabel, dearly.

Fred Oliphant was the next to take the stand.

Since the morning of the murder, some second sense had warned him that Edmond's death was somehow connected to the conversation they'd had in the study. Not for one moment did it occur to him that the years of mental and physical torment he'd once caused Sarah was to blame. His thinking was, that, with the police involved and rumours of a trial, and as there was no longer a master on the estate, it would be best to distance himself, and try for other employment. He had returned to the woman he knew he could always rely on, to the one who would never turn him away, to his ex-wife Annie, at the orphanage. At first she'd appeared to welcome him, then she changed, repeating to him what Edmond had told her about Sarah being abused. He had vehemently denied it. Annie, seemingly preferring to concern herself with Lady Isabel's reputation than delve into the mire of whether Edmond was telling the truth, said he could only stay on one condition. "If there is a trial," she warned, "if you so much as breath a word against Lady Isabel, or even hint at the secret of that girl's birth, I will report everything that young Sir Edmond told me. And don't think I wouldn't dare, 'cause I would. You'd never be employed by anyone respectable ever again. You just keep your trap shut!"

So, in the witness box, the wounded ex-soldier, attempted to, and succeeded in, eliciting great sympathy from the courtroom when he spoke of his long association and affection for the accused, describing how saddened he had been to discover her on the morning after the murder, "sleeping with the sheep and covered in blood".

As the last person to see Sarah before her disappearance, Annie, herself, was called.

Asked what she knew of Lady Sarah's state of mind towards her husband on the morning of her visit, she calmly committed perjury. "Lady Sarah seemed to be as happy as any new bride could be expected to feel." Since she'd spent a lifetime keeping Lady Isabel's secret, she was not about to undo it now.

Marshall Hall asked if she could therefore explain the Lady's disappearance.

"No," she answered. Then told the court of her son's telephone call, and how she had relayed to Sir Edmond the news that Sarah was staying at the Strand Palace Hotel in London.

"And what was his reaction?" asked the lawyer.

"He said he'd go up to London the following morning and fetch her home."

Reggie Oliphant was then called. Asked who his informant of Sarah's whereabouts had been, he answered, grinning, "It was me fiancee, Miss Mary O'Reilly."

Mary's appearance in the witness box caused a mild sensation. Looking delightful with a blue brimmed hat tilted over her eyebrow, she told of her friendship for the accused when they'd been at the orphanage, and later, while in service. She explained the reason for the alias 'Miss Annie Walsh' in the Hotel Register – confirmed by the said Register – and for her visits to the hotel, "was that Lady Sarah had had an abortion".

At this there were jeers and mutterings of censure from the public gallery.

Asked if she knew who had performed the operation, Mary answered, "No."

"And did Lady Sarah," asked Sir Edward, "confide to you if her husband was aware of this illegal abortion?"

"Yes, she did. She told me he did not know of it."

"Thank you," said he. "If my learned friend has no further questions, you may step down." Mr Curtis Bennett shook his head. "Call Dr Rebus Simmons."

Dr Rebus Simmons was the police medical expert who had examined Sarah on the day she was taken into custody. He concurred with Mary's testimony. "A recent abortion would be consistent with my examination," he announced. "Illegal abortion methods are notoriously tawdry and dangerous. They are frequently followed by puerperal depression, and, in some cases, by apoplexy, which is what I believe occurred in this instance. Especially if, as would seem to be the case on the night of his return from London, his late Lordship, unaware of his wife's situation, had demanded his conjugal rights."

Sir Edward Marshall Hall had previously had two interviews with Sarah in Southampton gaol, but, as was his prerogative, he'd decided not to subject her to cross-examination by the Prosecution by putting her into the witness box. Instead, he called a second medical expert, the German psychiatrist, Doktor Emile Kraepelin.

This eminent gentleman was exceedingly impressive. Stout, with a short grey beard, he wore pince-nez, and spoke with an accent, but in a surprisingly soft, almost genteel manner. Under questioning, he revealed that he'd made a thorough psychiatric evaluation of the accused to determine her mental health, and deduced she was suffering from dementia praecox. When asked to explain that condition to the court, he shrugged in a European fashion, and with an emphatic and earnest professionalism, elucidated thus: "Dementia praecox describes a number of characteristics. Hallucinations, delusions, a decreased attention to the world, lack of curiosity, thought disorder, lack of insight and judgement, also emotional blunting. I believe that the disease has its onset in early life – praecox – and leads to an irreversible impairment of cognitial behaviour functions – dementia."

The time arrived for Sir Edward to sum up his case. The suave figure rose to his feet (encased in highly-polished black shoes and cream-coloured spats). With a wide friendly face under his lawyer's wig, he argued that Lady Sarah had killed while in a "subconscious state of epileptic automatism. That in consequence of her severe mental and physical defect she was unable to appreciate the nature of the wrongfulness of her act. She had possessed a flawed mental functioning, and did not realise or understand the consequences of her actions". He cited the 'McNaughtan Rules', referring to the case of Mr Daniel McNaughtan, who had attempted to assassinate the Prime Minister, Robert Peel in 1843. He had killed Peel's secretary but was found 'Not guilty by reason of insanity'. The criminal justice system had thereafter adopted the legal precedent established by the McNaughtan decision. "Therefore," he concluded, "I ask the jury that they bring in a verdict of 'Not guilty by reason of insanity'."

Justice Avory, summing up the case for the jury, commented sceptically on the defence plea of insanity. "It is not every fit or start of passion," he said, "that can justify the killing of another, but must be the total loss of reason and incapability of reason in every part of life." But he warned them against any show of bias. "It is your duty," he concluded, before dismissing them, "to concentrate wholly upon the guilt or innocence of the prisoner."

The jury retired, and Annie breathed a sigh of relief that the secret of Sarah's birth, and of her true relationship with Edmond remained undisclosed. Annie had not been so greatly mystified by Sarah's behaviour in the dock as the general public and the other witnesses. Though Sarah's impassive countenance, without any outward show of grief or remorse, was entirely opposite to her character, Annie had realised some months ago, that all was not as it should be. Back in August she'd visited her, in the Victorian reception hall of Southampton prison.

Sarah had greeted Annie with a warm smile when the warder had released her to sit at the visitor's table. "Ma Cox! Hallo. How good to see you. How long did it take you to get here?"

"About two hours," answered Annie, who'd intended making the visit for weeks, but, feeling apprehensive, and not knowing quite what she would say, had put it off. Then, mindful that Sarah had no one else who would care enough to visit her, she'd come. "I came on the train from Lymington," she explained. "How are you getting on, lass? You've been in my thoughts so much lately."

"Who are all these people?" Sarah said, looking around at the other prison visitors. "I haven't invited them. There'll not be enough food to go round. How did they get here?"

Annie shrugged. "They've come to see their families, I suppose."

"Did her Ladyship invite them?"

Slowly it began to dawn.

Sarah turned to a big woman at the next table who was wearing the same prison gown. "This is my neighbour," she said, introducing Annie. Leaning forward, she whispered to the woman's male visitor. "Excuse me, but I'm a Princess."

"And he's the Shah of Persia, ducks," said the woman. Turning to her boyfriend, she added, "Nutty as a fruit cake! That's the kind of thing we have to put up with all day!"

Sarah didn't appear to be disconcerted by the woman's remark, she merely turned to Annie with, "You're lucky to catch me in. I've been out all day. I went to Egypt. I went right inside a pyramid," and her face beamed.

So Annie had not been exactly shocked by Doktor Kraepelin's diagnoses, but the final words of his evidence resonated guiltily in her mind. *"I believe the disease has its onset in early life"*. Worms of guilt and shame squirmed in the pit of her stomach as she glanced across at Fred.

She recalled the painful morning last June, when Edmond had come to see her and asked about Sarah's birth. When she'd been forced to admit the truth to that upright and charming young gentleman, and he, in turn, had repeated to her what Sarah had told him of her childhood suffering, of her sexual abuse at the hands of Fred. Annie's scalp had tightened across her scull in horror and disbelief; her stomach had twisted and lurched. Having refused for the past eleven years to admit such an abomination, Edmond's words forced her to confront her demons. *I don't, I can't believe it. Fred could never have done such a thing! Never. Could he? Did he? Did I never guess? God, forgive me ... if I did... how could I ever have admitted it? I couldn't. I didn't dare. It would have meant sending him away. That darling wee bairn that she was! I could never believe it ... not of my own Fred ... father of my sons ... Oh, no God! ... it was just a ...a feeling, not really a suspicion. He always was sex mad, I knew that well enough ... but I never knew it for sure ... not until... Sarah's pretty, eight-year-old face appeared.*

"I don't like Mr Fred playing with me, Ma."

"Tell him to leave you alone, then."

"He lifts my skirt and does nasty things."

"Now you stop that, missy! Don't you dare tell wicked lies like that about your elders."

"But he does, Ma!"

I grabbed that cane and beat the living daylights out of her. Beat her so hard, I did. Beating myself I was, for allowing it to happen. Weak, vain creature that I was. I should never have taken him back. Vanity, Lord, vanity. Grateful I was, that he still wanted to be with me. May God forgive me.

Everyone in the courtroom stood as Justice Avory re-entered.

The tension rose when the jury filed back. The first juryman stood to read out the verdict.

Annie glanced across at Sarah.

She was looking up at the window, a slight frown on her forehead, seemingly intrigued by the stained glass or some bird she'd noticed on the other side.

The juryman spoke. "Not guilty by reason of insanity."

The public gallery erupted in a hubbub of disapproval, cheers and relief. Mr Garner- Stevens came forward to shake hands and congratulate Sir Edward. George and Mrs Walsh sat stunned.

Seemingly impervious, Sarah was led down to the cells.

Annie watched from her seat, her grim, weather-beaten expression fighting to control her emotions. *Whatever will become of her now?*

Fred came to her side and quietly took her hand. "Let's go home, lass."

Annie shook his hand away. Standing up she looked at him full and square.

"No. No more. You and I are finished, Fred."

Puzzled he frowned at her. She looked at him for a long moment, then turned away, walking out of the courtroom alone.

Following her trial, Sarah was transported from the court cells to a mental asylum, where she remained incarcerated for many, many years to come.

Epilogue
London, March 2007

Since the explanation of my connection to this story in the Preface, I have tried – without success, I notice, as I re-read what I've written – not to allow my own voice to intrude. Although I don't know exactly what happened to Sarah next, I do know a little, and as I seem to be the only one left who does, the time has come for me to conclude the narrative as myself.

First, I should tell you a little about myself. I am the grandson of Lady Isabel's sister, Lady Beatrice Bragington Curram. I was born in June 1932, in Brighton. My mother, Phyllis, was a milliner, and my father, Bernard – whom I scarcely knew, for he died when I was eight years old – worked for The Liverpool and Victoria Insurance Company. There are no titles around these days, the baronetcy became extinct upon Edmond's death, and my grandfather's title was not hereditary, he had been knighted for his services to science.

Ever since I was a little boy I seem to have known I had a rich aunt. My mother used constantly to tell me so. "One day," she'd say, "when our ship comes in, we'll be rich." Which was her euphemism for either her marrying again – a millionaire, hopefully – or me inheriting a fortune from this wealthy aunt.

I never knew quite where this mysterious lady was, or how she fitted into the family. She was certainly not among my mother's army of brothers and sisters, all eleven of whom I knew

272

well. As an only child I used to join each one of them – and my cousins – in turn, for summer holidays from boarding school. When I asked Mother exactly who this rich aunt was, she was vague. "Some cousin of your father's," she answered. "I do remember your father once telling me, that, when he was a boy, his mother had taken him to tea with his aunt, old Lady Kingsford in Kingsford Hall, and this girl, Sarah, was waiting table as a servant. The family were all furious she was the one who got everything when Edmond died."

Intrigued, I wanted to ask my Father more, but as he had dumped my Mother four years prior to his death, he was not around for clarification.

Once, on Brighton pier, Mother and I had our fortunes told. The gypsy looked at my palm and said, "There's a legacy coming your way, lad. Inherit a fortune, you will." As a teenager, you can imagine the effect that had. I became even more interested in the whereabouts, and, in particular, the health of this unknown aunt.

I pressed Mother for details. She explained, "When your father died, I went to see a lawyer about getting some money from his estate. This was his opinion," and she showed me an embossed headed letter, signed, 'Hugo Ball, solicitor.' It explained in convoluted legalese that, on the death of Sarah Kingsford, I, along with any other legitimate surviving members of her family, would be entitled to an equal share of her estate, provided she did not make a Will to the contrary. I remember pointing this last part out to Mother.

"So she could, in theory," I said, "leave it all to a Cat's Home!"

"I suppose she could," said Mother, gloomily. "She is in an asylum."

"What!" I cried. "Why? Where?" But Mother said no more, for in those days, one didn't talk to children about such things, at least, my mother didn't. Great, I thought, so now I have a crazy, rich old aunt! There's all the more likelihood of her leaving her fortune to a Cat's Home.

"No," said my Uncle Ralph, clarifying matters for me later in Worthing, where he lived in a bungalow with his wife, my Auntie 'Pop-Goes-Your-Heart'. My uncle was a retired naval officer, my father's only surviving brother, and a far more stolid person than my emotional mother. "The financial affairs of anyone in an asylum are looked after by a body called The Court of Protection," he explained over the dining table, spread with papers and old photographs. "Her accounts are submitted to the Income Tax annually, and I, as next of kin, have to sign that state-ment. Eventually, as you're the next in line," he continued, "You will have to take over that responsibility." He showed me our family tree – which I have decided not to include among these pages, for some people, like 'Harry' in "When Harry Met Sally", like reading the last pages of a book first. So if you'd accidentally seen the family tree before you started, you'd have known the outcome too early – so you'll just have to take my word for it, that this dotty aunt, or rather, second cousin of mine, was, in fact, the wife of my father's cousin.

My dear Uncle Ralph died in 1974, and I duly took over the annual signing of accounts with the help of the accountant. That accountant was Mr Garner-Stevens, who had retired, and was working from his home in Worthing. Our business was usually conducted by letter, but I did visit him once, and, though reticent about his former clients, he did, when pressed, remark that both the Lady Kingsfords were "exceedingly charming ladies". He, too, died some years later, leaving many questions that I'd like to have asked him, unanswered.

As I examined the accounts, I saw for the first time the exact amount of investments and property involved. To me, an actor, who was sometimes in work and sometimes not, with a wife, two children and a mortgage on a semi in Wandsworth, it was a fortune. But so, too, I could see at a glance, were the annual asylum fees from St Andrew's Hospital, Northampton, where she was now in residence.

In 1975, I received a phone call from the Matron of that establishment. I clearly remember her words. "The clouds have cleared," she said. "Lady Kingsford is going through a comparatively sane period and is asking about her relatives. Yours in the name I have on file. Would you be at all interested in visiting her?"

"Very much so," I answered.

A date for tea was arranged, and a week later I drove my Volkswagen Beetle up the A1 to Northampton – my wife had been called away to work that day, so I was obliged to take along my daughter, Louise, who, at the time, was a pretty little girl of eight. Never mind, I thought, having a child around might interest Sarah and ease our first meeting.

To my surprise the asylum was a grandiose Edwardian mansion, with well-kept lawns and gardens set in beautiful parklands. It had been designed by Gilbert Scott, the architect of St Pancras Railway Station, so it enjoyed listed building status, boasted John Clair as a former inmate, and in 1887, when it was known as Northampton General Lunatic Asylum, I was amused to read in the literature, it accommodated "both private and pauper patients for the Middle and Upper classes."

I made myself known to the Matron, and she took us along to meet Sarah.

In a high-ceilinged dormitory with church-like windows, standing alone by a locker between the beds stood a tall, gaunt lady with an unattractive Eton crop.

"Sarah," said the Matron, approaching her. "This is your relative Roland, who's come to see you with his daughter, Louise."

"We shook hands politely and Matron suggested we go for a walk in the gardens.

Sarah looked like something out of a 'Miss Marple', Agatha Christie play, old-fashioned, middle class and deeply respectable. She wore a light brown suit, heavy stockings and sensible shoes. Her age was indeterminate, her skin unlined, she could have been in her fifties, sixties or seventies. "Who are you?" she asked. "Who was your father?" As we walked past the School of Occupational Therapy building and I tried to explain our connection, my daughter took her hand. "Oh no!" she said. "You must never hold hands. That's the centre of your being," and without pausing she continued rather surprisingly with, "I said that's no place for the rose secateurs, they shouldn't be left there, they should be put away with the garden things."

She was indeed very curious, seeming to me dry and charmless, but then, what are the rules of social behaviour when your head has been in the clouds for over fifty years? She didn't seem to know that World War Two had occurred, and was principally concerned about some garden clippers left somewhere years beforehand. There was this great gap in her memory; it was as if the last fifty years had never happened. However, we struck up a strange kind of friendship, I was fascinated by her and her story, and, of course, from her point of view, I was the only link she had with her family, and of a generation that knew nothing of why she was there. I could tell she liked me and was kind of proud of me – for I was appearing on television quite often in those days – she wanted to know my birthday, and later, over tea and cakes, said she hoped I would come and see her again.

I visited her several times after that, and we frequently corresponded, mostly by cards and short notes. As I write, I have the birthday card she sent me that year before me, written in her large childish hand. She had no knowledge of her own birthday. Once or twice she mentioned the word "home" to me, and I wondered what had become of it – the place I have called Kingsford Hall. I looked for it among her list of properties in the Court of Protection's annual accounts. It was not there. I supposed it must either have been bombed in World War Two, or have been sold to liquidize cash for the Trust Fund needed to pay years of expensive hospital bills.

After about eighteen months the Matron suggested to me that Sarah was well enough to be discharged. By then the hospital bills exceeded the income produced by the Trust, and my wife and I spent a panicky couple of weeks wondering if we could look after her, and whether we could afford to convert our garage into a Granny flat. We need not have worried. Matron tactfully told me that Sarah had "regressed". The clouds had descended again. Further visits were discouraged and pointless, she was back in her own world. I continued, with the help of a new accountant, to look after her affairs under the aegis of The Court Of Protection. The hospital generously waived their increased fees, and we paid just what the sadly depleted Trust Fund annually produced.

Twenty-two years later, she died at the age of ninety-eight. On her death certificate it said: "Said to have been born on: January 1900." I went to her funeral as I've described, and later, in the memorial gardens at St Andrews, planted a rose bush in her name. Seventy-nine years in asylums, I pondered – for Northampton had not been the only one – seventy-nine years of what? What could have been going through her mind during all those years? What happiness could she have known? The illegitimate orphanage girl, hired as a servant by her mother, married the lady's son, her half-brother, who, on his death had inherited his fortune, was ostracised by the remaining family, and went insane. It was like something out of a Victorian novel. It was then I promised myself, that one day, I would try and write her story.

With her death I naively imagined the finances would be plain sailing, but, oh no! Because I was only a relative by marriage and not a blood relative – little did they know – I was not allowed to administer her estate. The Treasury Solicitor on behalf of the Crown now undertook that. So began my twelve-month battle to inherit what little was left of her fortune. Copious letters, family trees, certificates of birth and marriage went to and fro; certificates of my birth, my father's, my grandmother's birth and death, all unearthed from St Catherine's House in the Aldwych.

Over the years, I had periodically received letters from a distant cousin of mine in Missouri, USA. He turned out to be a farmer, the great-grandson of the gentleman I have called the Reverend Ralph. His constant question was, "Is Sarah yet living?" and I knew, that if anything was ever going to be forthcoming from the Treasury Solicitor, I was going to have to share it with him. Which is exactly what happened. There wasn't much left, but it was sufficient to pay for a loft conversion on my new home, the one I'd had to buy when I started a new life after my divorce. Which reminds me...

After Sarah died, St Andrew's Hospital sent me a small package: "Patients Valuables Deposited With Hospital. One yellow metal ring." It was her heavy gold Italian wedding ring. I put it on the fifth finger of my left hand. It fitted perfectly. I have worn it ever since, all the time I've been writing this novelization of her story.

THE END